Mattie

M. Ann Rohrer

BONNEVILLE BOOKS
AN IMPRINT OF CEDAR FORT, INC.
SPRINGVILLE, UTAH

ISBN 13: 978-1-4621-1111-4

Published by Bonneville Books, an imprint of Cedar Fort, Inc.
2373 W. 700 S., Springville, UT, 84663

Distributed by Cedar Fort, Inc., www.cedarfort.com

LIBRARY OF CONGRESS CATALOGING-IN-PUBLICATION DATA

Rohrer, M. Ann, 1947-
 Mattie / M. Ann Rohrer.
    pages cm
 ISBN 978-1-4621-1111-4
 1. Grief--Fiction. 2. Fathers and daughters--Fiction. 3. Self-realization in women--Fiction. 4. Christian fiction. I. Title.
 PS3618.O496M38 2013
 813'.6--dc23

                         2012048377

Cover design by Angela D. Olsen
Cover design © 2013 by Lyle Mortimer
Edited and typeset by Whitney A. Lindsley

Printed in the United States of America

10 9 8 7 6 5 4 3 2 1

I DEDICATE THIS BOOK TO MY DEAR GRANDMOTHER MARTHA Ann Sevey Wood (Mattie) for whom I was named and to my mother, Marene Robinson Wood, who repeatedly told me that I should be a writer; to my family and friends, who might recognize some of the events, circumstances, and sayings that I borrowed from their lives; to Clarence and Anna Turley for their wonderful book, *History of the Mormon Colonies in Mexico*; to Grandma and Grandpa Wood, who, without their history of courage and indomitable spirit, there would be no story.

PART ONE

1902

MATTIE POUNDED HER PILLOW, THEN ROLLED OVER AND stared at the ceiling. She hated the interfering throngs of people. She hated the mountains of food. She hated the stupid whispering downstairs.

She hated God.[1]

Gentle rains made little difference in the suffocating heat this first day of summer, yet eleven-year-old Martha Ann Sevey shivered. The pungent smell of death, mixed with sweet carbolic acid and saltpeter, seeped through the high-ceiling parlor below. It wafted up through the wood floor right into Mattie's bedroom, invading her olfactory senses. Worse than the odor was the ghastly vision of her father (she refused to think of him as "the body"). Laid out on a board supported by two sawhorses, he was covered with rags drenched in the offensive mixture. To slow the body's decay, her mother had explained, which conjured dreadful pictures in Mattie's young, imaginative mind.

Her father never quite recovered from pneumonia. The wet spring had not helped. Racking coughs became increasingly worse until one night he coughed not at all. Two days he had been dead, yet to Mattie, it felt like years.

More happened in one hour than in a month of Sundays. From the moment he died, pandemonium descended upon them—something about Mexican law. Mattie's mother had called it "moratorium," which meant they had two days to bury her beloved father. Each moment required decisions. Friends and acquaintances dropped in throughout the day and night, bringing food, sewing burial clothes, whispering solemn condolences. The house overflowed with family. Harmless jangle among the children gave way to quiet politeness. Even Moe was subdued.

Today her father would be buried.

The older boys from Chupe had not arrived in time to say their good-byes. At least they were here for the funeral. Her father would be long buried before Mahala got word in California.

Mattie tried several positions before settling on her side. Dark shadows danced across the window. She wondered if her brothers in the other room slumbered as though the world had not changed. Beside her, Phoebe and Lola inhaled and exhaled in steady rhythm with the *drip, drip, drip* that fell from the eaves. In the other bed, Minerva and Nellie—Leuna between them—snored lightly. A low rumble of conversation floated up from below, where men sat by turns to keep father bathed in that awful mixture and to guard him against scavenging rats.

Mattie shivered.

Trying to block the macabre, she focused on happier times.

Her father, taller than average, a most handsome man with soft sage-green eyes under undisciplined eyebrows, would often peer down at her, deep in thought, while he stroked his beard that reached down to the first button on his shirt. The dark whiskers were streaked with silver, the same color as his hair, as if a few rogue strands had escaped their rightful place to take up residency in the cascading bristles. Soft spoken, even to his animals, George Sevey never scolded, though he did reprimand, which was pain enough.

Twice the age of her mother, her father at age seventy was old enough to be her grandfather. Mattie was entirely oblivious to the disparity. His advanced age with so young a family was due to the law of plural marriage. Not every Mormon man had multiple wives—in truth, less than one-fifth. As it had in the Old Testament from time to time, plural marriage was a sacred call from a prophet of God to the most faithful and morally upstanding. George Washington Sevey was one of those men.

With hundreds of others, he chose to colonize land in the northern part of Mexico in the state of Chihuahua, purchased by the Church from the Mexican government. To stay in Utah, George's first choice, meant probable arrest, a lengthy sentence, and confiscation of his property by the United States.

Colonia Juárez, one of thirteen settlements, was sandwiched in a gorge not more than a mile across and two hundred feet deep from the valley floor. Hills flowed down from the northeast to the desert plateau. On the southwest, they gave way to the rugged Sierra Madre. The Piedras Verdes River wound its way through the middle of town with cottonwood, walnut, sycamore, ash, and black willow marking its banks. During the dry season, a wagon could easily cross. During the monsoons, it was impossible. The community built a wagon bridge and a cabled footbridge commonly called the Swinging Bridge.

The town resembled southern Utah communities, which Mattie had never seen but had heard about in detail from her mother: wide streets and a grid of narrow irrigation ditches that gave life to each parcel of land. One to two acres was deeded to every man where he built his home of native adobe, faced with red brick, the gabled roofs covered with sheets of galvanized tin. In no time, the town became a verdure of orchards, kitchen gardens, and farms.

Religion was a way of life for the Mormons, not a list of Sunday rules to be set on a shelf during the week. Buildings for church and school took first priority, doubling as cultural halls where plays were performed and Friday night dances were held when it was too cold to have them outside.

Phoebe, George's first wife, chose to stay in Panguitch, Utah, with their grown children who ran George's prosperous sheep ranch. Margaret (Maggie), his second wife, and Martha, the youngest wife, with three young children—which eventually totaled eight—between them, went to Mexico. A good provider, George Sevey built two homes, one on Main where Martha lived with her eight children: Tom, Lee, Bill, Nellie, Moses, Mattie, Lola, and Leuna. Bill (William Exile) was the first Mexican—born when the family still lived in covered wagons in the sweltering Chihuahua desert and were waiting for final approval from the Mexican government to possess the purchased land. [2]

Maggie lived in a ranch house up river several miles with her children, George F., Minerva, Phoebe, and Leon, until she died. By then, George F. was married and lived in Chuichupa (Chupe for short)—a rugged day's ride up the mountain. He ranched with Mattie's two brothers: Tom who was married, and Lee, who wanted to be married.

Because she had been so young, Mattie could not remember Aunt Maggie other than an occasional scene. Sitting at her table pretending to eat rice pudding, which Mattie could not force past her throat; George F.'s birthday when Aunt Maggie cheered both sides when a little water fight turned into an outright dunking in the river; Aunt Maggie showing off her new baby boy. Maggie's first three children could be found under three tiny mounds in a busy cemetery in Panguitch. Mattie did not remember their names, if she knew them at all.

Shortly after Leon's birth, Maggie succumbed to cancer. Her husband rushed her to Utah, where she could get better medical care, but she did not survive the journey, dying just a day before they arrived. George Sevey buried Margaret Nebraska Imlay Sevey in Panguitch beside the three little mounds. Her living offspring she left to her sister-wife, Martha.

Martha welcomed Maggie's children, loving them equally without delineating between families. In return, they affectionately called her Mother instead of Aunt Martha. "Twins on father's side" were Maggie and Martha's children of the same age. By no wish of his own, born of love and respect, all the children, even the married ones, addressed George as "Father," never Pa or Papa.

Mattie reflected, not for the first time, on her walk with her father just a month ago. Moe's shenanigans had proffered the opportunity. Never did she think she would see the day when she would be grateful for her brother's teasing.

On a quiet Saturday afternoon, while her mother was visiting a friend, Mattie and Phoebe were deep into the mending, paying their just dues for a recent misconduct.

"If we had chosen a willow," Mattie sighed, "we would be off playing with our friends."

Phoebe looked up. "But a willow hurts."

Mattie stuck her hand into the mending basket, pushing aside the socks. She hated darning socks. Suddenly, one of the socks seemed to come alive, wrapping itself around her hand. Mattie's scream bounced off the walls as she shook her hand in a wild frenzy. A length of scales flew into the air and landed softly in Phoebe's lap. Phoebe jumped to her feet, her intermittent squeals colliding in discordant harmony with Mattie's clamor. Dumped unceremoniously to the floor, a surprised serpent slithered frantically to safety, sending Phoebe up on her chair with a single leap.

Nellie, packing a heavy broom, and Minerva, armed with a rolling pin, burst through the parlor door.

Mattie and Phoebe stared at their older sisters.

They stared back, weapons at the ready.

From her elevated perch, Phoebe stifled a giggle.

Mattie winced.

Nearly fifteen, Minerva never failed to pounce on an opportunity to prove the vast discrepancies between her, the young woman, and Mattie, the mere child. Despite her best efforts, Mattie was painfully accommodating in providing such proof. Large round eyes, the color of sage in spring, pled with the earth to open up and swallow her in one big gulp.

Pointing toward the tall basket, Mattie said meekly, "Snake."

Minerva lowered the rolling pin, her disapproval resting heavily upon her two younger sisters. "I'm guessing it isn't a rattler."

Mattie glanced at Phoebe, who worked her lips between her teeth, making her appear as toothless as poor old Sister White. "Garter . . . I think."

Nellie hid a smile behind the business end of the broom.

Minerva rolled her eyes. "Heavens to Betsy, Mattie. A garter? We thought someone died."

Mattie's face turned a light shade of pink, matching the ribbons that tied her French braids up into large loops that reached down to her shoulders.

Minerva fumed. "How many times have we told you to stop screaming at nothing?"

Nellie followed Minerva out of the room, chancing a comforting smile aimed at her mortified sister.

Mattie blinked back tears. It wasn't about snakes. It was about being startled. She hated being startled. Mattie could face the fiercest dog, stand up to the biggest bully, and squash the ugliest bug, as long as she could see it coming. But let something, however small or insignificant, surprise her, it was heart pummeling screams followed by hot humiliation.

Phoebe, superintending from her usual safe place high off the floor, directed Mattie to look over and under everything in the sitting room, even the rag rugs made from hers and Phoebe's old dresses. They argued that if a snake were under a rug, it would show. Phoebe insisted, and Mattie acquiesced. Sure enough, no snake. Finally, under the cushion-covered settee, curled up on the floor against the wall, Mattie found the little gray coil. Going to the open window, she bent low, setting the garter free among the yellow sunflowers.

"We scared you, didn't we, Mattie?"

Mattie's head snapped up. The familiar voice belonged to her little brother, Leon.

"Afraid of a little ol' garter?" That all-too-familiar voice belonged to her not-so-little brother, Moe.

Her brothers' grins nearly split their faces. A vein, like a length of blue rope, popped up in Mattie's neck as the puzzle clinked into place like a bolt in a spring-loaded barrel.

"Moses Thatcher Sevey," she seethed. "You . . . you . . . brat!"

Although Mattie credited her brother with many imperfections, brat topping her list, Moe was guilty of only one—being a twelve-year-old boy who lived for raucous reactions from the fairer sex.

And Mattie never failed him.

Both boys headed toward the backyard, disappearing around the corner of the redbrick house. Leon, the little darling of the family, imitated Moe's raucous laugh.

Hell-bent on revenge, Mattie grabbed several cold biscuits left over from breakfast off the sideboard as she ran through the kitchen to the back door, ignoring Phoebe's dire warnings of "waste not, want not" and the threat of another Saturday of mending, or worse. Mattie stepped through the door just as Moe came barreling around the corner, paying more attention to who might be chasing him than to who might be waiting for him.

The first biscuit hit Moe right between the eyes, exploding on impact, bringing Moe to a sudden halt. "Take that, Moses Thatcher!

Racing behind, Leon slammed into his brother, sending both of them to the ground in opposite directions. "Moe did it. Moe did it," Leon yelled, crawling to safety around the corner.

"You little twerp!" Mattie hollered after him.

"Mattie loves Alonzo. Mattie loves Alonzo," Moe taunted.

Mattie's momentary satisfaction with her aim turned a shade of truthful mortification. Then a deeper shade of indignant rage. The second biscuit caught Moe on the back of his retreating head as he ran toward the orchard.

"I hate you!" she screamed as a third biscuit fell short of its intended target, crumbling as it hit the ground.

Leon, giving Mattie wide berth, followed his brother. "Mattie loves Alonzo."

Alonzo Skousen was Moe's friend, but he tended to notice Mattie, and Mattie tended to notice that he noticed. However flattering the attention, it mortified her. She would rather suffer a hundred pranks than be teased about Alonzo.

And Moe knew it.

"I hate you, Moses Thatcher Sevey!" Mattie yelled to the entire orchard. Trees in perfect rows, heavy with small green nubs that promised amber, fuzz-covered peaches, stood in mocking silence.

Phoebe said, "You can love a seven-year-old, but you better not trust him."

Mattie glared at her, daring her to giggle.

Phoebe didn't dare.

"Blast it!" Mattie shouted for lack of another biscuit.

"Here, here." Although not a loud voice, it was commanding. Mattie whirled to stare up, up, up at her father, who leaned heavily on his cane. "Now what's got you in such a dither, child?"

Hands behind her back, Mattie looked down, worrying a pebble with the toe of her shoe. "Moe hid a snake in the sewing basket, Father."

"I see." George Sevey pulled at his long beard. "And you set out to even the score a little?" Had he been able to hold Mattie's gaze, she would have been relieved to see the familiar twinkle.

She nodded. "I threw a biscuit at him."

"*A* biscuit?" he said.

Surveying the evidence littering the ground, Mattie didn't see the smile that lifted his heavy mustache at the corners. "Three biscuits, Father."

"Ah. Waste not, want not, Mattie."

"Yes, Father." Mattie looked for her sister who had been standing by the kitchen door. Phoebe had vanished.

"As you know, Mattie, while we can choose our actions, we cannot choose the consequences."

"Yes, Father." Mattie could hardly bear the disappointment in her father's tone. Why hadn't she listened to Phoebe? Would she never stop to think before plunging in up to her neck in consequences?

"We shall discuss this with Mother."

"Yes, Father." Mattie knew that meant another hour of mending—or a few seconds with the willows.

"And what about Moe? He deserves some consequences," she said.

"I will deal with Moses and Leon."

Father had been privy to a lot more than Mattie first thought. "Oh, Leon is not to blame, Father. He was only following Moe."

"Nevertheless, Leon must learn that he must think for himself. Don't you agree?"

Mattie thought about that. "Perhaps Moe should suffer two consequences."

"Two?"

"One for being horrid to me and one for being horrid to Leon."

"Horrid?"

Mattie nodded, remembering the taunts about Alonzo.

"I see."

Mattie had no idea that what her father saw was the epitome of femininity—at least on the outside. On the inside, she was much like her brother, who had only himself to blame for her excellent eye.

George Sevey was about to speak when he was overcome with a fit of coughing. Immediately Mattie went to him. She hated to see him racked with spasms that came all too frequent as of late.

Wiping his face with his handkerchief, Mattie's father smiled down at her.

"So you hate Moses, do you?"

Mattie's lip lifted at the corner. "Not really, Father."

"I thought not. *Hate* is a strong word, Mattie, destructive. Usually it says more about the person who is saying it than the person about whom it is being said."

While Mattie agreed with her father, she had no idea how one went about changing one's feelings.

He winked at her. "Besides, you and Moe will most likely come to be great friends one day."

Mattie screwed up her face in disgust.

Her father chuckled. "Walk with me to the Swinging Bridge, dear? Perhaps you can practice your aim on a more challenging, albeit less worthy, target than your brother."

They slowly made their way under a ceiling of young cottonwoods and maples dressed in new spring green. Father's hand rested on Mattie's shoulder for support, only lifting to wave at a neighbor or a friend in a buckboard passing by, stirring up dust that would turn to mud when the rains came.

They crossed the Swinging Bridge, Mattie bouncing and swaying, but not too enthusiastically, for her father's sake. The Piedras Verde, not even a river really, was a shallow tributary. On this day, it was a gentle, trickling stream. Come monsoons, it became a raging flood spanning about forty feet.

"I love May," Mattie announced, breathing in spring. "I want to get married in May."

"I hope you don't mean this May!"

"I'm only eleven, Father!"

"Yes, of course. Perhaps next May."

"Oh, Father, you're teasing me."

His moustache rose at the corners.

Mattie smiled. "Will I marry someone who already has a wife?"

He tried to smile through another coughing spell.

Mattie only knew plural marriage. The entire community consisted of polygamists who had come to escape the persecution in the States. If the law caused conflict in other families, it was not discussed. Her mother and Aunt Maggie had been good friends, running their separate households seamlessly. Mattie was too young to remember that her father divided his time equally between families. It seemed she saw him every day, and where he slept was unimportant.

"No, Mattie, no more plural marriage. God has revealed it to the prophet, President Wilford Woodruff."

Because she was so young, the news had little effect on Mattie, one way or the other. "I want you to perform the marriage, Father, like you have for others.

"Like I did," her father corrected. "I'm no longer the bishop, remember?"

Mattie looked at him. "Well, then you must at least give me away. I'll have a garden wedding, and we will walk on a path of rose petals and you'll—"

"Child."

"You will, Father, won't you?" Mattie searched her father's face. He looked at her, solemn and sad. A robin chirped its familiar song, and from a distant pasture, a horse whinnied. Industrious bees hummed nearby, searching for blossoms.

Finally, her father smiled. Patting her shoulder, he said, "Nothing would please me more."

One month later, Father was dead.

Turning on her side, Mattie pressed against the ache in her chest. She knew Father was about to tell her that day that he was not going to live to see her wedding day, and she had not wanted to hear it. The Bible said God would answer prayers if one asked with enough faith. Mattie had followed instructions perfectly, with no doubts, and believing with all her heart. She had asked God to make her father well. Indeed, she had left God no choice, commanding Him.

She had taken Father's promise to mean that God would answer her prayer.

Mattie remembered their last visit, just a few nights ago.

"Martha Ann." He rarely called her by her full name. "Did you know your mother didn't want to name you after her?"

Mattie didn't.

"I insisted. You look like her." He coughed. "You're a good daughter, Mattie. I'm proud of you." Her Father gave her hand a reassuring squeeze. If it's to be rose petals, Mattie," he coughed again, "you best wait for July." He winked. Mattie had actually smiled then. "Your wedding . . . I'll be there . . . in spirit. You'll know."

"You mustn't talk, Father."

Her prayers had been in vain. God had let her down. *Trust*, her mother had said. *God knows best.* How could she trust someone she hated?

"Do you really hate God, Mattie?" Her father's voice whispered in her mind. *"Hate is a strong word—destructive."*

No. Mattie could not hate God any more than she could hate Moe. But if God intended to do things His own way, never again would she bother with trying to change His mind.

The window grew light, showing slithering rivulets spilling over the edge of the windowsill like the flood of tears that slid unnoticed onto Mattie's wet pillow.

1904

MATTIE AND PHOEBE KICKED A ROCK BACK AND FORTH between them, disturbing piles of dry leaves that rained down on the dusty, dirt road. When the rock went too far astray, they chose another rock small enough not to hurt their toes but large enough to travel the distance. The twelve-year-old sisters were part of a string of children spread out a mile from stem to stern on their way home from school. Daily, they trekked three miles to school and the three miles back home.

Just ahead, Alonzo Skousen and Silvestre Quevedo and her brother Moe stopped occasionally to challenge their rock-throwing skills: who could throw a rock to the other side of the bank; who could hit the dead branch; who could skip a rock across the water. Silvestre, who lived with his family next door to the Sevey ranch, usually won. More brother than friend, he and his siblings attended the "Mormon" school, where they became as proficient in English as they were in Spanish. Sadly, it didn't always work the other way around. Although Mattie's brothers were fluent, Mattie and her sisters knew just enough of their second language to get by, and their accents were terrible.

Alonzo lived in town. Most Fridays he was excused from his own chores at home to accompany his good friends, Moe and Silvestre—and if the truth be known, to be close to Mattie. Hardly a Saturday went by that Alonzo didn't show up late in the afternoon, his freckled face split in an ear-to-ear grin, and stayed until the Sevey children were called in to get ready for bed.

Phoebe giggled. "Alonzo's looking again."

Mattie blushed and pointedly turned her back on the fire-red-haired boy, pretending to check the stragglers, Nellie and Minerva, who brought up the rear, herding the younger children who were inclined to dawdle. Alonzo was as bold as Mattie allowed, and she didn't allow much beyond conversation and an occasional whirl around the floor at the Friday night dances. When Mattie turned back, Alonzo's attentions were mercifully elsewhere.

Wiping at her face, she smeared dust with perspiration caused by unseasonably warm October weather and the exertion of the long walk. Touching her tongue to her lips, she eyed the near-stagnated pools in the riverbed and might have stopped for a drink had it not been for the animals she knew were upstream who drank from the same river—or worse.

She swallowed, yearning for a long, cool, refreshing drink from the well that awaited her at home.

It had been a year ago that Mattie and her siblings first made this thirsty trek. To help make ends meet, Mattie's mother had rented out the two-story house in town, moving the family to the ranch up river, where she managed twelve cows that produced enough milk and cheese for her family of eight with enough left over to sell. It was work, and no member of the family, however young, was exempt from doing his part.

Bill, just eighteen years old, had the lion's share. With advice from his older brothers, and faithful support from his neighbor and hired hand, Javier Quevedo, Bill, with Moe's help, managed the orchards and worked at building up the ranch stock.

Minerva, Nellie, Phoebe, and Mattie took on the roll of milk-maids, assisted by Moe when he was available. Lola, Leuna, and Leon fed the animals and gathered eggs. Summertime chores included making jerky, curing and smoking hams, weeding, harvesting, and bottling produce from the kitchen garden. The list seemed endless, and it didn't include all that was required to keep a household running—washing, carpet beating, making feather tics, mending, and sewing. Just thinking about it made Mattie weary.

Every day the family was up before dawn "choring." After chores, they washed, changed from work clothes, bolted down their breakfast, and walked three miles to school, only to walk back, change back into work clothes, do more chores, eat, and go to bed.

Except on Fridays.

Mattie loved Fridays. Instead of going to bed, the family attended the community dance at the grade school, or in warmer weather, the bandstand by the river in the center of town. On Saturdays, Mother allowed the children to sleep until sunrise before rousting them out of bed to take care of the bawling cows. Besides milking, Saturday was washday and house-cleaning day, culminating with a lively neighborhood game late afternoon into early evening, depending on the time of year. When they were called in for the evening, it meant weekly baths in a big steel tub in front of the old wood stove, a blanket hanging over a wire to give a little privacy. The older children helped the younger children. After baths, the family gathered in the sitting room where Mother read from the Book of Mormon or the Bible. As of late, one of the older children played the roll of reader, Mother's eyes not being what they used to be.

Sunday—blessed Sunday—was a day of rest except for milking and feeding animals. After morning chores, the family attended church while a lovely pot roast cooked at home. Sunday dinner was another of Mattie's favorites. Perhaps the mouthwatering aroma of cooked meat made everything taste so good. Perhaps it was the anticipation of her mother's fruit pies, or suet pudding smothered in lemon sauce, or fresh strawberries and peaches with cream.

Mattie's mouth watered, as she was suddenly aware of how hungry she was. From outside, she could smell fresh-baked bread. First the pump. Moving the handle up and down, cold, clear water rushed out filling a tall milk bucket. Mattie filled the dipper and drank deeply.

"Save some for the rest of us," Phoebe said.

"I could pour this over my head and love it." Mattie put water in a wash pan that sat on a rough-hewn stand and handed the dipper to Phoebe. While Phoebe drank, Mattie splashed her face with water.

"My turn," Leon said, running up to his sisters.

"Yes," Phoebe said. "You do need a good face wash."

"Uh-uh! I meant a drink."

Grabbing him before he could get away, Mattie held her howling brother while Phoebe doused his grimy face. Calming him with a nice cold drink, the three of them headed for the kitchen door, leaving Minerva and Nellie, who had just arrived, to superintend Lola and Leuna at the pump.

***

"'Bout time," Moe said. "Don't want to be all day milking, so hurry it up."

Phoebe harrumphed.

Ignoring Moe and refusing to look at Alonzo, who would surely grace her with a heart-stopping smile, Mattie breathed in the aroma of salt-rising bread not long out of the oven wafting harmoniously with a big iron kettle of simmering pinto beans. Mother made the best beans: never hard, flavored with garlic and onion and ham hock, when available, or a dollop of pig lard.

"I thought I heared something." Their mother lumbered into the kitchen. Strictly speaking, Martha Sevey could not hear. Scarlet fever had left her deaf since childhood, and it had marked her speech with poor grammar. Nevertheless, she always seemed to appear at a sound and never failed to know what was being said—if she were looking at you.

"Hello 'Lonzo. Good to see you." Mattie knew that her mother approved of Alonzo as Moe's friend. However, she would have been mortified had she known how well her mother understood Alonzo's feelings for Moe's pretty sister.

"I see you found the bread and molasses." Martha's round face crinkled in a smile directed at the older boys.

"I want some too." Leon rarely waited to be asked anything. "With lots of butter and lots of molasses."

"I hate molasses," Leuna said, just coming in with her sisters. "I just want butter."

"You love Mother's ginger cookies," Lola pointed out. "They have molasses in them."

"Uh-uh."

"Heavens to Betsy, Leuna," Minerva scolded. "We call them ginger cookies so you'll eat them."

"Uh-uh," Leuna said again, in vehement denial.

Lola giggled.

"I swan," Martha said. "It must a been a hot walk today." She stacked thick slices of bread on a heavy, earthenware plate and put it on the table along with a bowl of home-churned butter, molasses, and honey. "This oughta keep your spirits up 'til supper." She chuckled.

In the absence of conversation, for it could not be called silence with all the chewing and smacking, Mattie braced herself for what she knew was to come next, and she really didn't want to share it.

"Any reports?" There it was. When Mama asked for reports, she wanted to know if they had behaved at school. There was no need for privacy. What happened at school was common knowledge among the children.

A chorus of "no" erupted despite full mouths. It sounded more like grunts and groans than speech.

"Dickey Joe pushed me, and I fell down. But I didn't cry." Leon puffed his chest.

"Why'd he be doin' a thing like that?"

"I beat him at marbles, and he said I cheated."

"And?"

"And what?"

"Did ya cheat?"

From the expression on Leon's face, it was clear that his mother might as well have asked him if he would rather be a girl.

"Mama! I won fair and square, and he got mad and pushed me."

"You taunted him," Minerva said in a tone that dared Leon to contradict her. "It made him angry."

Leon said, "Mama says nobody makes us mad. When we get mad, it's 'cause we choose to be mad."

Mother said kindly, "That's right, Leon. But the Bible says 'blest are the peacemakers.' That means 'tis important to be good winners as well as good losers."

Leon studied his bread, "Yes, Mama."

"May we be excused, Mother?" Moe never said Mama. That was just for girls and little boys.

"Any reports?"

"Was a perfect angel today." Moe grinned at his mother. His sisters rolled their eyes, although it was true that Moe had not met with any trouble—and usually didn't, except at home.

Martha smiled. "Well, don't go lettin' that halo slip."

Alonzo laughed out right along with the rest of the children. Moe made an exaggerated show of securing a halo firmly on his head.

"Go on, now, 'fore I give you what for." Martha laughed at her fourteen-year-old son who stood taller than she was. Leon followed, licking his fingers.

"How about my little gals?" Mother said, looking at Leuna and Lola. "You got somethin' to share?"

"I won the spelling bee." Lola glowed. "Teacher gave me an apple."

Leuna grimaced. "I didn't win no bee," she said. "But Sally shared her oat cake with me, and I let her have half of my dried peaches."

"That's grand, child. I'm proud a both a you." Leuna brightened at that.

"Phoebe?" Martha asked.

"I outjumped Lizzie Straddling at double Dutch."

"And t'were you a good winner?"

"Well, I didn't taunt her, if that's what you mean. But Lizzie was none too happy about it. She's held the record until today."

"You certainly can't control how someone acts. You just do your best and let the consequence follow."

Mother turned her gaze to Mattie.

"We learned a new song at school," Mattie said. "'Red River Valley.'"

"Wonderful. You can teach the children, and we'll sing it together." Her mother smiled. "Anything else?"

Mattie looked down at her bread, knowing exactly what her mother was fishing for.

"Sister Clayton was the trouble," Phoebe said, coming to her sister's rescue. "She hit Mattie on the head with the yard stick again."

"What was you doin'?"

Mattie might not have been so nervous had she known that her mother didn't care much for Velma Clayton's methods of discipline and had tried to approach her on the subject years ago to no avail other than to make trouble for the younger Sevey children that followed.

"I wasn't *doing* anything." Mattie's green eyes danced indignantly. "Allie asked me a question about the assignment, and I was trying to help her."

"Did you done somethin' earlier to make her s'picious of you?"

Mattie looked at Phoebe who stared at her next bite of bread. "Probably," Mattie said quietly.

"You see. You go makin' a reputation for yourself and that gives cause for Sister Clayton to always be thinkin' the worst."

Mattie nodded.

"Yer teacher means well, Mattie."

"But Jesus wouldn't hit little children," Phoebe said, her mouth full.

"Jesus doesn't talk out of turn either," Minerva snapped.

"Thank you, Minerva." Mother's look made Minerva turn red. Mattie glanced at Phoebe and then at Nellie. They nearly erupted into giggles.

"Well, after all said and done, you oughta be grateful, Mattie."

Mattie looked respectfully at her mother. "Yes, Mama."

Martha allowed her smile to stretch her face. "Grateful that you got two whole days not to worry 'bout teachers. Heaven knows they's relieved they don't got to worry 'bout you."

This unleashed a wave of pent-up giggles. Even Minerva smiled. Mattie felt a rush of love for her mother and threw her arms around her ample middle, Mattie's fingers barely touching in the back. Somehow Mother always made things right.

Well, almost always.

***

Alonzo made it his duty to help Mattie lock Queenie's head between two sliding boards over the feed bin. With Queenie firmly in place with enough hay to keep her mind off the goings at her back, Mattie sat on a three-legged stool that Alonzo held in place and put a bucket between her knees. Queenie swished her tail. Mattie turned her head away just in time.

"Oh, no you don't," she said, swatting the cow's rump. "You be a good girl." Grabbing a teat in each hand, Mattie squeezed her long fingers and pulled. Alternating streams of milk hit the inside of the empty bucket, creating a hollow rhythmic beat interrupted only when she reached for another teat. As the bucket filled, the pitch changed. From the symphony around them, each milker could tell how close to full the other buckets were. It was always a race, although morning milking was usually silent, everyone still half asleep. At evening milking, the conversation flowed as freely as the milk, a harmonious time when Minerva wasn't trying to be important and Moe wasn't trying to be annoying. And almost every Friday, they had an extra hand.

Alonzo was solicitous at every opportunity, his attentions were a wee bit flattering and, at the same time, irritating to Mattie. What did he think she did the rest of the week when he wasn't around?

"Here, Mattie, let me get that for you." Alonzo traded his empty bucket for Mattie's full one, emptying it into the milk can before sitting down to another cow.

Mattie groaned, glad she couldn't see the others grinning at Alonzo's chivalry. Mattie's bucket modulated the halfway mark when a ruckus on the other side of her cow culminated with sharp gasps coming from Moe.

"Whoa! Whoa! Whoa!"

Mattie looked under the belly of her cow. The stool that Moe had been sitting on was on its side and the bucket had overturned. Several generations of cats lapped madly at the lake of milk disappearing quickly into a carpet of straw. And poor Moe, pinned on his back by the cow's hind leg, stared up at its switching tail directly over his head. She wasn't sure which would be worse—having the cow's full weight on Moe's stomach or it taking that moment to relieve itself. Not sure whether to save her own milk bucket or to save Moe, Mattie froze.

"Please don't." Moe coughed, trying to move the bovine hoof while it chewed its cud indifferently.

Almost instantly Alonzo appeared, grabbed the Jersey's leg above the hoof, and forced it up and away from Moe's stomach. Moe rolled sideways out of harm's way. Mattie looked at Alonzo with new respect. Her eyes went back to Moe. He was up on all fours, breathing hard.

Just then, a yellow stream issued from the cow pooling where Moe's head had been seconds before.

They all stared.

No one spoke.

The cow mooed soulfully.

Perhaps it was the ludicrousness of the moment or abject relief that what could have happened didn't—the stream being the lesser of the two evils—that great wheezing guffaws escaped from behind Mattie's hand. The others joined in, no one laughing harder than Moe.

1905

SEATED ON STRAIGHT-BACKED, HARD WOOD BENCHES, THE old folks watched as several generations swished around the bandstand.[1] Flaming torches cast their bouncing shadows against the backdrop of towering cottonwoods. Mattie had no idea what a beguiling picture she made standing alone on the periphery of the dance floor. Dark brown hair, held in place by two large combs, spilled thick and heavy down her back and curled slightly at the ends, complementing the delicate contour of her budding femininity. The dance was the last activity of what had been a day of raucous games and delicious food launched by a parade celebrating Pioneer Day. Grandmother Thomas, who had walked most of the distance from Illinois to Utah as a young girl, had been prominently displayed and cheered by the crowd as she rode with queenly dignity on the wagon seated beside Bill.

Mattie was named for her grandmother, but Mattie, who was all legs and arms and taller than most boys her age, was unlike seventy-year-old Martha Ann Thomas, who was soft-spoken, graceful, and stood no higher than a young child.

Grandmother's recent arrival from Salt Lake City had not been the only change in the Sevey family.[2] Leon had gone to live with George F. and Anna to be big brother to their young children. Last year, Tom had married Isabelle Johnson—a beauty from Chupe, and Minerva had married Ben Johnson, who lived in town. Lee was promised to Bessie White, their wedding date set for after harvest. And from the looks of things, Mattie thought with arched brow, watching Bill and Keturah skipping to a polka, Bill showed every indication of following suit.

"Hey, *little* sister." Almost sixteen, skinny, and just beginning his growth spurt, Moses Thatcher never missed an opportunity to point out his meager advantage. "I thought I would never get a chance to dance with you, sis."

Mattie smiled at Moe's changing voice that held a promise of rich bass tones. "I was just waiting for you especially."

Moe grinned at the deliberate fib and led his sister to the dance floor. Hand in hand, they whirled in a fast polka. To dance arm in arm was verboten. Such impropriety, even for brother and sister, would cause old Naomi Packer to convulse, unable to recover until she had duly reported their scandalous misdeed to their mother or, if necessary, the bishop.

The music, compliments of the Peter Wood family as it was at every function, made even those who weren't dancing tap their feet to the lively rhythm. The younger boys, William, Lehi, and John, fiddled furiously. Brother Wood, as if it were a natural appendage of his mouth, made beautiful sounds with the clarinet. Even Roberta, not yet five, clapped her hands, keeping impeccable rhythm while Lucy, the oldest daughter, provided flawless accompaniment on the piano. Enos Wood, Lucy's fifteen-year-old brother, dark eyed and olive skinned like his sister—and too cute for his own good— breathed skillfully into a harmonica.[3]

Ene (rhyming with bean, short for Enos) was and always would be the bossy, boisterous boy who had commandeered the hide-and-seek game years ago. Mattie had just turned ten, not long after father had died. Her mind drifted back to that night that the indomitable Ene Wood became more than just a name.

"He doesn't speak," Silvestre said. "He thunders."

"That's Ene Wood for you," Alonzo said.

Mattie felt hot indignation toward the outsider. "Who invited him?"

"I think he's sweet on Dell," Phoebe whispered, looking toward Dell Taylor.

"When Sister Wood comes to visit Sister Taylor, Ene comes to protect her.

Mattie said, "Protect who, Dell or Sister Wood?" The girls giggled.

Eleven-year-old Ene said, "You girls listening?"

Mattie glared. "We close our eyes, clog our ears, count to a hundred, and yell 'ready or not.'"

"Or in your case, you count to ten, ten times."

Dell Taylor giggled.

Mattie's temples throbbed. "How many sleepless nights did it take you to figure that one out?" It was something she had heard Minerva say. Annoyingly, this seemed to please the boy. He threw his head back and let go with a genuine guffaw that Mattie was sure had been heard clear to the border that separated the United States and Mexico at least a hundred miles away.

"You do have brains in the cute little head, after all." Ene grinned. "But don't sneeze. You'll lose them all."

There was no smile on Dell's face this time, and Alonzo didn't look any too happy either. He stepped forward with clenched fists as if saving Mattie from Saint George's dragon.

"I'm counting, Ene Wood, and you'd better start running," Alonzo said.

The group scattered.

Irritated at Alonzo's well-intentioned gesture that prevented her from proving herself to Ene, Mattie ducked behind a bush. Peering through the leaves, she fumed to find Ene Wood standing within a few feet of Alonzo. Although not cheating, it was risky. If the counter did not remember to disqualify anyone that stood that close to base, the bully boy would be home free the minute Alonzo yelled "ready or not!"

"Ninety-seven, ninety-eight . . ." Alonzo counted.

Say it! Mattie willed silently.

"Ninety-nine, one hundred."

Say it, Alonzo.

As if on cue, Alonzo hollered, "Anybody ten feet from base is it. Here I come, ready or not."

"What are you grinning at?" Moe asked, jerking Mattie back to the present. "You look like the cat that swallowed the mouse."

She wanted to laugh at Ene as she had that night, but she dared not look at him. Instead she looked at Moe and shrugged. "You're a good dancer."

Moe grinned and whirled his sister around the floor.

It was maddening how over the years Enos Wood played Romeo to every Juliet, assenting or not. From his usual vantage point in the band, Ene's brazen wink at every girl was welcomed with giggles or demure smiles. Loath to be numbered among his conquests, Mattie pointedly did not look toward the grandstand, counting herself lucky that she had only Ene's officious eye to avoid rather than the displeasure of his impertinent company.

His only redeeming qualities were his mother's beautiful flower gardens and, of course, the Wood family music. Otherwise, he was just a gun-packing, horse-racing, no-good flirt; a view wholeheartedly embraced by Alonzo, excepting the good looks of course.

The music ended, and Moe steered Mattie toward her friends, Allie Accord and Maudie Croft, who stood with Phoebe.[4] "Thanks for the dance, sis. You look pretty tonight. Too bad Alonzo isn't here to see you."

She blushed both for the compliment and the reference to her beau and usual escort who had gone with his family to El Paso. Moe surprised her on occasion with uncharacteristic sentimentality, and she loved him for it. His soft green eyes were much like her father's. Glancing at his square jaw, razor scraped as evidenced in three places, Mattie wondered what Moe would look like with a long white beard.

"You're welcome, Moses Thatcher."

While waiting for the next set, Mattie visited with the girls. A strand of hair waved across her face in a gentle caress. Turning her head expertly so the gentle breeze would force the rebellious lock back to its original place, she surreptitiously stole a glance at Ene.

To her utter mortification, he winked.

***

The August sun, still high in the sky, beat down unmercifully, bearable only in the shade of the cottonwoods that lined the banks of the three-foot-wide irrigation ditch that ran through town on the east side of the valley. Mattie sat rigid, her lips pursed. In her lap was a letter bearing the return address of Chuichupa. Behind her, the terrain ascended four or five hundred feet, scorched and barren. She stared, not seeing the peach orchard that sloped gently toward the road and home. She did not hear the gentle trickle of water or the soft hum of buzzing bees searching for ripe fruit from which they might rob a bit of nectar. The letter rose slightly with a breeze and then settled again. Mattie glanced at it but did not touch it.

When they had learned that Leon was "serious ill" with scarlet fever, Mother and Minerva left immediately for Chupe, leaving Grandmother Thomas in charge at home.

Martha's first letter showed her desperate struggle between hope and despair. "We hardly know how to pray for our dear Leon. I feer these unmerciful fevers will make livin' worse for him than dyin'," she wrote. Martha would know. Scarlet fever had left her deaf when she was a girl, and she was one of the lucky ones.

As much as Mattie loved Grandmother Thomas, she resented the older woman's harping on the power of prayer and the importance of faith and resented even more how she talked about Leon as if all that prayer would make him well. Mattie knew that prayer had no such power. As if to prove her right, Mama's second letter arrived. "Our dear little Leon has passed and now rests in the arms of his waiting mother."[5]

Mattie glanced at the letter. Old bitterness caught in her chest like a day-old biscuit swallowed whole. She squeezed her eyes shut and tried to block the picture of ten-year-old Leon laid out on a board. Almost, Mattie could smell the stench of carbolic acid.

𝟣𝟫𝟣𝟢

LUXURIATING IN THE PREDAWN BREEZE WAFTING THROUGH the open window, Mattie pulled her covers up to her chin. Although southern Arizona was known for its intolerable summer heat, Bisbee's seven-thousand-foot elevation in the heart of the Mule Mountains kept the thermometer hovering around highs of seventy-five and the lows one or two points either side of sixty.

Mattie lived with her sister Nellie and her husband, Parley McRae. After the quiet rural existence of Colonia Juárez, where horse and wagon was the only mode of transportation, the hustle and bustle of one of the largest cities between San Francisco and St. Louis was a shock. Bisbee proper, sandwiched between several canyons that spread like fingers on a hand, was a booming economy owing its success to copper mining and the El Paso/Southwestern Railway. Bisbee Junction was located south of Warren and Lowell— suburbs of Bisbee beyond the copper mine. For those who didn't own one of those newfangled motorcars, which was nearly everyone, the station was accessible via the streetcar that ran every thirty minutes beginning at 5:30 a.m. and ending at 2:30 the next morning. Several times a day a sharp staccato whistle bounced up the gorge, announcing the train's arrival and departure to Bisbee's general population of twenty-five thousand.

Lying between Tucson and the Mexican border, the place had been known as Mule Pass not so long ago, a watering hole for the

Indians and the cavalry who chased them. Hearing the story from Parley so many times, Mattie could repeat it word for word.

"Then one day," she said in a whisper, mimicking Parley's expressions and hand movements that never wavered from one telling to the next, "a smart lieutenant saw that he was surrounded by green rock and figured it to be copper. Word got out and an enterprising prospector staked a claim and named it Brewery Gulch. In a drunken stupor, the old boy lost his claim in a poker game. The fellow who won it sold it. The buyer?"

Here, Parley would pause dramatically before continuing.

"DeWitt Bisbee," he'd finally say, when he was sure he had the listener's attention. "And the rest is history." Mattie laughed Parley's laugh, albeit much quieter since all was still dark in the house.

From Mattie's window of the McCraes' rental in the low-income neighborhood, first light revealed the canyon that still went by Brewery Gulch. Not only did the water hole lose its innocence to the seedy community still boasting fifty saloons, it also was prostituted by criminals who fled to the safety of the lawless territory—some of them famous—or infamous as Parley would say: Crazy Horse Lill, Black Jack, Red Jean, Doc Holliday and his mistress, Kate Elder—now Mrs. Kate Cummings. Still a resident of Bisbee, the woman purported to be a paragon of rectitude, though rumor had it in some circles that she still maintained a brothel at Brewery Gulch.

Bisbee's seedy strip was off limits to the reputable, and Mattie would never dream of going there. Nevertheless, it was fascinating to have the Wild West mere blocks away.

Most of Bisbee's construction made its way up the sides of the canyons, including residences with a flight of never-ending steps for convenient access—if you could call climbing up a thousand steps convenient. The main businesses, all within walking distance, were located on the floor of the canyon or the next level, one flight of steps up: the opera house, the library, both hospitals, the Copper Queen Hotel, and Mattie's all-time favorite, Phelps Dodge Company Store where she had purchased her first ready-made dress. The Country Home Bar and Hermitage was one of these, a comfortable boarding house and public diner for those who could not afford the elegance of the Copper Queen. Mrs. Abernathy, owner and head cook, impressed with Mattie's qualifications and work ethic, offered her a job.[1]

Mattie soon learned that the "head cook" only made pies, two woman having been hired to bring the rest of the menu to life. If the stocky, rotund employer had a first name, Mattie didn't know it. She imagined it would be something like Implacable Constance, Gracious Theodosia, Virtuous Parthenia, or Imperial Victoria. Regardless of her name, Mrs. Abernathy tolerated no nonsense from customer and employee alike.

"The workday starts at five," she said. "We serve breakfast to our boarders and get them out the door by eight. By nine, you start upstairs. There are ten rooms. You will make beds, dust furniture, empty trash, give the rugs a good shake, and sweep out the room. Monday is washday. The washwoman will take care of that, but you do need to bring the linens down and put them in the cart on the back porch. Clean linens are in the closet at the end of the hall." Mrs. Abernathy waited a few seconds to see if Mattie had any questions. "As to the men's personal things, they see to that themselves."

Mattie nodded politely as Mrs. Abernathy continued.

"Monday, Wednesday, and Friday, you will clean the bathing room." Mattie was led to a spacious room, probably a bedroom once. Yellow starched curtains hung at the window. On one side of the room stood a porcelain, claw-foot tub, and a multicolored rag rug graced the floor by its side. The other wall supported a tabletop basin that sat on a wood pedestal just below a generous mirror in a gilded frame. And next to the basin was a contraption Mattie had only heard about.

"We call it a water closet," Mrs. Abernathy said in answer to Mattie's raised eyebrows. "Some of our guests still use the privy out back if the bathing room is occupied."

"Mother would love this," Mattie breathed.

Mrs. Abernathy smiled. "As a Hermitage employee, Mattie, you are welcome to use these facilities on your off hours."

"Hot water and everything?" Mattie asked unable to suppress her enthusiasm. Electricity was not new to Mattie, but indoor plumbing was a novelty. At Nellie's and Parley's house, it was cold water piped to the kitchen, good old chamber pots, outhouses, and Saturday night baths in steel tubs with water heated on the stove.

"Right from the tap." Mrs. Abernathy beamed. "Competition and all that."

Leaving the bathing room, Mattie paid close attention as her stout employer continued down an invisible checklist. The Hermitage was closed on Sunday except for the bar and light fare under the supervision of the bartender, a tall, redheaded, barrel-chested Swede named Frank, who doubled as the bouncer. Belle Kettering, the other housekeeper and kitchen assistant, took care of the lower floor. (Mrs. Abernathy failed to mention Belle was a blonde beauty with a drippy southern accent.) Bernice someone-or-other would help Mattie learn the ropes before taking her leave. Mattie would be expected to wait tables at the noon meal that was open to the public from twelve to two. Strict propriety was to be observed with the guests, who were mostly men. And could she start next Monday?

Mattie blinked, realizing a response was finally necessary. "A . . . yes. Monday is perfect."

"I expect you'll do splendidly." Mrs. Abernathy gave her a Theodosia smile. "We'll give it three months, see how you like us."

That was over a year ago. And Mattie liked the Country Home Bar and Hermitage just fine. Nevertheless, she did get a little homesick from time to time. And this was one of those times.

Sitting up in bed, she hugged her knees to her chest. Except for her mother, she missed Phoebe most.[2] Not the redhead Alonzo. He had pled ardently with her not to leave Mexico. A wave of guilt washed over her. Both families assumed they would marry. When Alonzo pressed Mattie to set a date, she was not so sure.

Shaking off the moment, she hurried to dress, unaware of the forthcoming events that would mark her much like a callus marks the hand. While painful in the getting, they would strengthen her character, broaden her perspective, and restore her faith—if they did not destroy her first.

***

A lone rider, whiskered and covered with days of trail dust, dismounted and tied his horse to a low bush. Stretching his stiff legs, he felt much older than his twenty-eight years. A lanky afternoon shadow belied his medium height and muscular form. He leaned heavily against a large, sun-baked rock, hot to the touch. Removing his Stetson, he passed a hand over his sweaty forehead. Under a cloudless sky of cobalt blue, he squinted against the brightness at the reddish hue of the Mule Mountains. As his eyes gazed further upward, Manzanita brush gradually gave way to juniper and oak. Tipping his canteen, he drank deeply, letting the tepid water run over his face and curly hair, washing away dirt-streaked perspiration, an extravagance he could afford now that he had only a few miles to go.

Necessitated by the need to disappear from Houston without witnesses to point a finger in his direction, the man had been forced to the inconvenience of horse instead of rail, surfacing where he could lose his past—Arizona Territory. Nobody asked questions, and Bisbee offered a life of respectability while within easy reach of the more appealing life of women, booze, and gambling. And Mexico was just a hop away when things went bad.

Replacing his Stetson, the man caught the movement of a leggy tarantula about four inches long. Fearlessly, it slinked to a stop in the traveler's shadow.

"These sun-scorched hills crawl with life forms not even God could love," he sneered. The conjecture applied more to him than it did to the fauna of the mountainous desert. But, as humanity is wont, the relevance was lost, especially on this man who grinned down at the hairy critter that was missing one of its legs. "You've seen some action, you old coot. I'll bet it was some female." Then, it occurred to him, that the "old coot" probably was female. "Femme fatale," he hissed, his handsome face turning hard. "Aren't you all?"

Visions of several dames came to mind, the latest, a Texas beauty. Ella Mae, just seventeen-years old, promised to love him forever. Just one mistake, and blind love turned into a full-scale inquisition.

"She won't try men's patience anymore," he said to the creature at his feet. "Heck, she won't do anything anymore." He laughed and took another gulp of water, swished it in his mouth, and spat it with perfect aim at the tarantula.

The arachnid reared up defiantly. Like its two-legged enemy, the ends, however dangerous or cruel, always justified the means. For the big spider, it was survival. For the man, it was amusement.

"Here's to femmes fatal," he said, pressing lightly on the body of his furry foe, enjoying its desperate struggle to escape. Finally, the killer slowly brought all his weight to bear, squeezing, cracking, crushing, until all grew still.

"You aren't too smart, madam," he said, his tone cool and even.

***

There was not room for two on the narrow staircase shoulder to shoulder, especially when one of the two was a broad-shouldered man. Furthermore, it was awkward being in close quarters with a handsome man Mattie did not know but with whom she was indirectly intimate by virtue of having to clean up after him and serve his meals. And awkwardness turned downright unsettling when faced with the likes of Carter Jackson, whom she referred to as "Room Number Ten," a mysterious and unsmiling man she guessed to be about thirty.

"Excuse me," she said, not quite meeting his eye.

Turning to one side, he tipped his Stetson. "Ma'am."

Mattie hurried down the stairs to the dining room, her face hot as red glowing coals in a wood-burning stove. Surely the man noticed—not that she wanted his notice.

Nor did she want Belle's notice, whose discerning eye missed nothing despite delivering a plate of biscuits to table four as Mattie entered the diner.

An older woman of twenty-one, Belle Kettering was experienced in more ways than Mattie cared to know. Although different as a domesticated mare and a free-roaming Mustang, an affection of sorts had sprung up between them.

"You're as red as cherries in snow, honey," she said, joining Mattie in the kitchen. "Some man try to smile you into somethin' funny?"

"He wasn't smiling," Mattie said. "And it wasn't funny."

"I do declare. You definitely are as spotless as today's wash." Belle's multisyllabic vernacular made a masterpiece out of the word *definitely*.

Mattie found it endearing that, mistaking innocence for naiveté, Belle was serious about protecting her friend from the wiles of the world—Belle-speak for men, with four times that many syllables.

"Depends on who's doing the wash, honey," Mattie said, grinning, mimicking Belle's southern drawl.

Belle laughed her signature raucous laugh. She would have continued Mattie's education had Mrs. Abernathy not ambled into the kitchen looking every bit like a Constance. What would the boss say if she knew that Mattie assigned monikers to her as circumstance demanded?

All business and efficiency, the older woman's magnificent chest rose and fell as if she had just reached the summit of a thousand steps. Tables were assigned by number, and each waitress was assigned certain tables, with Mrs. Abernathy helping with coffee refills and orders from the bar. During the lunch rush, the effort was a little too taxing for the owner of the Country Home Bar and Hermitage.

Mrs. Abernathy's soft brown eyes surveyed the younger women over wire-framed spectacles held in place by a little button nose. "Number seven and number ten want coffee," she puffed. "And that tweak of a man at number three is hollering his head off."

"Yes, ma'am," Belle and Mattie said in unison.

As Belle left the kitchen with coffee, she gave Mattie a look that said the interrupted conversation would continue later. She hummed "Let Me Call You Sweetheart," as she usually did when she thought Mattie obtuse to the intentions of the opposite sex.

Mattie rolled her eyes as she picked up the next order from the cook's counter.

"Whew," Mrs. Abernathy mopped perspiration from her round face. "I'm getting too old for this," she said, and then returned to the more sedate task of greeting and seating customers.

Nodding in Mrs. Abernathy's general direction, the cook said, "Age got nuttin' to do with it."

Guilty of thinking exactly the same thing, Mattie, balancing three plates, turned toward the dining room to hide her smile.

"Miss, miss." It was Mrs. Abernathy's "tweak of a man" dressed in a tailor-made suit. Mattie fervently wished Mrs. Abernathy had seated him in Belle's section. Since he had arrived he had grown to be more obnoxious than his usual self.

Mr. Big Stuff, as the waitresses referred to him, was a regular on the train between St. Louis and San Francisco. He condescended to take his meals at the Country Home Bar once or twice a month, although his quarters were at the Copper Queen, which he never failed to mention. What the vociferous gnome lacked in stature he compensated for in self-important bluster and a giant thirst that made his eyes a little too bright and his disposition a whole lot rude.

His kind was especially onerous during the lunch hour when the whole town of Bisbee turned out for a veritable feeding frenzy. Even visiting VIPs who could afford to stay at the Copper Queen found their way to Mrs. Abernathy's fresh pie, made daily. It irritated Mattie to have to take the brunt for variables over which she had no control: food too cold, service too slow, the wait too long—and all with a smile and polite apology as if it were her fault.

Generally, customers were good natured, but it only took one "tweak of a man" to ruin the day—or disconcerting customers like room number ten, who had just taken his seat in Belle's section. Mr. Jackson, never far removed from his Stetson, said little beyond please and thank you.

Then there was that fellow who came for lunch a couple of times a week. Mattie's eyes darted toward JT Jones, also seated in Belle's section, thankfully. Just looking at him left Mattie breathless. If she had to actually talk to him, she might faint. Belle certainly had no problems carrying on a conversation with any man, no matter how devastatingly handsome. And JT Jones was no exception.

"Miss," Mr. Irksome demanded, as if he expected Mattie to drop the three plates she carried and rush to his side. Mattie nodded in his direction, with what she hoped was a pleasant expression while thinking he was an imbecile.

"Here you go," Mattie said with a genuine smile for two miners with identical dusty hat lines across their foreheads.

"That pipsqueak give you any trouble, Miss Mattie, and we'll box his ears."

"That's a comfort, Karl." Mattie grinned, setting down steaming plates. Regulars since before she arrived in Bisbee, Lars and Karl eyed their food, practically smacking their lips: potatoes, gravy, thick steak, cooked rare, and a stack of buttermilk biscuits.

Karl picked up his fork almost before the plate had settled. "My stomach's not so sure my throat ain't been cut."

"Thank you, Miss Mattie. Not a moment too soon," said Lars.

"The third fellow better hurry up before his food grows cold," Mattie said, placing a third plate on the table.

Karl, the larger of the two winked at her. "You know I aim to eat 'em both."

Mattie grinned. The customary banter rarely varied. "Dare I ask if I can get you anything else?"

"This'll do, Miss Mattie, till Mrs. Abernathy's strawberry pie."

"Will that be one pie or one piece?"

"I'll see when I get there." The big man flashed a friendly, tobacco-stained smile.

"And the usual for you, Lars." Lars always finished his meal with coffee, apple pie, and a dollop of whipped cream on each.

"The usual," he said around a mouth full of steak.

"Girl! Girl!"

With a raised eyebrow, Karl nodded toward the man as if to ask if it was time to box his ears. Mattie laughed. "Not yet, Karl."

"Your feet stuck in cold tar?" the impudent little man sputtered. "I have a train to catch! Bring me another drink." It would be his third on top of whatever he had when he arrived. "And I want it today. I got a train to catch."

"Yes. You mentioned that." Mattie forced herself not to stomp her way to the bar.

Belle sidled up to her while she waited for Frank to pour the drink. "You want I should take care of him?"

"What would you do, throw this drink on his head?"

"Exactly." Belle chuckled.

Mattie sighed. "You know the rules. Customer is always right."

Belle arched an eyebrow. "Not always, honey." To Frank she said, "Keep an eye out."

"Always do, lass."

Mattie took the drink to the red-nosed customer.

"Anything else, sir?"

He leaned toward her conspiratorially. "I have a very comfortable room at the Copper Queen," he said in a low tone. "How about you meet me later."

Mattie wondered about the train he had to catch but refused to give any importance to so impudent a suggestion by the evil little troll who was grinning at her like a crocodile imagining his next meal.

"I have money," he said, misinterpreting her hesitation.

"Not nearly enough." The storm that raged in Mattie's chest might have blown itself into a harmless breeze had she turned on her heel in that instant. Her unfortunate hesitance due to politeness, however, unleashed a full-blown tempest.

Before Mattie could blink, the man grabbed her and pulled her down on his lap. Mattie's scream silenced the lunchtime din. The scene slowed frame by frame, like a movie projector stopping every second, allowing scrutiny for every sordid detail.

***

Mattie grabbed the iced beer and emptied it over the man's head. The carefully groomed comb-over suddenly hung in long wet strings curtaining his red face and exposing a large bald spot. Mattie stifled a giggle. The man's mouth moved in exaggerated motion with a string of words she hardly heard. He pushed. She stumbled. Strong, unseen arms prevented her from crashing into a table. Suddenly Karl appeared with Frank close on his heels, each grabbing an arm of the raging customer.

"This will cost you your job!" he screamed.

Mattie glanced at Mrs. Abernathy, who looked every bit like a

Victoria. She pointed toward the door with the dignity of a royal mandate. Frank and Karl complied, ushering the furious little man out the door.

Then, all was silent.

Every eye turned to Mattie. Mrs. Abernathy, now looking like a Theodosia, smiled her approval. Carl and Frank grinned. Belle winked, giving her thumbs up. Shockingly, even Carter Jackson saluted her stiffly, almost smiling. Two puzzled cooks stared from the kitchen door.

When slow motion finally gave way to real time, the diner had erupted in whistles and cheers and showed no intention of subsiding.

"I don't think it's going to stop until you acknowledge them," a deep voice said in her ear.

Mattie had forgotten the solid form still behind her. Turning, she gazed into deep pools of translucent blue that belonged to none other than JT Jones. She stepped back, afraid that she might fall helplessly into his arms and weep.

"What do I do?" she stammered.

He grinned. "Bow or something."

With aplomb she did not feel, she bowed to her approving audience with a melodramatic flourish, delighting Belle. Applause and whistles grew louder. Mattie mouthed her thanks to Frank and Karl. Slowly the diner resumed its normal lunchtime clamor as the patrons went back to the business of eating.

The large clock on the wall told Mattie that what seemed like forever, from start to finish, had taken no more than a few minutes. She let out a long breath as she turned to her protector. "Thank you," she said, not trusting her voice to say more as she fell once again under the spell of electric-blue eyes.

***

Mattie's indomitable spirit had excited the attention of one dangerous man from Texas. But Mattie was blissfully unaware. With lunchtime rush over, she allowed herself to be ushered to a quiet corner.

"James Thornton Jones, at your service."

Mattie held out her hand. "Martha Ann Wood." She winced inwardly. She never used her full name, not unless she had to.

"Pleased to meet you Martha Ann Wood. That was quite a performance."

"One I hope never to repeat," she said.

"If that little spit of a man had tried that in Brewery Gulch, he would have been shot on the spot."

"Mr. Jones, if I'd had a gun, I might just have done the job myself."

JT Jones laughed. "You are quite a lady, Martha Ann Wood."

"Please, just Mattie."

Mr. Jones grinned. "And I'm just JT."

JT didn't board at the Hermitage—a pity. Mattie liked that his hands were smooth, that his clothes didn't smell of farm, that he never put himself forward despite the effects of his beguiling smile and remarkable good looks, both of which he seemed completely unaware. From that time on, JT Jones was a regular, coming even on Saturday to eat a late lunch with Belle and Mattie.

***

With church and southern-fried chicken behind them on a late August afternoon, Mattie and Nellie sat on the porch, enjoying the cool relief from the last few hours spent in a hot kitchen. Nellie held one-year-old Naomi, who nodded sleepily. Wanting none of their women talk, Parley played solitaire in the front room where the cross-breeze blew in from the front door and out the back.

Mattie and her sister talked of home. Nellie was excited that they were just a little more than six months away from a place of their own in Lowell. The sisters dreamed of going to the opera one day, wishing they could go see *Naughty Marietta* playing for another week, although, technically, the performance was an operetta, not an opera, which was even better. Operettas weren't so heavy—and usually in English. Finally, the conversation got around to Mattie's work at the Hermitage.

"Did that troublemaking customer ever try to come back?" Nellie asked.

"Haven't seen him. Doesn't mean he won't someday." Mattie and Nellie laughed at the possibilities of next time, and the happy consequences of the first time.

"And your handsome banker?"[3]

Mattie turned to Nellie, doe-eyed. She knew the conversation would roll around to the one topic she wanted to discuss most. She just wasn't sure how Nellie was going to take it.

Nellie set her lemonade on the side table and shifted Naomi to the other shoulder. "From the long silence, I would say big sister is sticking her nose where it doesn't belong."

"Of course not," Mattie said, laughing. Where to start? Belle had made a play for JT until time proved that JT's preference was for Mattie. Belle was gracious about losing out to her friend. Even Mrs. Abernathy seemed pleased. The Saturday lunch date blossomed into an official courtship. Mattie requested that JT give her a little time to break the news to her sister and brother-in-law before he came calling.

Mattie said, "We still have lunch on Saturday, but . . . Well, it's not a threesome anymore. Belle says she 'ain't gonu be no third horse in the harness no more.'"

Nellie laughed. "That woman does have a way with words."

Mattie smiled. "Yes, she does."

"And how do you feel about JT's preference?"

"Oh, Nellie. I like him a lot. I think I love him."

"Do you and he have an understanding?"

Mattie took a deep breath. "Yes. Matter of fact, JT has declared himself and wants to come courting."

"My, this does sound serious indeed. Parley and I better have a look at this chap." Nellie laughed.

Mattie realized she had been holding her breath. "Oh, Nellie, really?"

"We insist. How about dinner next Sunday?

"Thank you, Nellie. I know you'll love JT."

"If you do, we do." Nellie smiled, rocking slowly, and patting her baby, each woman lost in her own thoughts. "Mattie," she said, "forgive me for asking, and you don't have to say anything if you don't want to, but . . . I always thought you intended to marry Alonzo Skousen."

Mattie absently shooed a mosquito. In the distance a dog barked. The red hills were beginning to cast their long shadows.

"I thought so too," she said in a low voice.

***

As he was wont to do, Room Number Ten looked as if he were going to speak. Mattie forced herself to meet his eye defiantly. He would scowl, shake his head, and walk away. The man was disquieting. There were things that didn't quite fit. For instance, Mattie expected him to be a slob, but Carter Jackson's room never failed to be immaculate. Perhaps he was trying to hide something. Nellie just laughed, saying that an immaculate man was the object of admiration, not suspicion. Even when Mattie confessed to her sister that she had caught Mr. Jackson watching her, Nellie brushed it off, sure that he was not the only man at the diner who watched her. Which was true, but other men didn't scowl in the process.

Wishing Carter Jackson had taken up residency in one of Belle's rooms, Mattie knocked tentatively at his door, waited for a moment, and knocked again. Hearing nothing, she let herself in leaving the door open—house rules—and began her Saturday cleaning. Unlike the other rooms, there was little sign of residency, except a smattering of wood shavings on the floor and a straight-back chair slightly askew where the occupant had pushed away from the secretary. Framed by a metal headboard, a patchwork quilt spread smooth over the mattress was tightly tucked in on each side, exposing the bedsprings. The secretary, armoire, and chest of drawers, all of solid pine, punctiliously concealed their contents. Yesterday's downpour left the streets a mucky mess, most of which Mattie was sure had been carelessly tracked into the Hermitage. But not room ten, where the occupant had obviously made an effort to clean his boots.

Mattie wondered if she was silly for distrusting a man who showed marks of good character, just because he rarely smiled and kept to himself. Mrs. Abernathy seemed to have no objections to the man, not that they discussed Mattie's objections. How could she when Mrs.

Abernathy referred to Carter Jackson as "that nice Mr. Jackson"?

Mattie brandished her broom, beginning under the secretary before returning the chair to its proper place. It never took long to put the finishing touches to number ten. A few passes under the bed produced a little dust and a newspaper cutting beginning to yellow. She scanned it before deciding whether to toss it or store it. A tingling sensation spread over her head like a little army of biting ants. She hated to think what Carter Jackson would do to her if he knew she had read this incriminating piece of evidence.

The hollow *clomp, clomp* of boots told Mattie someone was coming. Just as the paper floated to the floor, Mr. Carter stepped in. Seeing Mattie, he tipped his hat and said he'd come back later.

Only when he had left did Mattie realize she had been holding her breath. Quickly, she shoved the paper under the bed and finished sweeping.

"You look like you saw a ghost, Mattie." Belle's blue eyes showed real concern.

"Not now," Mattie whispered, glancing at Mrs. Abernathy. "Over lunch."

Belle scowled. She didn't want to join Mattie and JT for lunch. She'd just have to swallow her pride, for Mattie's sake.

Mattie gave her hands a thorough scrub and put on a clean white apron. Unlike a weekday, Saturday's demands were not enough to take her mind off her discovery. The knowledge of it burrowed in her chest. No matter how deeply she breathed, her lungs refused to fill. When Carter Jackson walked in and sat at one of her tables, she refused to look him in the eye for fear he would find her out.

Feigning thirst—for it wasn't thirst that made her mouth feel as dry as Bisbee's hills on a hot, windy day—Mattie went to the kitchen and lingered a few minutes over a glass of water while she demanded compliance of her insubordinate nerves.

Fixing a smile on her face, Mattie delivered an order to table five before speaking to the man with a white Stetson. "What can I get for you?" she asked, in what she hoped was a casual voice, her eyes focused on the pad of paper in her hand.

"Enchilada plate and an order of beef tacos, please."

"Anything else?"

Carter Jackson hesitated—too long.

Mattie looked up to see that he was scowling at her with an intensity that made her shiver. Her smile slipped. He knew. From down deep, Mattie commanded an unwavering, defiant gaze.

Suddenly, Carter Jackson shrugged and looked away. "You have any ice today?"

Mattie could only nod stupidly, sure that he had not been thinking of ice.

***

"A murderer?" Belle's whisper was harsh.

"Shhh!" Mattie looked around the near-empty diner. Frank smiled over at the three friends who were working their way through beef tacos, tamales, beans, and rice, although Mattie had made little progress.

JT laughed. "Because Jackson doesn't smile?"

"Jackson isn't even his real name. The paper clipping says its Jeremy Williams. He killed Ella Mae somebody and disappeared."

This time, she had JT's attention. "Was there a picture? ¨

"No picture."

"Then how do you know Jackson's the man?"

Mattie said, "I feel it. And today, he was acting more suspicious than usual. I think he suspects that I know."

The three of them stared at one another. Finally JT said, "I think I should report this to the sheriff. Let him handle it. And in the meantime, Mattie, be very careful."

***

"I'll see ya Monday." Belle held the door for Mattie as she stepped out into the September afternoon.

Mattie shaded her eyes against the sun. "Doing anything particular tonight?"

"Wish I could say yes, but looks like it's home alone for me if I'm lucky. Those gals I live with can get right wild."

Mattie smiled at the irony of Belle Kettering calling anyone wild. In the beginning, Belle had seemed as foreign to Mattie as legs on a snake. Under all that crass, Mattie had discovered that Belle, like herself, had fears and dreams, making her and Belle more alike than different.

On impulse, Mattie felt for the music box in her pocket. She had intended to give it to Belle earlier, but the excitement of the new light shed on Mr. Jackson pushed it right out of her mind.

"Belle, I hope you won't be embarrassed, but I have a little gift for you." Mattie held out a small silver box not much bigger than a pocket watch.

"Oh, Mattie, this must'a cost a month's earnin's."

"I have a confession. I got it at a much-reduced price because of the scratch on the underside. I hope you don't mind."

"I wouldn't have noticed if you hadn't pointed it out."

"Press that little latch." Mattie pointed to a small button.

Obediently, Belle complied. The top flipped open. A rendition of "Let Me Call You Sweetheart" trickled from the box one plinking note at a time.

Belle giggled. Then, her eyes softened and became misty. "This is the nicest thing anyone's done for me." She gave Mattie a quick hug. "Now I gotta get before I cry."

Those were the last words Mattie would ever hear Belle speak.

***

Her strangled body was found behind a saloon in Brewery Gulch early Sunday morning. There was no sign of a struggle, and no one had seen or heard a thing. Mattie and JT answered countless questions, as did Mrs. Abernathy and the boarders at the Hermitage. The two women who lived with Belle had been out for the night, but they swore that she'd been home with a pile of mending when they left with no intentions of going anywhere.

It was not the first murder in Brewery Gulch, but it was the first time it was someone Mattie knew. Mrs. Abernathy said Belle had no business wandering around Brewery Gulch, "which was no place for a proper young lady."

Though she was unwilling to admit it, Mattie's anger at Mrs. Abernathy's unkind judgment came partly because Mattie herself was torn between blaming Belle and defending her. Blame freed Mattie from vulnerability, assuring that such a thing could not happen to her if she did not invite it. But blame also bred guilt, like bitter bile, burning in her throat, and Mattie tried to bury it with passionate defense for her friend.

Mattie blamed Carter Jackson. He might have lured Belle to Brewery Gulch on some pretense or had just dumped her body after the fact. JT said he had reported Jackson to the sheriff. In the meantime, JT cautioned Mattie not to take chances after dark.

She was disappointed when she was unable to keep their Saturday lunch date. While she was deep into training Sally Goodall, the new housekeeper, JT had eaten alone. Before he left, he told Mattie he would have to cancel for the evening as well, something about work. They had planned to go to the fair, but truth be told, Mattie wasn't ready for lively entertainment. It had only been a week since the tragedy, and a quiet evening at home suited her.

Leaving the last of the cleanup to Mattie and Sally Goodall, Mrs. Abernathy ran her few errands. Mattie tried hard not to resent Belle's replacement so soon hired. Mrs. Abernathy had settled quickly on the drab, matronly widow. Mattie suspected that her boss purposefully chose someone who would not attract attention from the opposite sex. And scandal. Sally Goodall certainly fit that bill. She was a pleasant woman, but she did frown on JT, and that alone was a great mark against her.

The diner was empty. Mattie wiped down the tables and swept the floor. She nearly jumped out of her skin when she turned to see Carter Jackson standing close, holding her in a cold stare.

Mattie knew the routine and stared back. Only this time the man spoke.

"I know it's none of my business, Miss Wood, but I feel duty bound to warn you that you might be in great danger."

Mattie felt the blood drain from her face. She gripped a close-by chair for support. Was he threatening her?

Gathering up all the courage she could muster, she said, "Mr.

Jackson, I can assure you that I am perfectly aware of the dangers."

Carter Jackson's eyes grew angry. With an even voice, he said, "I don't think you do, Miss Wood." He turned and stomped out of the room.

"That man gives me the absolute shivers," Mattie said to Sally, who came lumbering out of the kitchen.

"He's a solemn one, that one." Sally followed Mattie with a broom.

"To call him solemn is being kind," Mattie said.

"He's come on hard times." Sally bent over her ample middle to push her sweepings onto a page of an old newspaper and then folded it carefully to keep the garbage from falling out.

"Hard times?" Mattie asked, annoyed that Sally would defend the man.

Sally stood, leaning heavily on the table for support, and headed for the kitchen with her unsavory parcel signaling an end to the conversation.

Taking the garbage to the back lot, Mattie emptied it on to a charred pile. Striking a match, she held it to a crumpled piece of paper until it lit. The fire flared, gained momentum, and then spewed black smoke. Deeply disturbed by her encounter with the man from room number ten, she watched until the blaze died to a smoldering heap.

Several times she ventured to talk to Mrs. Abernathy about Carter Jackson, but JT said it would only worry the woman, and what could she do. Even Nellie thought there was nothing to worry about since the sheriff had been apprised. Obviously, the clipping proved nothing. And why darken a man's reputation unnecessarily. Jackson or not, it would be a relief when Belle's murderer was finally behind bars.

***

Mattie returned to the kitchen, smelling of smoke. "I'll go have my bath," she said to Sally.

Sally nodded.

The grandfather clock on the far wall struck two just as a distant whistle announced the train's departure. *Right on time*, Mattie thought, disappearing down the long hall to the bath.

Reluctant to get down to the business of actually washing, she closed her eyes, luxuriating in the soothing water, letting her worries seep from her like whey through a cheesecloth. She was not sure why she opened her eyes. Perhaps it was a barely perceptible sound, or just a plain and simple premonition. From the tub, she had a direct view of the door. The door handle moved. At first she thought she imagined it. Then it moved again, slowly. Down and up. Mattie felt a chill run down her spine.

"Sally?" Mattie called. There was no answer, but there was a hint of a shadow lurking under the door.

"Occupied," Mattie called again, a little louder. Had she forgotten to flip the "occupied" sign on the door?

Then, as if some big animal was trying to butt its way in, the door shuddered, straining against the lock. Some one wanted in badly. *Jackson*, Mattie thought, *or whatever his real name is*. She imagined Sunday's headline: "Woman Drowned in Public Bath."

Mattie pulled the plug and the water started draining. She would not be that woman.

"Occupied!" It was not quite a scream but shrill enough that she hoped Sally Goodall would hear it.

Abruptly, the shadow receded. All was quiet.

Mattie dressed in record speed despite shaking hands and watery knees. Once dressed, she was afraid to open the door. What if he was standing just a few feet away? She would scream bloody murder, that's what she would do. Scream and claw her way, using every trick Moe had taught her.

Taking a deep breath, Mattie pulled the door open, letting it swing wide, steeling herself for the worst. The hall was empty. The sign on the door read "occupied."

Squaring her shoulders, Mattie made her way tenuously down the hall toward the kitchen, expecting any moment for a door to swing open disclosing a villain who might grab her and pull her into his dark den of iniquity. Or worse.

"Nervous as a polecat," she whispered, using her mother's

words. Rounding the corner, Mattie practically bumped into Mrs. Abernathy.

Mattie screamed. Mrs. Abernathy jumped.

"I'm sorry, Mrs. Abernathy. You startled me." Mattie hated being startled. To her mortification, tears gathered in her eyes.

Surveying Mattie's wet hair, her eyebrows rose high on her forehead. "Where's Sally?" House rule number twenty. No bathing without another woman on the premises.

"I left her in the kitchen."

"I'll have a word with her on Monday." Mrs. Abernathy smiled. "I saw that nice boy *friend* of yours."

Mattie blushed.

"My, but doesn't he have the nicest hair?" Mrs. Abernathy went on. "It seems such a waste to keep all those curls under a hat all the time."

Mattie agreed but was not about to admit it to Mrs. Abernathy.

"By the way, you will need to sparse up room number ten for a new customer. Mr. Jackson left on the two o'clock today and won't be back."

Mattie blinked. Carter Jackson on the two o'clock? Then who nearly broke down the bath door?

***

Unlocking the front door of the McRae house, Mattie found a note on the kitchen table.

> Gone to the fair. Won't be home until close to midnight. Naomi is at Clare's. If you and JT have no plans, come and join us. If you decide not to, leftover chicken is in the icebox.

Mattie smiled at the note. Nellie had become a very thoughtful sister. If she knew that Mattie would be sitting home alone, her older sister would have made a list of precautions: lock the windows, latch the screen doors, and after dark, shut and bolt the front and back doors. Still feeling a little spooked, Mattie had no inclination to argue. She latched both screen doors. She might have bolted the heavy wood doors as well, but it had been an unusually warm September day, and the cross breeze felt nice.

Over a supper of cold chicken, potato salad, and bowl of sug-ared peaches, Mattie mulled over the newly acquired information from Mrs. Abernathy, who unlike Sally Goodall, had no qualms in sharing all she knew about poor Mr. Jackson. Mrs. Abernathy's nar-ration was interrupted at frequent intervals to swear to the truth of it, assuring Mattie that it was not gossip when information was true and repeated out of deep concern and admiration for another.

"That Carter Jackson, why, he's an upstanding man, I'll swear to that," Mrs. Abernathy said. "He's got a heart of gold, bless him, spending his free time, and heaven knows there is precious little of that, visiting sick children at the Copper Queen Hospital. It's true, Mattie. And him looking to all the world so unfriendly. Why, Mrs. Charleston, a particular friend of mine, you've met her, claimed that he has excellent whittling skills and could whittle just about any toy a child could wish for."

That explained the wood shavings on the floor, Mattie thought.

"Why, he delights those little folk so unfortunate as to have to keep to a hospital bed—which makes what I'm about to tell you very sad, and every word is truth.

"Mr. Jackson's youngest boy, there are two, has been ill for some time and the doctor suggested a drier climate. That's the very reason Mr. Jackson came to Bisbee, to get established so he could bring his wife and sons here to live, to help his poor ailing boy. It was nothing more than a race against time."

At this point Mrs. Abernathy clucked her tongue and wiped her eyes.

"I can barely take the grief, and I'm sure you'll feel the same, Mattie dear, when I tell you that Mr. Jackson lost the race."

"Are you telling me his little boy died?" Mattie asked.

Mrs. Abernathy nodded. "He got word this very morning. That's why he left. Can you imagine, after all his kindness to children, and then to lose his own."

As it had then, shame washed over Mattie again as she sat over her dinner. She had unkindly suspected the poor man to be a killer, trying to get into her bath when he had been miles away on a train headed for Houston to bury his young son. If it weren't so tragic, it might be funny.

So that was why the man was so solemn. It was worry. No wonder the sheriff didn't arrest him. He was not guilty.

JT was going to laugh at her. He was right. Just because the man carried a news piece didn't make him guilty. Why did Mr. Jackson carry that yellowed newspaper clipping? What did he know? He might have told her had she given him the chance. He did say she was in danger. Mattie shivered, remembering the incident in the bathing room. She should have told Mrs. Abernathy. Monday, she would tell her. Tomorrow, she would tell JT. And tonight, she would confide in Nellie and Parley.

Robbed of her appetite, Mattie carried her few dishes to the sink and retired to the secretary in the front room to write letters. She thought of Alonzo. More guilt. She would write him about JT. She owed him that.

Night came too early, turning the sky to inky blue. There would be no yellow moon pushing up from behind the hills for several more hours. A chorus of crickets chirped and an intermittent breeze rushed through the screen door. The light of a single kerosene lamp cast Mattie's shadow on the wall. Only the rhythmic ticking of the clock interrupted the silence. It was almost nine when she looked appreciably at the stack of letters and flexed her fingers. Phoebe and Tom would be surprised to hear from her. One more letter. Alonzo's letter, and she would call it a night.

A knock at the door cut through the silence. Mattie jumped. *Nellie and Parley must have cut their evening short*, she thought. "I'm coming!" Mattie called, pushing back her chair.

"It's just me, Matt, JT."

Mattie flushed with pleasure. "JT." His smile, beguiling as ever, left her breathless.

"I saw Mr. and Mrs. McRae at the fair. Thought you might like some company," JT rushed on. "We could visit on the porch."

Just like him. She smiled to herself. *So proper.* Mattie stepped out onto the porch. JT pulled her close. Not very tall for a man, she stood eye-to-eye, acutely aware of the warmth of his arms around her. Even in the darkness she imagined flecked lines in his eyes like miniature sticks floating in pools of ice tea. Her heart thumped against her chest with such force she wondered if JT would notice. Mattie resisted brushing a lock of curly hair off his forehead where it always flopped lazily, unless he was wearing his Stetson. He leaned forward and kissed her. Mattie wanted to sing.

"I have something for you," JT whispered. He pulled a small object from his pocket. Mattie heard a click and the familiar tune, "Let Me Call You Sweetheart."

A tingle started at the base of her neck, crawling up into her scalp. Was this the same music box she had given Belle? And if it was, how had JT come to have it? Mrs. Abernathy said she had seen JT this afternoon. Where had she seen him? Was JT the man at the bath door? Was he the danger that Mr. Jackson warned her about? Was JT Belle's murderer?

Her heart screamed no. But what did she know about James Thornton Jones? That he stopped her heart with his blue eyes and lovely smile. That he was polite? That she thought she wanted to marry him?

If Mattie had been so far wrong about Carter Jackson, it was conceivable that she was just as wrong about James Thornton Jones.

She panicked.

"You don't like it," JT accused, suddenly angry. Mattie had never seen him angry. And she couldn't see it now, but it she could feel it in his grip and hear it in his voice.

Mattie willed herself to melt into his arms. "Oh, yes, thank you. It's lovely. I like it very much." It was the truth. That's why she had bought it for Belle. Mattie forced herself to give JT a convincing kiss.

"That's more like it," he said, his voice thick. His kisses were demanding, hungry, and almost angry. "I love you, Mattie. Marry me. Marry me tonight."

"Tonight? JT, my sister would never forgive me. Besides, who would marry us at this hour?" She had to get away. She had to look at the bottom of the music box even though Mattie knew in her heart it would not make a bit of difference in her new convictions. "Can't we wait until tomorrow, at least?"

JT dropped his arms. "Let's take a walk, Mattie. The moon will be up in an hour. We can go up the steps and watch it from there."

"I'd like that," Mattie said. "If you'll wait a minute, I'll get a wrap." Willing herself not to hurry, Mattie reached the screen door, stepped in, and latched it behind her. Next to the kerosene lamp, with shaking fingers, she examined the little music box to find a little, familiar scratch.

"Didn't count on you knowing about the music box," JT drawled.

Mattie jumped. "You killed Belle."

JT answered with a sinister sneer.

"And Ella Mae?" Mattie's voice was barely a whisper.

"Pretty smart, aren't you?" His handsome face turned hard. "Femme fatal, my dear. You all are."

Mattie shuddered. She found herself unable to think of him as JT, if that was even his name.

"You never talked to the sheriff." It was not a question.

JT laughed a raucous laugh.

"And I think Carter Jackson suspected you."

"You are dangerous," JT said smoothly. "I should have taken care of you in the bath."

The confession did not shock Mattie. It all fit. Why hadn't she seen it before?

Suddenly, JT yanked at the screen door, nearly pulling the latch free. Another yank and it would give. Mattie slammed the heavy door, sliding the bolt into place. Her thoughts swirled. "The back door!" She rushed toward the kitchen. Remembering that she had not checked the bedroom windows, Mattie prayed that the latch on kitchen screen door would hold if JT reached it before she did.

Sure enough, her bedroom window was open. Pushing it firmly down, she fumbled at the lock, willing her shaking hands to obey. The lock finally slipped into place just as a shadowy figure appeared.

Mattie raced to Nellie's room. "Please, let the window be locked," she whispered. It was.

She ran to the kitchen. JT's muscular form was just a dark spot huddled on the other side of door. Somehow he had cut the screen and was reaching for the latch.

Mattie slammed the heavy wood door with vicious force and threw the draw-bolt into place. JT's blasphemous howl told her she had smashed his hand.

The door handle moved fiercely. Mattie stepped away, both hands pressed against her thudding chest and watched as JT battered the door as he had that afternoon in the bathing room. This door, being much heavier, gave no indication that it might suddenly swing open.

Paralyzed with fear, tears streaming down her cheeks, Mattie closed her eyes, willing herself to think.

"Mattie, Mattie." JT purred through his pain. "Open the door, and we'll talk about this calmly."

"Like you talked to Belle?"

"Come with me, Mattie. We'll go away together."

"Your only chance is to run for it, James Jones, or whatever your name is."

"I plan to do just that." JT laughed.

"Parley will be here any minute."

"That won't work, Mattie. I talked to him before I came, remember?"

"If anything happens to me, they'll know it was you." Mattie's voice was shrill.

"On the contrary, my virtuous little friend," said the smug voice on the other side of the door. "I bade them an early good night and checked into my room. Even my renter thinks I'm sound asleep."

Mattie shuddered. She knew his scheme would work—had worked. His renter verified that JT had retired early the night that Belle was killed. Mattie silently begged God to bring Parley and Nellie home.

Cold sweat ran down her back. She would make a run for it. But where? The neighbors? She dashed the thought as soon as it came. If they were home, they would have come by now, having heard her scream.

Could she outrun JT the mile to the boarding house? Would anyone be there on the night of the county fair? It was a long shot. Did she dare risk it? Did she have a choice?

Mattie went noiselessly to the front door and opened it. She screamed when a looming shadow appeared before her. Again, the latch on the screen door saved her, but just.

"You can't get away, Mattie." JT's chuckle on the other side of the door froze her blood.

"Dear God, help me," she breathed. Mattie realized that she had been praying nonstop almost since JT arrived. Would God hear her after so many years? "Heavenly Father," Mattie whispered. "Help me know what to do. I don't have a lot of time, God," she added. "I need help now."

On impulse, Mattie extinguished the lamp, plunging herself into darkness. She placed the lamp out of easy reach, then made her way in the dark. *Hide*, she thought, heading for the bedroom. No, that would be a trap. The space between the secretary and the wall close to the door. Her hiding place allowed a vantage point beyond the table to a shadowy view of the sitting room, the hall entrance, and the doorway leading from the kitchen. The only possible way in was through a window. Shattered glass would reveal his position and she could make a break for it. She hoped it would not come to that.

The ticking clock had turned ominous, counting the minutes until . . . what? She ached for what could have been between her and JT—and repulsed by what was. Nausea threatened like a rising storm. Mattie swallowed. Who would believe that James Jones was mad? Mr. Jackson would believe. It seemed like days instead of hours that she had practically defied poor Carter Jackson to speak to her. Sure now of what he meant to have said, she wondered if she would have believed him.

No. Even now, she hardly believed.

Mattie strained at the night sounds and started at every creak, trying to identify each one. Were they human made, or was it the cooling house? Mattie stared into the darkness until her eyes ached. JT could be on top of her before she saw him. The moon would be up in a little while. But if she could see him, he could see her.

Mattie's cramped legs screamed for relief. She needed to shift her position. Casting a precautionary glance in the direction of the hall and then toward the kitchen door, studying the shadows, she froze. He was there. She knew it.

Dear God... The words clamored in her head so loud she feared JT would hear. Not daring to breath, Mattie wondered how he had gotten in.

Straining, if she didn't look right at it, she could made out a dark form, black on black, moving toward the hall, halting each time the floor creaked. She counted the duration of each pause before the shadow slinked forward. Two hundred. Choking back her terror, she rehearsed a plan. Once he disappeared around the corner, she would count to three hundred, giving him ample time to be well inside a bedroom before she made a break for the front door.

Avoid the chair, throw the bolt, open the door, and run. Mattie rehearsed it mentally over and over with a nagging apprehension that she was forgetting something.

The inky form disappeared. Mattie counted. When she reached three hundred, she rose, gave her legs a moment to adjust, hurried to the door, successfully circumventing the chair, and threw the bolt. In the deathly silence, it sounded like thunder. Jerking the door open, she ran, slamming into the locked screen. The impact threw her backward and broke the latch. Mattie scrambled to her feet. JT caught her, twisting her arm painfully behind her.

"If you scream, I'll kill you," he hissed.

Mattie groaned.

JT pushed the big door shut with his foot. "Latch it," he commanded, pushing Mattie close enough to reach the lock.

Mattie slid the bolt into place. In one quick move, JT turned her around, letting go of her arm to grip her neck and shove her against the door with brutal force, kissing her hard.

Remembering JT's injured hand at his side, Mattie reached for it, wrenching it with all her might while at the same time biting his lip and raising her knee, connecting with his soft places. Groaning, he loosened his grip. Mattie pushed with all her strength and ran.

The moon had finally risen.

Heading for the back door, she tasted blood, whether his or hers, she could not tell. Just as she reached for the bolt, JT caught a handful of her skirt and jerked her toward him, but not before she had taken hold of a solid log from the wood box that sat beside the door.

Using the momentum, Mattie swung hard at her attacker's head. There was a sickening thud and JT staggered backward.

In an instant, Mattie was at the front door. This time, she had better get away. If JT caught her again, she wouldn't live to tell the story.

She wrestled the bolt, threw the door open and shot past the screen door right into a dark form that suddenly loomed before her. Mattie screamed. Just before succumbing to black oblivion, she wondered where they would find her body.

***

It had been two months, and still Mattie felt as cold and barren as the winter scene visible through the parlor window. She longed to be whole, to be warm, to laugh.

To pray.

She had helped decorate the Christmas tree, but she didn't see it. She didn't smell the fruitcakes baking in the oven nor did she hear Nellie humming "Silent Night" as she worked in the kitchen.

The wooden rocking chair creaked a monotonous rhythm as Mattie hugged Naomi[4] to her, as if the child's pure innocence could somehow seep into her own soul. It was a precarious lifeline that Mattie clung to, a tenuous thread between sanity and madness.

The child shifted her head and settled in against Mattie's chest. Holding the baby was about all Mattie had done—all she wanted to do. If nightmares and flashbacks were not terror enough, Mattie's waking hours were full of the same, hard as she tried to force her mind elsewhere—a difficult task when just breathing took almost more concentration than she could muster. To no avail, she closed her eyes against the memory of that night. She stroked Naomi's downy hair, a gesture that would keep her in the present no matter where her thoughts might take her.

A telegram from Houston, compliments of Carter Jackson, had reported that James Thornton Jones had left a long blood trail from Arizona to South Carolina with an equally long list of aliases, William James Dyer being his real name.[5] He died when he set fire to a building. Had he not been trying to get away from the sheriff, he might have escaped, as did hundreds of others who fled the blaze that destroyed Brewery Gulch and part of Main Street.[6] His accidental death saved him from his imminent hanging.

Maybe death was too good for a murderer. Sometimes she wondered if death for her would be sweeter than the living hell she suffered. She felt cheap. And guilty—guilty that Belle had died instead of her. Why hadn't she seen what Sally Goodall had seen? What Mr. Jackson had seen? Why had God allowed this madman to shatter their lives?

It was Parley she had crashed into that terrible night. Bouncing off him, she hit her head. He claimed that the porch railings suffered more damage than she had. But she could see how shaken he was. After all, Parley witnessed her terror; heard her defeated scream; and held her thrashing arms when she was just the other side of consciousness.

Nellie hovered, pleading with Mattie to eat, rushing to her bedside when nightmares came, holding her when the tears wouldn't stop, following behind her picking up the pieces as Mattie tried to help with chores. Neither Nellie nor Parley dared to leave her home alone. The night at the fair was the last time they had gone out together.

And Mrs. Abernathy? The woman's accusations against Belle caused Mattie to feel that she too stood accused. She could hardly blame the old lady. How could Mrs. Abernathy think Mattie guiltless when Mattie herself could not? Although kind and willing for Mattie to keep her job, Mattie could not face a public who would shake their heads behind her back in compassionate accusation.

Mattie no longer referred to the man as JT. If she had to call him anything it was Mr. Dyer. A sociopathic stranger. How could anyone so handsome, so beguiling, so kind, be so evil?

And fool her so completely.

Mattie hugged Naomi. As if feeling her need, the baby stirred, her warm hand coming to rest on Mattie's neck just under her chin.

Mattie sighed a long, heavy sigh. Having the ordeal behind her was not the same as having *put* the ordeal behind her. That was another matter. A matter that seemed impossible.

A tear trickled down her cheek. "Dear God," she whispered into Naomi's downy hair. "Will I never find peace?" Mattie would not have called it a prayer. What came next surprised her.

"Ask for that which is right and ye shall receive. Knock, and it shall be opened unto you."

Long since buried, the scriptures came to her mind as if spoken. "Ask and ye shall receive." She was afraid to ask, having tried it once to no avail.

"Ask for that which is right." The silent voice came again.

"Ask for what is right?" Mattie pondered that for a minute. "Wasn't it right that I wanted Father to live? And Leon?"

The answer came. "Of course it was a good thing. But it was not the best thing."

Mattie thought on that. Father was an old man, had lived a good life. She realized that for him, death was a gift. And Leon? Young Leon? Was death a gift for him?

"My ways are not your ways." The unspoken thought pierced her heart. Perhaps "things that are right" are not always understood, Mattie reasoned. Perhaps "right" means being in harmony with God's will, not forcing God to my will.

"Dear Father, what is thy will?"

"Ask and ye shall receive." Not exactly the spoken word, but again, it might as well have been.

Mattie thought of that night, when she had prayed desperately that God tell her what to do. Thoughts came to her so naturally; she didn't even realize He was answering her prayers almost before she could get the words out. Would He answer her now?

Her heart quickened. She was afraid. She didn't think she would survive if God turned His back on her now. She would not survive on her own.

She stopped rocking. "Heavenly Father, I can't do this by myself, and I don't know how much longer I can last. I need thee. Help me. Please."

The warmth began as a small spot in Mattie's heart as if she were finally absorbing virtue from the sweet purity of the baby in her arms. But Mattie knew differently. The feeling spread through her like a warm, thawing breeze. She hardly breathed for fear she would stem the flow. Tears streamed down her cheeks, tears that come from gratitude. God was listening.

"Thank you, Father," she said.

It was a start.

1911

"MONTEREY!" THE CONDUCTOR SANG. GATHERING HER carpetbag and reticule, Mattie stepped onto the platform. She pulled her cloak close against the chill of the February drizzle.

Having been only three years old when Mahala married and left home, Mattie knew her sister and her husband only from their wedding picture, not to mention that seventeen years had changed Mattie some too. How would they ever find each other among the melee of travel-worn passengers, petulant children, and matronly females, crying their hellos on each other's ample shoulders?

A well-dressed man in a smart fedora worn at a rakish tilt waved and shouted ineffectually over the hiss and belching of the train as he made his way toward her. Not until he removed his hat did Mattie recognize Alonzo Skousen.[1]

No longer the farm boy who had come to visit her in Bisbee less than six months ago, Alonzo was decidedly elegant. His reddish-blond hair, cropped short, was slicked back in the popular style and glistened with pomade. His suit was tailor made and set off by a striped, stiff-collared shirt and a wide conservative tie. She could only stare. He looked marvelous.

Alonzo grinned. She thought he might kiss her. "Hello, Mattie." He smelled faintly of apples—the pomade, of course.

"I . . . I was expecting Mahala, or . . . or Bennett."

"They wanted us to have time alone." While Alonzo's face pinked up at this, his twinkling green eyes clearly showed he agreed. The handkerchief in Mattie's hand suddenly twisted into a messy knot.

"Besides," Alonzo said, "your sister figured I'd have no trouble recognizing you."

Mattie smiled. "I certainly didn't recognize you. At least, not at first."

"I gathered as much." Alonzo grinned again. "You haven't even said hello."

Mattie laughed, her face turning a flustered shade of red. Perhaps because she wanted to make up for her rudeness, or perhaps because Alonzo had once more become her dear friend, Mattie threw her arms around his neck, giving him a chaste kiss on the cheek. "It is good to see you, Alonzo. You look devastatingly handsome."

Alonzo laughed. "That's even better than hello." Placing Mattie's arm in his, they made their way, along with the cluster of humanity, to the luggage car. While he went in search of a porter, he left her guarding a heavy trunk and several boxes Nellie had packed with Mattie's bridal trousseau and gifts for the Hancocks.

Mattie took stock of her surroundings. The depot had little to recommend it other than an expansive backdrop of a cerulean sea. To the east, nature's benevolence was evidenced by the same verdant magnificence she had witnessed since arriving in California.

Missing the desolate desert portion of the costal state, having passed through it at night, Mattie had awakened to scenic splendor. Bright orange poppies accenting an endless carpet of green gliding by her window reluctantly submitted to imposing pines that snaked wildly as if trying to escape the trunks that held them fast. Now and then, patches of blue ocean peeped through the canopy of cypress trees that stood like large umbrellas against the misty sky. The passing pageant included acres of plowed earth ready for planting. Large, rustic signs identified each farm and the produce it would grow: rhubarb, strawberry, artichoke—whatever artichokes were. Mattie wondered if Mrs. Abernathy had ever heard of artichokes. Surely Parley had. He knew everything.

A sudden tinge of homesickness poked at her. She missed

Naomi and baby Jack and the peace they inevitably brought to her troubled heart. Mattie smiled, remembering Naomi's first step and the day she tried to say "Aunt Mattie." It came out "Ammie." But not for long. By the time Jack[2] made his appearance, Naomi was speaking in clear paragraphs.

Paradoxically, Jack's birth marked the one-year anniversary of that terrible night. Mattie chose to make Jack's arrival another sweet gift of healing instead of a dark memory. September became a month of celebration of new beginnings, another step toward wholeness.

Mattie quailed at the emptiness of life without children. Her eyes misted at the very thought. One day, she would have her own sweet babies, God willing, to provide harmony in her life when perverse happenstance intruded upon her. With marriage on the horizon, that day was not far off. In the meantime, Mattie hoped the Hancock children would fill the void as had Naomi and Jack.

Mattie had been surprised when Alonzo showed up on her doorstep, not long after Jack was born, en route to California. His successful contractor/builder uncle from Monterey had offered him a job. By the end of the week, Alonzo, ardent as ever, officially proposed marriage.

And Mattie had accepted.

She had nearly refused Alonzo. Gratitude at any level is not love. But Mattie knew she could trust him at face value, no surprises, despite his little show of elegance just now, which had left her quite speechless with admiration—in truth, a little more than admiration.

Mattie smiled. Perhaps it was best, after all, that Alonzo came to meet her alone.

***

As if her thoughts had summoned him, her faithful friend and future husband appeared followed by the biggest man Mattie had ever seen. His black arms resembled tree trunks, and he stood about as tall.

"Sorry it took so long," Alonzo said. He motioned to the porter. "This trunk and these boxes. I've got a car over there.

Taking her arm, Alonzo shepherded Mattie off the platform to one of several Model Ts in the parking area, all black.

"This is yours?" Mattie asked.

"Nah. It belongs to Bennett. He insisted I bring it, and I didn't put up much of an argument."

While Alonzo handed Mattie into the motorcar, the porter hefted her trunk and the boxes effortlessly into the boot. Mattie thanked the man. Alonzo tipped him. The porter offered to crank the starter. Alonzo gave him another dime, and he crawled under the steering wheel. After a few false starts and a couple of pops, the motor finally rumbled to an agitated idle. Saluting his thanks to the porter, Alonzo patted the dash. "Ocean View, Old Boy."

Old Boy was the name of one of Skousen's horses that pulled their wagon ever since Mattie could remember. She laughed. The car jerked forward, and they were on their way to the Hancock residence.

"This is the first time I've ever ridden in one of these things."

Alonzo grinned. "For all their technology, they aren't much more comfortable than Pa's buckboard and sure as heck not much faster, at least not in this traffic."

Mattie giggled. "I was thinking the same thing."

Alonzo gave her a knowing look that said they often thought the same thing. How could they not? They were cut from the same big piece of cowhide.

***

Alonzo stopped in front of a modest, two-story home perched on a shelf just above the beach. Contrasting with purple bougainvillea and shocking pink roses, the house gleamed white even on a gray day. Tall, white lilies bowed their heavy heads while peach-colored gladiolus were forced to attention by long stakes. The green lawn, interrupted by a flagstone walk, spread from the white fence toward the back on both sides of the house. A matronly woman looking very much like Mattie's mother came flying through the ornately carved door and down the flagstone walk as fast as her round, fleshy body allowed.

"Mattie, Mattie, you're here. Welcome to Hancock's cove." The woman gave Mattie a fierce hug, breaking the embrace to look at her. "You're here," Mahala said again, brushing away a tear. "And look at you. A beauty, for Pete's sake." Mahala hugged her.

Alonzo's envious grin was not lost on Mattie. She promised herself that the next time she was wrapped in his arms, she would reward him with more than a quick kiss on the cheek.

***

Mattie and Mahala quickly fell into comfortable camaraderie. And though more formal than Parley, Bennett was welcoming and accommodating. Mattie immediately loved the children, and they fell in love with her.

Seven-year-old Emil reminded Mattie of Leon at that age, full of adventure and imagination. However, Emil had no impertinent brother to teach him how to torment a younger sister. He did, nevertheless, rebel against Aileen's self-appointed authority. At age five, she was an exacting supervisor. Emil's lack of cooperation matched that of Melva's, who at one and a half, answered to no one. Yet she was quickly forgiven, being the baby with a charming smile.[3] Only three-year-old Floyd remained faithfully subservient to Aileen's dominion.

When Mattie was not with Alonzo, and the older children were in school and the younger ones were napping, she and Mahala made wedding plans. Mattie made her notes and lists as fast as Mahala dictated: trim the rose bushes; weed the gladiolus; paint the fence; make appointment with the bishop; shop for white shoes, white stockings, and white lace for the girls' dresses. Pick up wedding dress and new hat. Make appointment with photographer.

Mattie could readily see that Aileen came by her supervisory talents rightfully. Not that she objected to any of Mahala's well-meant plans, except for the money—and that objection was overruled thanks to Bennett's generosity and Alonzo's newfound wealth. Mattie was grateful not to have to decide anything, grateful not to have to think at all. It made it easier to ignore the subtle uneasiness that kept whispering that she was on a fast train to disaster.

Needing to make life stand still, if just for a moment, Mattie hazarded a visit to the beach, as she was wont to do more and more often as of late. Watching the living water meander in and meander out gave her a chance to catch her breath. She never dared to stay long. The solitude was too dangerous.

Staring out to sea, Mattie concentrated on her wedding dress: a simple, high-neck, long sleeve, straight pattern cut from white satin that required nearly a hundred tiny pearl-like buttons down the back. Cleverly romantic, Alonzo gave her a pair of pearl studs with a matching drop pearl necklace from pearls they had dug out of real clams. It was he who suggested a garden wedding, weather permitting. The only thing Mattie knew about their honeymoon was that San Francisco was the destination. The rest was a great surprise.

Their wedding day was set for on April 23 at one o'clock in the afternoon, giving the fog a chance to burn off. What Mahala called a light lunch would be served after the ceremony: shrimp cocktail, crab legs, clam chowder, rolls, olives, sweet pickles, wedding cake, mints, nuts, orange frappé, and anything else that she might think of.

Mattie learned from her sister, who learned from her ladies garden club, that *frappé* was an exotic French word loosely meaning crushed ice, or in this case, a frothy drink made from slushy orange juice and vanilla ice cream.

The exotic menu was a far cry from the homespun food that a farm girl was used to: potato salad, cabbage slaw, corn on the cob, fried chicken, lemonade, apple cider, bread and cheese, a big pot of pinto beans, and good solid fruitcake.

The short guest list included the Hancocks, Uncle Jeb Skousen and family, and a few of Alonzo's friends and coworkers, along with Mahala's closest friends who were helping in the kitchen.

Mattie pulled her shawl close and let out a long sigh. Marriage had always seemed so far in the future, like the end of the world. Suddenly, it loomed just weeks away.

***

With its name so boldly and beautifully displayed on all sides, surely propriety demanded the mention of the streetcar's name in its entirety—which she did for the first few days. Finally capitulating, Mattie joined the rest of Monterey in calling the Pacific Grove Street Car, Incorporated, simply "the Car."

On this afternoon, it was the Car that deposited Mattie and Alonzo at the zoo. After an unhurried inspection of all the exhibitions, Alonzo insisted that Mattie pose for a picture. That's how she found herself tenuously, and regrettably, perched on the back of a giant ostrich, taking instructions from a dictatorial photographer with sun-leathered skin while Alonzo grinned at the three of them.

Mattie was the essence of femininity in a wide straw hat, smartly decorated with silk flowers and held in place by a matching silk sash that tied in a charming bow under her delicate, square jaw.

"Take the reins in your right hand and let your left hand drape at your side," the man commanded. The reins wrapped around the ostrich's beak and fastened at the back of its head, draping down its feathery back within easy reach. Mattie thought it absurd that a bird, no matter how large, wore an apparatus reserved for horses.

The photographer motioned impatiently to his left. "That's too far back. Move your hand forward about six inches. Now look this way. Good. Good. That's it. Hold."

The essence of femininity rolled her eyes at the photographer. Alonzo guffawed.

Mattie smiled.

The photographer snapped the picture.

***

Cannery Row, lined with small white cabins, was a tourist attraction now.

"Japanese fishermen used the cabins," Alonzo explained, "back when there were fish to be had in the bay." Mattie noted on a plaque that fishermen had come not only from Japan but also from Switzerland and Russia.

On a warm, late-March day, with shoes in hand, Alonzo and

Mattie strolled on the beach. Water swirled around their ankles, washing the sand from between their toes. A rogue wave surprised them, wetting Mattie's hemline and Alonzo's pant cuffs. They made their way to an outcrop of rocks where they sat until their clothes dried. Mattie gazed as perpetual blue water disappeared over a humped horizon.

"I pretend that if I could get out to that line where the ocean meets the sky, I could look over the edge into a great abyss."

Alonzo laughed. "You're about five hundred years too late."

"What if the ocean tipped toward us, like an enormous pan of water?" Mattie shuddered. She had never seen a body of water larger than the streams and ponds back home. The sheer magnitude of the ocean gave rise to a hint of panic.

"It does sometimes, I hear, or something like it. They call it a tidal wave."

"How awful!" Alonzo's claim might not have been so disconcerting if the Hancocks didn't live on the beach. To keep her mind from going down that unsettling path, she focused on nature's beautiful display.

Unlike the calm, lapping water at Hancock's cove, these waves crashed against the reef, sending a spray high into the air. White sailboats dotted the blue ocean, their soft wakes drawing lines in the water. Moored a little closer to shore, three clippers bobbed on graceful swells. A spider web of ropes zigzagged between three bare masts like tall crosses one in front of the other. Low-flying pelicans skimmed the ocean's rippling surface for unwary prey. Seagulls landed gracefully on the beach, bravely demanding morsels from their observers.

"From the position of the sun and the sounds of my growling stomach," Alonzo said, "I'd say its lunchtime."

"Now that you mention it," Mattie said. "I'm famished." Carrying their shoes, they walked barefooted to the wharf. No longer used as a dock, it now housed a cluster of stores and eateries. They settled at a table that looked out toward the ocean.

"Let me guess." Alonzo pretended to think. "You'll have clam chowder."

"How perceptive." Mattie grinned. Before coming to California, she had never heard of clam chowder. Now she ordered it at every opportunity.[4] Even Mahala humored her, serving it once a week and insisting that it also be added to the wedding menu.

Although a panoramic view could be seen from any point in Monterey, Mattie liked the wharf best. Water lapping on all sides, she felt as if she became part of the scene, no longer a mere observer. It filled her with a sense of awe and contentment that masqueraded easily as love. Sitting close so that her shoulder touched Alonzo's, Mattie ate her hot clam chowder.

The day's tour finally ended late afternoon at Pebble Beach. They dug for clams to take home to Mahala and found a few shells to add to the children's collection, and Alonzo showed off his crab walk, reminding Mattie of their childhood when Moe and Alonzo would do the craziest things just for a laugh.

The clouds gathered and a westerly storm brewed as the crimson sun descended slowly into a molten sea of gold. Mattie and Alonzo huddled close while they watched the spectacle that never ceased to leave Mattie in awe.

Inexorably, the swells advanced, rising high, then bowing low, crashing on the beach, and causing the ground to shudder. The wave roiled inland, growing increasingly shallow, finally slowing to a stop, only to recede and begin again.

Mattie never tired of the phenomenon and didn't want to leave until the last of the sun disappeared below the horizon. She leaned in a little closer to Alonzo, who put his arm around her to shield her against the bracing breeze.

"I love you," Alonzo said, bringing Mattie's hand to his lips. "I've loved you ever since I can remember."

Mattie laughed. "Ever since you can remember? You were eight. A little boy doesn't know anything about love."

"Well, I know now." Alonzo's kiss flowed through her like a warm illusory stream. She let it drown the disquiet that lay deep in her heart. *Just homesickness*, she thought.

She might have exhumed the truth to see it for what it really was except for overwhelming distractions: Alonzo's dauntless devotion, sightseeing, Mahala's endless, effervescent wedding planning—not to mention the enchanting children.

Soon, the undeniable truth would be brought to the surface, forcing Mattie to choose between heartache and heartbreak.

***

The first day of April did not begin well. Mattie awoke shivering and aching all over. Her throat felt as raw as one of Bennett's famous steaks. Even her hair hurt. Sunshine streamed through the window. The brass, twin-bell clock beside her bed showed one o'clock. Mattie gasped and bolted from bed. Alonzo was supposed to come for her at eleven.

The room began to spin. Mattie fell back into bed and groaned.

"Well, sleepyhead." It was Mahala looking as cheery as Mattie felt rotten. She touched Mattie's forehead. "You feel hot, sister mine."

"Alonzo . . ."

"He's come and gone." Mahala chuckled. "He looked stricken when I told him you were sick."

"It's just a cold."

"Yes, my dear, just a cold with a raging fever. I brought you eggnog to help get the medicine down." Mahala produced a teaspoon and a bottle filled with white powder labeled ASPIRIN. "This newfangled stuff sure works its miracles. You'll feel much better in a half hour or so, just in time for chicken noodle soup. Sorry it's not clam chowder at the wharf." Mahala came at her with a teaspoon of powder.

Mattie choked it down with eggnog working her way to the last drop. She shuddered.

As if the cosmos itself shuddered in her behalf, the Hancocks' house began bumping and grinding, making the four-poster bed dance like a puppet on strings.

"Earthquake!" Mahala screamed. "The children!"

Mattie had never experienced an earthquake, but she knew the drill. Grab a child and get out. Muster area, front gate.[5]

Forgetting her aches, Mattie headed for the children's room.

Mahala made it through the door on the second try. It took Mattie three times. Pictures fell off the wall. Drawers flew open. The hanging lights swung back and forth. Downstairs, Mattie could hear glass break. Finally arriving at the children's room, she went for Melva, who was deep into a nap. Mahala had Floyd. Emil was at school. "Aileen?" Mattie managed to ask.

"Backyard," Mahala said. "She'll know what to do." The two women didn't dare try walking down the stairs. Sitting, they practically slid to the bottom expecting any moment for the staircase to collapse. Shattered vases and china strewn the floor. That's when Mattie realized she didn't have shoes on. They had just scrambled through the front door when the tumult quivered to a stop. The rumbling roar that had announced the quake just seconds before it hit, like an approaching train, had grown louder, louder, and suddenly clamored off into the distance.

Mattie and Mahala stared at each other in the blessed silence.

"Somebody shaked my bed," Floyd said in a sleepy voice.

"Yes, baby," Mahala said. "I know."

They found Aileen, wide eyed and pale, waiting at the gate. "It was an earthquake, Mommy," she said in a quavering voice. "It made me fall down. But I did what we practiced."

Mattie hugged her stoic niece, wishing there were someone who could do the same for her. She hoped to never experience another earthquake as long as she lived. In defiance, a short-lived aftershock gave the earth a good hard shake. Mattie held her breath, but an enduring upheaval never came.

What did come was worse.

***

While the sisters were still at the gate conferring with neighbors who had congregated, Bennett arrived, visible relief flooding his face to see that his home and family were safe. Alonzo arrived minutes after Bennett with news that the school was not harmed and that Emil was fine.

The men insisted the women wait until after a quick structural inspection before returning to the house—Alonzo's forte. Mattie, still in her robe, and wishing for a place to lie down, went with Mahala and the children to the backyard. The view opened up to a long beach that stretched fifty yards to meet the great expanse of various hues of blue, depending on the day. Hancock's Cove, the family's name for it, was about thirty feet straight down, almost from the property line.

Something was terribly wrong. Sinister. The water had receded leaving yards of exposed beach beyond the usual breakers. Mattie's eye followed it out. The surf, high, dark, and angry, surged forward to fill the void.

"Mahala!" Mattie's tone brought her sister immediately to her side. They watched as the sea kept coming, coursing over rock where they hunted starfish and tormented crabs, sluicing over dry sand up the rise where Mattie loved to sit and watch the waves, finally colliding with the embankment. As if angered by the impediment, the current spewed and swirled, higher and higher until it seemed the whole ocean filled the cove and threatened to spill into the Hancocks' yard.

Mattie stifled a scream. The great sea bowl had tipped.

***

The wave never breached the precipice, but just in case, Bennett had loaded his Model T with food and bedding, and they all had gone to higher ground.

By the time Emil arrived home from school, the water had crested. Emil, wide eyed and excited, thought the whole affair nothing but a grand adventure. His only objection was that the school hadn't crumbled to the ground or been washed away by the big wave.

The lower elevations in town suffered most: collapsed buildings, broken underground pipes, damaged bridges, flooded crops, grounded boats, a collapsed wharf. Mattie grew weak at the thought of being numbered among the casualties, which would surely have been the case if she had kept her date with Alonzo. How lucky they were to lose only china and glassware when some had lost their homes. And lives.

Now, added to her nightmares of being chased in the dark by a madman, she dreamed of giant waves that crashed against the house like a great frothy beast trying to reach its helpless prey, pummeling the flimsy wall of glass, the only hope that stood between her and certain death.

In her waking hours, the radio blared destruction and the rising death toll, which was as frightful as the disaster itself. So much devastation in so little time left Mattie feeling powerless, vulnerable, and introspective.

***

Alonzo was occupied from sunrise to sunset as a public servant in his construction company, Bennett as a volunteer. There was little to do outside of helping Mahala with the children—little to do and too much time to do it.

Time is a fickle friend at best—a callous enemy at worst.

It might fly blissfully by, leaving one breathless, wondering if by some quirk of the universe, one is shortchanged the usual twenty-four hours. Under such happy circumstances, one suffers few occasions of keeping one's own company, hardly aware of reality that is securely ensconced under layers of frivolity.

Or time might stand still. Silent. Stripped of blessed distraction, forcing dangerous forays into the deep places of the heart where lies neglected truth. Second by interminable second, painful revelation after revelation, truth is exposed in all its candor, for good or for bad, for happy or for sad.

The past few weeks, time had been Mattie's foe. Days passed like years. The nights fared worse. She had not slept well. Without Alonzo's constant presence to muddy the waters, just two days before her wedding day, Mattie came to heartbreaking realization.

She could not marry Alonzo.

Did she love him? He was kind, thoughtful, dependable, and handsome. He offered her the world. He was a dear, loyal friend. And yes, she did love him, in a way. How could one not love a life-long friend? But love was hardly the issue. She had been living with a growing impression that marrying Alonzo was a mistake. She prayed to know why, but on that note, the Lord chose to remain silent.

How does one tell a fiancé that he is not right for her? Or more accurately, that she is not right for him? She couldn't do it. She couldn't bear to hurt him. Then there was Mahala and Bennett and Alonzo's aunt and uncle. What would they think? How could she disappoint them?

Apprehension pressed upon Mattie like a hot humid day when the air is almost palpable, making it hard to breathe. At first light, she slipped away to the beach to her favorite knoll, one of the few things that had survived the flood, although slightly rearranged. Visits to the cove, which had been under twenty feet of water not so long ago, was not without anxiety, but she had to get away, to breathe. To think. To decide.

Mattie let her gaze flow out to sea. A clipper in full regalia, like an elegant swan in tranquil water, inched toward the horizon and slipped over the edge, the last vestiges of billowing white bidding her a final good-bye.

Soaring over the shimmering emptiness, seagulls gloated in screeching cacophony under fingers of gold and purple that reached toward the distant cerulean contour that met the brightening sky.

Just beyond the pounding surf, a piece of driftwood floated help-lessly, trapped in an unyielding current that was too strong to oppose.

A cool, pungent breeze touched Mattie's wet cheek. It was decided. Like the driftwood, it was useless to fight the current. Tomorrow, just as the sun reached its zenith, she would agree to be Mrs. Alonzo Skousen.

***

Brimming with one-sided chatter, Mahala dressed Mattie, secur-ing the dainty, satin-covered buttons one by one that began at the nape of Mattie's neck and ended well below her waist. Mattie stared at nothing in particular, unaware of her sister's anxious glances.

Guests were already gathering in the garden—Alonzo's aunt and uncle and family, a few friends, and the Hancocks. Mahala patted Mattie on the back at the last button.

"You'll do," she said, turning Mattie toward the mirror, addressing her reflection. Mattie forced a smile but was unable to hold her sister's gaze.

"You're awfully quiet," Mahala said.

"Nerves." Mattie didn't trust her voice with more than that.

"Mattie." Mahala's voice was gentle. "No one could be more pleased than I am to have a sister settled in California. But I would gladly sacrifice that joy if it meant your happiness."

Mattie looked her sister in the eye. "Am I so transparent?"

"For a while now. Bennett told me to stay out of it." Mahala smiled. "I think you better tell me what's going on."

The sudden sympathy crumpled Mattie's face. Great heaving sobs wracked her body. In Mahala's tender embrace, Mattie choked out the truth.[6]

"Your motives are noble, sister dear, but living a lie won't get easier," Mahala said.

Mattie hiccupped.

Mahala continued, "And a lie will hurt Alonzo a lot longer and more deeply than the truth."

"I didn't think of it that way." Mattie sniffed. "But how can I tell him?"

"How can you not?"

"He's going to hate me," Mattie whispered.

"Shall I have Bennett bring him?"

Mattie hesitated, but just for a second. "I'll wait on the beach." Reaching up, she removed her veil. "Help me out of this dress." Mahala once again began the arduous task of negotiating all the tiny buttons.

***

Attired in his black suit and good shoes, Alonzo's ponderous pace told Mattie what she could not yet see in his face. Her heart ached. When Alonzo reached her, he enfolded her in his embrace. Sobs shook her again.

"I can't, Alonzo. I just can't."

"I don't understand," Alonzo said in a hoarse whisper. The pain in his voice was no less than the pain that made her heart feel as if it might explode through the wall of flesh and bone.

"I hardly understand myself," she choked.

"Do you need more time, Mattie? Have I rushed you?"

Mattie's laugh was low and mournful. "Dear, sweet Alonzo. I've had a lifetime to think about marrying you. It never felt completely right, but one gets caught up with expectations, excitement, gratitude, and even joy. Alonzo, you've brought me great joy. You are a dear, dear friend. You're a wonderful man. I know you'll be a wonderful husband."

Alonzo's face paled as he waited for the inevitable "but."

"I'm not right for you, Alonzo."

"We can work things out."

"I want to go home, to Mexico."

"Mexico?"

"It pulls me. I belong there. Marrying me would cheat you of a wife who shares your dreams. It's a road that can only end in tears."

Alonzo's jaw muscles worked furiously. He turned his head to hide the pooling tears. *A road that has ended in tears*, she thought. She had seen him weep only once. He was twelve. His faithful dog, Scab, developed an unfortunate taste for chickens and had to be put down. And Alonzo had insisted on being the one to do it.

"Forgive me," Mattie whispered in a quavery voice.

"There's nothing to forgive. Have a good life, Mattie." He turned and walked away.

Mattie elicited a low, visceral groan, hugging herself, as if trying to keep her very bowels from spilling out into the sand.

***

"It's insane, you going back to Mexico, Mattie." Parley was adamant. "I tell you, Mexico is going to be a hotbed for a long time, and I mean right there in your backyard."

Nothing had changed in Bisbee, not even Parley. Nellie was a bit put out as well that Mattie was leaving the next day. With Alonzo's last farewell three days behind her, Mattie refused to be deterred. Mexico beckoned like a mother hen to a frightened chick.

"Don Terraza is powerful," Mattie said. "He'll protect us. Heavens to Betsy, he owns half the state of Chihuahua."

"Don't be silly," Parley said. "Terraza's properties have been confiscated by the new government, his big haciendas, everything. He's had to hightail it out of the country just like President Díaz."[6]

"Mattie, please don't go," Nellie pleaded. "We'll send for Grandmother and Mother and the girls, and you can all live here until things settle down."

Mattie smiled. "Lola's new husband might object to his wife leaving so soon after the wedding." Mattie wondered if Lola had struggled over her decision to marry.

Nellie grinned. "I keep forgetting our baby sister is married, but you know what I mean, Mattie. Please stay. We missed you so much. The children love you."

"I can come back," Mattie said to appease them.

"Maybe," Parley huffed. "You never know how things will go when war breaks out."

The political unrest in Mexico was overshadowed by Mattie's need to be home, and the next day found her boarding the train bidding another tearful farewell to another sister.

On the long silent trip, even the anticipation of home did not dim the picture of Alonzo's ashen face.

When she had returned to the house, all plans for a wedding had been neatly cleaned up, and the guests had disappeared along with Alonzo. Hoping to save him from humiliation, Mattie begged Mahala to rumor it around that Alonzo had called off the wedding.

Why did life have to hurt so much?

She remembered a summer day about a year after father had died. She was eleven. A splinter had lodged deep in her foot. When infection threatened, Mattie's mother insisted on digging it out. No matter how loud she wailed, how fervently she begged, mother did not stop until her foot was splinter free. When the wound was clean and bandaged, mother had hugged her and kissed her on the forehead.

"I know it hurt like the dickens, child. I hated doin' it to you. But what's pain if it saves your foot?"

Mattie sighed. Perhaps, given time, this moment too would be nothing but a distant memory well worth the suffering for having saved the foot.

***

The whole family had come to Juárez to welcome her home. They loved her tales of the flying contraption they called an airplane. She didn't tell them that Alonzo had taken her to Dominguez Airfield to watch it fly. Moe and Phoebe were the only ones who didn't treat her with kid gloves, and she was grateful. They made her laugh.

Now it was just Moe, Mama, and Leuna again, and Grandmother, of course. At eighty-two, Grandmother Thomas heard nothing, saw nothing, and said little that was intelligible.

Minerva and Lola lived in Juárez, an easy hour walk from the ranch, quicker on horseback. Mattie tried to visit at least once a week. Minerva's new baby girl was the main draw. It seemed that her sisters' children never failed to bring solace to her soul. The only thing worse than not being married was not having children, and perhaps she had lost her chance at both. Perhaps God intended that she never marry. Never have children.

Mattie stiffened at this. "If that be the case, Lord, just strike me dead now." And then she wondered how Alonzo was doing. Despite her best efforts, every thought eventually came back to Alonzo.

Adjusting to her old life and the euphoria of being home allowed little room for melancholy. Grandmother's condition had come as a shock and Mexico's primitiveness took some getting used to: no indoor baths or commodes; no electricity, at least not at the ranch; only horse and wagon for transportation, and the train of course. But home was home. Although smiling did not come easily, not yet, she was happy to be home, especially this time of year.

The cottonwoods were dressed in new foliage. Well-irrigated fields boasted thriving shoots—maize, corn, alfalfa, and green chili. The valley was awash with canopies of pink and white blossoms promising Red Delicious apples and Clingstone peaches.

Mattie remembered her girlhood fantasy of getting married in May. April was just as beautiful as May in California—Alonzo had pointed out.

And there he was again. Would it ever be otherwise?

***

May gave way to June, and Mattie began to feel as if she had never left home, except for intruding thoughts of Alonzo. And the nightmares, of course. She loved the solitude of the ranch, a far cry from the hustle and bustle of Monterey. She felt safe—no earthquakes, no tidal waves—even with the threat of war.

In Colonia Guadalupe, the water master was killed, and in Colonia Díaz, two men and a woman had been murdered, all Mormon Anglos.[7] Tragedy was not easily brushed aside. Incessant talk commanded every discussion. But it did not shake her security. More than likely, political unrest would end before it erupted into full-fledged war.

On the first day of July, Mattie felt strong enough to organize a box that had come with her from California, a box she had pushed under her bed instead of burning with the trash.

Her resolve faltered when she picked up a photo. From the back of that ridiculous ostrich, her own image looked out at her with a beguiling smile. A rush of sadness, like that awful tidal wave, surged upon her heart, swelling, swirling, until it spilled from her eyes. She put the picture away. She couldn't do it, not yet. She missed Alonzo; she missed Mahala, Bennett, and the children. She missed clam chowder.

Was she crying over clam chowder? Mattie actually smiled, promising herself to share the humor with her mother, who would laugh her head off.

For now, the picture went back into the box, back under the bed. Maybe another time.

***

"Is Grandmother awake?" Mattie asked.

"I jest put'er in the rocker." Martha stirred the water until the sugar dissolved. "Want lemonade?"

"Thanks." The cool drink traced a line from her throat to her stomach.

Martha smiled, handing her daughter another glass of lemonade. "See if you can get your grandmother to drink this."

Mattie found Grandmother, head back, eyes closed, her breathing more raspy than yesterday. Martha Thomas opened her eyes and looked vacantly at her granddaughter. A gray hue tinted Grandmother's pale face. *It will not be long before she passes to the other side,* Mattie thought, disturbed that she envied her grandmother just a little.

"I have something to make you perky." Mattie humored and cajoled until Grandmother finished the entire glass of lemonade. As she often did, while caressing her grandmother's hand, Mattie prattled on about Nellie, Parley, Mahala, Bennett, and the children, describing the beauty of the ocean compared to the dry mountains of Bisbee, carefully pushing away the memories of Mr. Dyer, which still made her shudder, and memories of Alonzo, which still tormented her heart. The older woman always stared through Mattie, giving no evidence that she heard. Then they sat in silence, Mattie still holding her grandmother's hand.

"Why does God let you linger so long?" Mattie whispered, more to herself.

"You always were a good one to ask why, child."

Mattie blinked, startled at Grandmother's sudden lucidity. Martha Thomas shut her eyes again.

"Grandmother?" Mattie whispered.

The elderly woman did not answer, and Mattie had about decided the whole thing was imagined when Grandmother's eyes came open again. She smiled at Mattie. "I suppose it's natural, wondering and struggling with what we can't understand, but asking God why He does things is like asking why it storms. It just does. It's life. But anger and blame bring only bitterness, child. Trust God. He's always there. You just have to invite Him in." Exhausted with the effort, she relaxed against the chair, her eyes shut.

Mattie closed her gaping mouth. This woman had not spoken two intelligible words together in months.

"I love you, girl."

"I love you too, Grandmother," Mattie choked out.

When Martha Thomas next opened her eyes, Mattie knew that her grandmother had slipped back into obscurity.

Grandmother Thomas died the next day, a stroke. Mattie's mother explained that it was quite natural for the mind to momentarily awaken. It had happened a few times before. But to Mattie, it was a miraculous gift.

Bringing out Grandmother's gift for close scrutiny, Mattie came to realize that while she had come a long way in trusting God enough not to blame Him for the storms, she was still trying to weather the difficult times alone. No wonder she couldn't get past Alonzo. The sorrow. The guilt. The whys.

"Forgive me, Heavenly Father," Mattie prayed. Familiar, sweet peace permeated throughout her like a bowl of warm chicken soup. Inviting God's comfort and solace seemed to be a lesson she had to learn over and over again.

"Thank you," she offered.

Next, she prayed for Alonzo.

***

Ruthie Greer slowly turned within the circle of women holding a quilt.

"It's beautiful," gushed Maudie, who was now Mrs. Walton Hall.

"I'm certainly glad it's finished." Allie Spilsbury rubbed her rough fingertips. "One more needle prick and my hands will be rough as Lem's."

"You don't fool me with your complaining, Allie Spilsbury. You're bragging on that husband of yours." Dell Whiting laughed.

Ruthie Greer folded the quilt. "I'll certainly brag on my husband, if he ever finds me." Her peaches-and-cream complexion turned the same color red as her hair.

Maudie threw back her head of curly brown hair and laughed. "I think he has, if Moe Sevey has anything to say about it."

"Well, he doesn't," Ruthie said, a sharp edge to her voice. Her hand flew to her mouth as she threw Mattie an apologetic glance. The room grew uncomfortably quiet waiting for Mattie's reaction. Mattie's only concern was for Moe's heart, but how could she, of all people, point a finger at Ruthie for breaking it.

Allie broke the silence. "We can't all be as daring as you, Maudie Croft," she said, using her friend's maiden name, her blue eyes dancing with teasing pleasantness. "Walton finally proposed to you because even climbing trees, he couldn't get away from you."

Her brown eyes twinkling, Maudie grinned. Even the casual observer could see that Walton adored his spirited wife. She threw a ball of yarn that caught Allie on her narrow shoulder. "Whatever it takes, girl. That's my motto."

The group of childhood friends burst into laughter, dissolving the tension in the room. A moment later, when no one was paying attention, Mattie mouthed a "thank you" across the room to Allie.

***

"Quilt's done, food's gone, sun is setting." Dell Whiting, tall and willowy, turned to Mattie.

Mattie envied Dell's blonde hair that shined like pulled taffy. "Must be time to go home." Dell lived a quarter of mile from Sevey's ranch, and she and Mattie had come to town that afternoon, both on the same old sorrel.

The western sky was a dusky blue when they said their good-byes, and by the time they reached the river crossing, a full moon crested the eastern hills. Horse and riders cast comical shadows as they plodded down the dirt road in the cool July evening. Dell and Mattie appeared as a single blob with two heads swaying rhythmically on what looked like a camel—a tired, long-necked camel.[8] The wraithlike image floated over rock and bush, growing short, suddenly growing long again, and then disappearing altogether when they passed under a leafy cottonwood. Mattie and Dell sang in soft harmony to pass the time. From the dark shadows, an unidentifiable sound silenced them.

Dell pulled the horse up short. "Did you hear that?" she whispered.

Mattie strained fore and aft, her neck tingling. She whispered, "Is it ahead of us or behind us?" Their horse whinnied. In the distance, another horse answered.

"Do you suppose that horse has a rider?" Mattie whispered.

"My guess is yes."

"Maybe we should hide in the river brush."

"If it's not too late," Dell said softly, nudging her horse off the road.

Then came a sound they both recognized as human—a loud, baritone guffaw.

"Doesn't sound dangerous." Mattie couldn't help but smile. It was a contagious laugh, one that seemed vaguely familiar.

Dell giggled and turned the horse back to the road. "All depends on your definition of dangerous."

"Someone you know, I surmise."

"Yes, but I thought Ene was in El Paso, which he very well may be. I've never known anyone with such a loud voice, especially his laugh."

"You're not talking about Enos Wood?"

"The same." Dell giggled again.

It had been a long time since Mattie had thought about the handsome, arrogant boy who was every girl's dream. If Dell was any indication, he still was. Mattie had managed to avoid Ene through high school, not too difficult with Alonzo hovering every minute. She ignored the stab of guilt that accompanied Alonzo's name and wondered where she might hide.

The rider chose that moment to emerge from the shadows into the moonlight. He was not alone. In light-colored clothing, on a horse black as Satan's soul, they appeared as a luminous floating mass.

Dell said with a touch of envy, "He's probably got Charlotte with him."

"Not Charlotte Redding? She's just a baby."

"Sixteen. And her mama practically has the wedding planned."

"Buenas noches, compadre," Enos boomed in a singsong timbre typical of the northern Mexico dialect.

"He thinks we are a man," Mattie whispered.

Charlotte sat sidesaddle and Ene rode behind, his arms conveniently around her, holding the reins.

Dell said, "I thought I was hearing you all the way from Texas."

"Dell Whiting?"

"Yeah. What are you doing home?"

"Just got back yesterday," Ene rumbled.

"Guess who else came home?" Dell said.[8]

"It's Mattie Sevey," Charlotte said quickly, her tone dripping with satisfaction at ruining Dell's surprise.

Enos chuckled. "Well, I'll be. Welcome home then, Matt."

"Thank you," Mattie said coolly, annoyed at him calling her Matt. Except for a few monosyllables, she allowed Dell to carry the rest of the conversation. Finally, bidding their farewells, the two shadows passed.

"Thought Mattie had gone off to marry that Skousen fellow?" It was not a question meant for Mattie's ears, and she would not have heard but for Ene's powerful voice. Indeed, Charlotte's answer did not travel the distance between them, but Mattie knew what she had said from the man's surprised response.

"He left her at the altar?"

Mattie smiled. The rumor started in California had finally reached Alonzo's hometown.

Mattie had not been able to see Ene's face in the deep shadow of his hat and wondered how the man might differ from the boy. He was old. Okay, not old, but at least twenty-three, and courting that silly Charlotte Redding—silly, but beautiful. And besotted. Obviously, some things hadn't changed. At least she would not have to suffer the likes of that man. Poor, poor Charlotte.

Dell broke the silence. "Did you know that we have Ene to thank for the new irrigation ditch in town?"

"Ene?" Mattie almost squeaked. It galled her that both she and Dell had been thinking of Enos Wood. That certainly would flatter him.

"Well, he didn't build it alone," Dell explained. "He was construction boss, but he did fine work. After that, he worked with the lumber camps and sawmills up in the mountains. He came back to finish school at the academy."

"He finished school?"

"And graduated with top honors. He speaks fluent Spanish, which makes him pretty popular around here. After he graduated, he went to Snowflake to help his Grandfather Flake—ranching or something."

Dell's high praise tore away at Mattie's well-nurtured, carefully guarded prejudice. It annoyed her.

"I see Ene still packs a gun."

"Who doesn't?" Dell said.

Mattie had no objections, of course. She meant it simply as an observation. Ene had always packed a gun. Only recently, since the war threat, Moe had taken to carrying a gun too. "So, when's the wedding?"

"Wedding?"

"You said Charlotte and Ene are getting married."

"I didn't say they're getting married. I said Charlotte's mama had the wedding planned. There's a difference. Charlotte is one of a long line of women just dying to have the honor of ending Ene's bachelor days. She thinks she's got him trapped like fly in a pot of honey."

"More like Ene is the honey trapping a poor little fly," Mattie said.

Dell stiffened, and an uncomfortable silence fell between the two women. Obviously Dell had a soft spot for Ene, if not in love with him. She was thinking of an apology when Dell said, "Whatever you might think of him, Mattie, Ene is a respected man around here." It was said without rancor.

"I was just trying to be funny." Mattie hoped that Dell believed her. "So why haven't you set your cap for the most popular, respected bachelor in town?" Mattie asked.

Dell laughed. "I don't like standing in long lines."

***

With produce ready for harvest, there was no procrastinating. A dozen empty bottles lined the sideboard, waiting to be filled with fresh peas, still in pods that filled the buckets to overflowing. And tomorrow would bring more. *Ugh*, thought Mattie, popping her first pod, spilling four little green balls into a large empty pan. They bounced jauntily, sounding like heavy drops of rain on a tin roof.

"Happy is the day when green peas cease to grow," Mattie said.

"Might as well not wish it away," her mother said. "If it's not peas, it's something else."

"Yes, Mother, but it will not be peas."

"You make an excellent point, sister dear," Leuna said, with exaggerated diction and a straight face. She had been reading Jane Austen's *Pride and Prejudice*. "I prefer larger produce myself. Hour for hour, there is much more to show for our efforts. More rewarding, wouldn't you agree, sister dearest?"

"Indeed."

The sisters looked at each other and laughed. The women conversed easily, and the time passed pleasantly. By and by, a "previous engagement" called Leuna to town, leaving Mattie with a handful of pods left to shell.

Mattie smiled at her mother. Although a large woman, Martha moved gracefully as if performing a dance, turning, swaying, and lifting, first to one side, then to the other. Even her hands, calloused and rough, moved deftly as she poured hot water into the bottles to the brim with green peas. Adding a dash or two of salt, she carefully wiped spills from the lip of the jar. With a long wooden spoon, she fished rings and lids from a pan of boiling water. Using a dish towel to protect her hands, she put the lids on the bottles and twisted a ring around each one, securing it tight, and placed the bottle in a deep pan of water for a water bath to seal the jars.

Fiercely proud of her mother, Mattie believed her to be the wisest woman in the world, second only to Grandmother Thomas. More than once her mother had smoothed away a moment of childhood humiliation, making Mattie laugh, allowing that if the incident had not happened, many would have sadly been denied great entertainment. Her encouragement came with just the right words, careful to allow Mattie her feelings, but never allowing her to wallow in self-pity.

Her mother was just the right medicine for what ailed her broken spirit.

"Mattie." It was the second time her mother had said her name.

Mattie looked at her mother. "Sorry."

"We got too much peas at the end of the salt. Can you run to Whitings' and see if they got some."

Mattie rinsed her hands in the wash pan, drying them on her apron as she slipped out the back door. Headed for the front gate on a dead run, Mattie didn't see the man as she rounded the corner of the house. She slammed into him, nearly knocking him down. His strong arms held her close, preventing her from bouncing backward.

Suddenly, she was at Nellie's house, the terror of that night crashing down on her. She tried to scream, but no sound came. Thrashing and writhing, she could not free herself from the iron grip.

"Hey, hey. I can't let you go until I'm sure you aren't going to fall and kill yourself."

Her arms grew still, but her heart continued to thud against her chest as she cowered in the security of a warm embrace that smelled of horse and leather. She trembled.

"I sure am sorry. Didn't mean to scare you."

Like the sun breaking through the last of the morning fog, reality burst upon Mattie. She was safely home, on her way to get salt for her mother—and wantonly standing in the embrace of a man who clearly meant her no harm. Leaning her head back, she found she was looking into the anxious, penetrating eyes of Enos Wood.[9]

***

Sister Whiting gave Mattie a generous portion of salt. "You okay, Mattie? You look a little upset."

Mattie considered an answer. By sheer willpower and the need to appear normal, she had continued on her mother's errand when what she really wanted to do was find a corner and weep. "It's just the heat," Mattie finally said. She was grateful that Dell was nowhere to be seen. Conversation was near impossible.

As Mattie hurried home, she tried without success to forget the dreaded flashback and the humiliation that Enos Wood, of all people, had witnessed it.

He was more handsome than the boy she remembered. He would, no doubt, have a good laugh at her expense with that Charlotte Redding, although he certainly had not been laughing at the time. She had probably frightened him as much as he had frightened her. There was some satisfaction in that.

What would Enos think if he knew that she kept a lamp burning all night, and that more often than not, she had inconsolable nightmares, not to mention flashbacks.

Mattie put the salt on the sideboard.

"You look heat stroked. Have some lemonade." Her mother gave her a compassionate look, far more compassionate than heat stroke merited. Mattie suspected that her mother knew the truth.

"Ene Wood's coming to supper."

Mattie choked on her drink.

Her mother did not look at her.

***

Ene showed up every day at the Sevey ranch, arriving late in the afternoon. Although he made no overtures toward Mattie, Ene fooled no one, especially not Martha, who disapproved as heartily as her daughter on much the same premise: Ene's wild side, rough around the edges, too handsome for his own good, and lacking industriousness.[10]

Industriousness, to Martha, was a nice way of saying Ene wasn't rich enough. While money was not a prerequisite to a happy union for Mattie, she didn't argue the point, mollifying her mother with assurances that Ene would grow tired of her guarded company and move on. To herself she promised that when he did so, their black-eyed, olive-skinned guest, who could pass for Geronimo himself if his hair were longer, would not take her heart with him as he had Charlotte Redding's.

In the meantime, Martha wouldn't let the devil himself leave her home hungry, and she continued to invite Ene to stay for supper. He never failed to graciously thank his hostess as if she had fed him roast beef with all the trimmings instead of bread, milk, and onions topped with last year's peaches.

Moe, enjoying the little drama, had no such reservations toward Ene. Moe enjoyed his company, and Martha conceded that was reason enough to welcome him.

Even Mattie thought the conversation more interesting when Ene was present. After swapping stories, invariably, the topic turned to war. It both fascinated and worried Mattie.

"The biggest problem is our own Mexican neighbors," Ene said. He had gained the trust of the locals who were quick to keep him informed. "They have a chance to make money off this war. The Fierro brothers, for instance, incite their people against us, and all for gain."[11]

"You don't mean Demitrio and Lino?" Mattie was incredulous. "They went to school with us, for Pete's sake. Demitrio even wanted to be baptized until Rachel Payne's parents wouldn't let her marry him."

Moe leaned back in his chair. "Maybe that's the problem."

"War changes the best of people," Martha said. "'Fore it's over, we'll all change, for good or for bad."

"Well, Quevedos are loyal and sympathetic," Moe said. "They don't hold with their people who take advantage."

"If Madero can keep his seat, the war will be over before it can get started," Ene said "As soon as he gets things settled here in Chihuahua, the action will be too far south to touch us."

"Let's hope," Moe said. "Sam Tenney told me some of his own workers have plundered his stock in the name of patriotism, then kept the stuff themselves instead of giving it over to the soldiers."

Martha shook her head, grateful for her kind neighbors.

Mattie began stacking the dishes. "Parley figures we'll have trouble right here in our backyard. Revolutionists won't get too far from the border because they'll want to raid US soldiers for guns."

"They'll want our guns too," Ene said. "If you have them, you'd better hide them."

"What good are guns to us?" Mattie asked. "Apostle Ivins told us to try to live peaceably and not take sides."

"That may be true, but the rebels might think twice before they cause trouble among us if they know they might die in the process."

Martha spoke. "'Postle Ivins don't say that we can't defend ourselves. He says not to take sides and fight against t'other. We're s'pose to try to get along with them if they's reasonable. 'Course, we got to use wisdom."

"Exactly right, Sister Sevey," Ene said.

Moe rubbed his chin. "We can only hope that whatever political faction is in power will be willing to protect us."

Ene laughed. "That won't be easy. Political power shifts from week to week." It was an exaggeration, but not by much. Madero had four generals: Inés Salazar, Pascual Orozco, General Zapata, and Pancho Villa. They were all ambitious men, as trustworthy as smiling crocodiles. And as dangerous.

Ene continued. "And they're short of funds. You can bet they'll lean on us pretty heavy. I think we're going to be looking at hard times if the war doesn't move south soon."

Wise insight for a man so young, Mattie thought, refusing to meet Ene's eye. And unbeknownst to her, very prophetic.

***

She heard him before she saw him. If she had known that Ene's business would bring him to the ranch this early, she certainly would have found someplace else to dawdle other than the orchard. Ever since Mattie had heard that Ene and Charlotte were no longer stepping out, Mattie had carefully orchestrated their encounters to include a crowd but now . . . She looked for an escape. Too late. Ene waved. Resigned, she waved back. Shamefully, her traitorous heart pounded.

"It's almost too hot in the shade," Ene said.

"That's August for you. Would you like a peach?" Mattie held out the large, fuzz-covered fruit touched on one side with a deep salmon hue, a sure sign of ripeness. "I don't know where Moe is; probably over there." Mattie pointed to the corral. "When you're done with business, come on in. Mother has lemonade in the icebox." Mattie tried to step past Ene.

Ene took the peach and grinned. "You are my business, Mattie."

Mattie flushed. She looked frantically toward the house. Where was Moe? Where was Leuna?

"I came to ask you to the dance this Friday."

"You're asking me to the dance?" Mattie moaned inwardly. Why couldn't she come up with a clever, dismissive excuse?

"Is that a yes?" Ene grinned.

***

As Mattie dressed for bed, her thoughts were on the Black Knight, as she referred to Ene. He was something that happened at the end of every day, riding off into the black night on a black horse.

On this day, against all that she knew to be wise, she had accepted his invitation to the dance, even agreeing to let him ride out to the Sevey ranch in his father's buggy to fetch her. Graciously, Ene had offered to bring Moe, Leuna, and her mother as well. Mattie acquiesced finally, knowing that Moe would welcome the ride, grateful that he would not show up smelling of horse at Ruthie Greer's door, however much good that might be.

Mattie struggled with the paradox that was Ene Wood. He was gun-packing, rough, and jovially boisterous, yet his manner was gentle. He never brought up that day when she had trembled in the security of his arms. His startling dark eyes seemed to look directly into her heart, and his baritone laugh, full of exuberance for life, drew her in.

Then she remembered Charlotte Redding. And how many broken hearts had he left in Snowflake?

"He's a fraud," she decided, "handsome and dangerous. He is cocksure he can melt me into a puddle like butter on a hot stove. Well, I'm a heartbreaker too, and I won't melt. I won't!" Mattie stamped her foot at the fat tabby stretched on the windowsill. The animal raised its lazy head to look at her.

She stuck her tongue out at the feline and crawled into bed.

***

The town gathered at the bandstand. The Wood family provided the music. Ene's mother was conspicuously absent, being large with child, her tenth, a fact not mentioned due to propriety. Women pretended to be sick when they were expecting, hiding the evidence as long as they could. In the last months, when binding made no difference, women appeared in public only when necessary. For all their secrecy, the experienced eye was not deceived. Only small children were not aware.

The Wood family performed admirably, despite being shorthanded most of the evening because Ene preferred to stay with his date. When he wasn't dancing with Mattie, he was giving his little sisters a whirl or waltzing with Mattie's mother. Mattie shook her head. She couldn't help but smile. Enos Wood was definitely a charmer, a real ladies' man. Tonight, however, all of his women were prudently family, hers and his.

Twirling to a fast polka with Ene, Mattie caught Charlotte's glare. Earlier, when Mattie had tried to be pleasant to Charlotte, the young snippet had turned her back. *Can't blame her*, Mattie thought. *Next time it might be me on the sidelines glaring.* Mattie vowed silently that she would never flatter any man by glaring in jealous rage. Especially not Enos Wood.

But Mattie had little room for guilt over Charlotte when she was filled with compassion for Moe. Her brother felt more strongly about Ruthie Greer than she felt for him. Poor Moe. Torn between guilt and compassion, Mattie couldn't be angry with Ruthie for hurting Moe. Hadn't she, herself, hurt someone's brother? How the Skousens must loathe her. Guilt stabbed at Mattie from every angle. Why did this love business have to be so painful?

"How 'bout I walk you home tonight?" Ene grinned. Provokingly, as it was wont to do of late, Mattie's heart leapt with acquiescence while the voice of warning scolded. She glanced through the crowd at Charlotte. "Don't be silly," she said. "Mother and Leuna can't drive the buggy home alone."

Ene grinned. "Moe offered to drive."

Whether from guilt or compassion, Mattie did not know, but the evening found her strolling toward home in awkward silence with Enos Wood.

The stars, like sparkling stones set in black velvet, seemed close enough to pluck from the sky. A choir of frogs sang inharmoniously as crickets fiddled in resounding accompaniment.

Ene mimicked the frogs perfectly, and Mattie laughed. He offered his arm when she stumbled, and reluctantly she took it, irritated to feel as if she had come into safe harbor.

"I hope your mother will be on her feet soon," Mattie said, grasping at straws for something to say.

"Her ninth baby died before it was a week old, nearly taking her with it."

"Boy or girl?" Mattie wondered how a mother ever got over the heartache of losing a child.

"A boy." His voice trembled, surprising Mattie with the depth of his feeling. "I'm afraid this time, she won't be so lucky."

It seemed strange to discuss with a man what some women dared not talk about even among themselves—strange and embarrassing. "Your mother keeps the prettiest garden in town," Mattie said, leading the conversation to a more comfortable topic. She had long admired the honeysuckle and trellises of roses, artfully arranged, covering the ugly cement embankment of the canal that backed the Wood home. The bird of paradise bordering the little rock house had transformed it into an inviting element of beauty.

Ene chuckled. "Believe it or not, that's Father's doing. He loves flowers. Guess I get that from him."

Mattie's mouth hung unflatteringly agape, and she was glad for the dark. Who would have believed that Peter Wood, the town tooth extractor, and his gun-packing son enjoyed the finer aspects of life. On second thought, she supposed it wasn't such a far step. Weren't they also musicians? Had her bias painted a painfully narrow view of Enos Wood?

Ene cleared his throat. "You don't have to tell me if you don't want to, Matt, but I think something terrifying happened to you that has you a bit on edge."

Mattie sighed. She knew this moment would come. Did she owe this man an explanation? "You startled me, that's all."

Ene was quiet. Then he said, "Yeah, you're right. I really shouldn't have asked. Forget it."

Perhaps it was the intimacy of the dark or the hurt in his voice. Whatever it was, her resolve dissolved like sugar in water.

She left nothing out of the telling, even jilting Alonzo. It poured out of her, the jarring ordeal with JT, her nightmares, her need to sleep with a lamp lit, the flashbacks. She even spoke of the old resentment toward God and how Nellie's children had helped restore her faith. And most disconcerting, she told him about her fears of being barren.

In the telling, the chink in Mattie's armor widened a little. She wondered if, in the light of day, how she would view this intimate moment. Would she blush? Would she be able to meet Ene's eye. Although she appreciated his compassion, and even his anger in her behalf, she was not about to allow a kiss.

Never that.

***

A carpet of red and gold leaves crunched under Mattie's feet as she walked down Colonia Juárez's main street. The large rust-colored mulberry leaves went into a basket for Minerva and Lola, who would arrange them artfully into a fall centerpiece.

Crossing the wagon bridge, Mattie had gone a block when she heard her name called.

"Mattie, dearie. Yoo-hoo!"

Mattie turned to see Alonzo Skousen's mother, with her usual condescending smile, motioning to her. Mattie hoped this wouldn't take long. Her sisters were waiting for her. More correctly, baby Maggie would be waiting. She looked forward to her weekly dose of baby. Now six months old, Minerva's third child almost wasn't a baby anymore.

"Hello, Sister Skousen," Mattie said. "It's nice to see you." Mattie silently asked God's forgiveness for her little white lie.

"Oh, Mattie, you'll never guess." The older woman barely contained her exuberance.

Mattie had a very good guess. Sister Skousen never spoke to her except to inform on Alonzo.

"It's very, very good news. Alonzo is married!" Sister Skousen practically sang it.

Mattie's first reaction was relief. Relief that Alonzo had found happiness, and relief from the weight of guilt she had been carrying since April. "I'm so glad to hear it, Sister Skousen. Please offer my best wishes to him when you write next."

Mattie practically skipped to Minerva's house where she was to meet Leuna and Lola.

"You'll never guess," Mattie said to her sisters, mocking Sister Skousen.

"Ene proposed," Minerva said. It was not a question.

"Don't hold your breath on that account," Mattie said. "Ene is looking for conquests, not a wife."

"What else would leave you so breathless?" Minerva asked.

"It's Alonzo. He's married!"

"Nooooo . . ." The women exhaled in trio their lips forming a perfect O.

"Yes. I just talked to his mother. She practically rubbed my nose in it. I clearly disappointed her when I didn't burst into tears."

"That's terrible. The old bat." Lola was indignant.

"Honestly, Mattie," Leuna said, "I don't know why you let people think that Alonzo dumped you."[12]

"I owe it to Alonzo," Mattie said.

"So?" Minerva waited expectantly.

"So what?" Mattie asked.

"So, how do you feel about it?"

"That she rubbed my nose in it or that Alonzo is married?"

Minerva looked exasperated. "You know perfectly well what I mean."

"My first reaction . . . blessed relief that Alonzo found a wife," Mattie said.

"And your second?" Lola asked.

Mattie grinned impishly. "I hope she's ugly." Lola, Leuna, and Minerva hooted. Mattie instantly regretted having said such an unkind thing. Sister Skousen did need to be brought down a peg or two, but not at Alonzo's expense. On the contrary, as she explained to her sisters, Mattie hoped Alonzo had captured a real beauty that would love him with all her heart.

Sundown cut her visit shorter than she would have liked. The warm November afternoon turned chilly as the sun dropped. Just as the last light turned a ghostly gray, Mattie and Leuna walked into the kitchen. Their mother was putting supper on the table and Moe was washing up.

"What, no Mr. Wood at our table tonight?" Leuna asked.

"Ene won't be comin' for a few days," her mother said. "'Tisn't good news, I fear."

Mattie almost laughed at the thought that her mother considered Ene's absence bad news.

"Sister Wood birthed her baby. She's doin' fine, but the baby . . . well, I'm 'fraid the baby didn't make it."

Mattie sobered. "This is the second time."

"I know, dear."

"How do women do it, Mother? I don't think I could bear it."

"You do what you got to do, Mattie, and somehow God helps you through it."

It was well after midnight, and Mattie still could not sleep. She cried for Ene's mother. She cried for babies past and babies future that would never have a chance at life.

***

On November ninth, Mattie turned twenty. In her honor, her mother butchered a chicken and Mrs. Quevedo made tamales. Leuna saw to the cake. Moe made an exaggerated show of gratitude for the event that finally occasioned a "decent" meal. Ene, as usual, was present. The extravagance and attention flattered Mattie.

After all the hoopla, Mattie made ready to return Mrs. Quevedo's basket and acknowledge her kindness.

"May I come with you?" Ene offered.

Mattie was glad she didn't have to make the trek alone in the dark, however short. "If you'd like."

Rafaela Quevedo graciously invited the couple in. It was a two-room adobe house with a dirt floor and immaculately cleaned. The aroma of the meal they had just finished, a blend of garlic, green chilies, and toasted tortillas, filled the cozy room. Rodrigo and Silvestre no longer lived at home, leaving only Susana and Pablo who were on the brink of adulthood. Javier Quevedo spoke proudly of his sons who had joined the revolutionary movement, yet he feared war as much as anyone. He and Ene conversed easily, and Mattie could see the unabashed respect that Javier had for him.

Rafaela beamed at Mattie's praise for the tamales . . . the best tamales south of the border. Mattie smiled when Rafaela addressed Ene as Don Enés. Mattie had never thought of him as a Don. Mattie scolded her softening heart. She was at that place where Ene had power to hurt her, and she didn't like it.

"Would you mind if we walked a little before going in?" Ene asked after leaving the Quevedos.

Mattie smiled to herself. Translated, "walk a little" meant "talk a lot." "If you'd like, Don Enés."

Ene chuckled. "You like the sound of that, do you?"

"Probably not as much as you do."

Mattie wondered if Ene's laugh was heard for miles around.

They stopped at the leafless cottonwood. Ene leaned back against the large trunk. Mattie pulled her wrap close against the cold November evening.

"Happy birthday.

"Thank you."

"Do you remember that time we played hide-and-seek under this tree?" Ene asked.

"I remember."

"Yes, ma'am. You were downright saucy, a little spitfire if I ever saw one."

"That's not very flattering."

"I was smitten."

Mattie laughed. "You're smitten with every girl."

"Hey," Ene said with mock injury. "Girls are smitten with me, with one exception, and I'm afraid she despises me. Do you, Mattie, do you despise me?"

Mattie laughed.

Ene said. "Ah. You give me hope."

"You can hope all you want, Ene Wood, but I won't be duped into being another one of your conquests to be counted and flung aside."

Once again, Ene's hearty laugh shattered the silent night. "Just for honesty's sake, I've been trying to dupe you since I came to town. But cast you aside? Never. As to who has been conquered will require a court of law to determine. I want to marry you, Mattie Sevey, and I've never wanted to marry anyone. I quake at the thought."

"That has to be the most unromantic proposal I have ever heard," Mattie said, her voice a whisper.

"Well, just how many have you heard?"

Mattie did not answer. This man could be infuriating.

"So, you haven't answered my question?"

Mattie said, "Yes, I despise you."

"That's not the question I'm talking about."

"It's the only question you've asked." Mattie would have laughed with glee had she known how easily she disconcerted the seemingly unflappable Ene.

In a dramatic sweep barely visible in the dark, Ene bowed. Taking Mattie's hand, he kissed it, then went to one knee. "Martha Ann Sevey, I sincerely pray that I have been successful in duping you to accept me as your future and faithful husband. I'm far from perfect. I can't think of single reason why you should say yes, except that I love you. I want to take care of you. Will you marry me?"

It was melodramatic, comical, except for Ene's voice that quivered at the last.

Mattie didn't laugh.

She looked into the deep places of her heart where truth had hidden once before and found that truth, indeed, was hiding again. This time, however, truth wrapped around her like a warm blanket.

For the first time, head and heart were not in bitter argument.

She could hardly find her voice. When it came, it was a trembling whisper. "Yes."

Ene stood and took both her hands. He said in all seriousness, "Is that a 'yes, if you'd like,' or is it a 'yes, I want to very much'?"

"Yes, I want to very much." Mattie laughed from pure delight.[13]

Ene exhaled in relief. He cupped Mattie's face in his hands and for the first time, he kissed her. Gently. Sweetly.

The indomitable Mattie Sevey melted like butter on a hot stove.

PART TWO

1912

"MAY I KISS THE BRIDE?"

Mattie grinned. "I would be plumb put out if you didn't."

Moe gave his sister a chaste peck on the cheek. "You glow like a lightning bug in July."

Her hand flew to her face. "It's just the heat.

"In February?" He laughed.

"Oh, why don't you go help crank ice cream?" It was not a question.

At that moment, the front door of the three-room house swung open. The Bills, one Ene's brother and one Mattie's, each carried a cylinder of ice cream to the sideboard.

"Looks like I'm too late," Moe said, grinning, "but I'll do the honors. You look like you could do with something cold."

"You going to rub ice cream on my face?"

"Not a bad idea."

Mattie punched her brother lightly on the arm. She had to admit, in the crush of people gathered in Jane and Peter Wood's little house, ice cream on the face might actually be refreshing.[1]

In the dim light of kerosene lamps, mother and mother-in-law scurried to keep up a perpetual flow of a sumptuous chicken dinner, hot bread, and an endless assortment of salads while their daughters worked feverishly over a pan of hot water to provide clean dishes.

Peter Wood and his children dominated a corner of the room, each with their musical instrument. Ene, breathing intently into his harmonica, met her eye and winked, transporting Mattie to another time years ago when she had spurned such charm. As they did then, Ene's eyes danced with mirth. Was he remembering too?

Smiling at her new husband, she tugged at her ear, their private sign for "I love you." He signed back before getting down to the serious business of his harmonica.

If anyone had told her when she left California that she was coming home to marry Ene Wood, she would have jumped off the train.[2] Now, here she was, Mrs. Enos Flake Wood beaming with the sheer pleasure of a private moment shared across the room with the very same.

The wedding ceremony, which had taken place at the church, had been simple albeit slightly larger crowd than the guests who had gathered in California for the wedding that didn't happen. Today, just family alone made up the bulk of seventy guests. Even her father had honored his promise to be with her on this special day.

As she waited to march down the aisle, she felt his touch on her shoulder like a gentle breeze. She could almost see his benevolent smile under his bushy mustache and long beard.

"Are you here, Father?" She whispered.

"I'm here, child." The words came to her like a soft breeze. His presence had continued with her until the bishop pronounced her and Ene husband and wife. "You have chosen well, my little Mattie," the voice spoke in her mind. Then it was gone.

Mattie wondered if she had imagined it all until her mother, hugging her congratulations, said quietly, "Your father was here."

Remembering the sweet emotion, Mattie teared up.

"Ice cream for the beautiful bride." It wasn't Moe. It was Ene. She hadn't noticed that he had left off playing. Checking to see if there was another Ene, Mattie glanced at where the family continued their music without the harmonica.

"Sure hope those are happy tears," Ene said.

She smiled. "Very happy tears."

"Here's to happy tears." Ene lifted his bowl of ice cream in a toast. Mattie did the same. They laughed.

Life was about to offer precious few occasions for happy tears, though tears would be shed. For now, the bride basked in the warmth of her groom while the future loomed ever threatening, ever challenging, ever changing.

***

In the early morning, nippy for May, the horses stamped impatiently while Mattie bid her farewell to her mother and brother, who were leaving for the States: Martha, to visit her daughters; Moe, to escape the heartbreak of seeing Ruthie Greer marry Tobias Jones, although he would never admit it. What he did admit to was that his mother needed a traveling companion, and with Ene willing to oversee the orchards, there was no reason for Moses not to leave.

Mattie knew Moe felt guilty about abandoning them in the midst of political unrest, which was gathering momentum. She hugged her brother. "I'll miss you, Moe."

He grinned. "I'll miss you too, little sister. Be careful." Turning to Ene, he shook his hands. "Old man, good luck with the farm. It's all yours now."

"When you get Mother Sevey settled, go to Snowflake if you haven't found anything," Ene said. "My grandpa can help you get a start."

Mattie tucked a frayed quilt around her mother and kissed her cheek. "Give my best to Mahala and George and Nellie and Parley. And kiss the children for me."

Martha smiled. "I'll do jess that." Her eyes glistened, her smile quivered, but her voice was strong. "Now you and Ene don't let no grass grow under yer feet," she said, forcing a strong voice. "Leuna's 'spectin' ya out to the ranch today. 'Sides, I ain't comfortable, her bein' out there alone."

Mattie nodded, not as successful as her mother at keeping her voice from quivering. "I'll miss you terribly."

Martha patted her daughter's hand. "Take care, child. I'll be back 'fore you know it."

Mattie watched the wagon bounce and creak its way down the road. While she would miss her mother, her heart ached for Moe. She knew how painful it was when carefully laid plans didn't work out.

Her thoughts brought up another painful failure of carefully laid plans; she still was not pregnant. Panic tied her innards in knots each time her flow issued, maddeningly punctual and most decidedly unwelcome. She was being silly, she knew. It took Nellie a year to conceive. Mattie had been married only three months.

Then again, what else might she expect? Except for their wedding night, she and Ene had shared a room with Roberta and Rose, Ene's little sisters, and sometimes the bed as well. And if that wasn't enough to subdue conjugal liberties, Ene's brothers, Lee and John, men in their own rights, slept in the next room with young Clarence. Even if Mother and Father Wood had offered their semiprivate circumstances on a small bed in the corner of the kitchen that also served as the sitting room, it hardly lent itself to connubial bliss.

Guilt washed over her like dirty laundry water. However inconvenient, the Woods had freely and unselfishly provided what they had. She was an ungrateful wretch to complain, and she hadn't until this moment, when fortuitously, on this very day, their circumstances were about to change. The ranch house, twice the size of the Wood's home, would be shared with just one person—Leuna.

Mattie waved her last good-bye as the wagon carrying her brother and mother turned north to begin its ascent up the Dugway.

***

By midmorning, linens, quilts, and dishes were stored away in their new home. Mattie stretched her back, looking around. She had never considered the ranch house as particularly spacious, but after living cooped up in a little house with twelve people, she thought it a mansion.

Leuna was gone to town, not due back until late afternoon. Seventeen, she had blossomed into an even-tempered woman like their mother and a pleasant and helpful companion. She would probably be married soon if her beau, Cliff, had anything to say about it.

"Where do you want this, Matt?" Ene appeared in the doorway, effortlessly carrying another trunk.

"Our room." Mattie followed to superintend.

Ene sat the trunk in the designated spot. When he stood, he was so close Mattie could see her reflection in his dark eyes. He grinned. "We're alone."

"So we are," she demurred.

When Ene kissed her soft and full on the lips, Mattie's heart began its usual flutter. He pulled her close, his kiss more demanding. "Enos Flake Wood," she breathed, "you're terrible."

"Yes, ma'am." With one deft move, Ene closed the bedroom door.

***

Even though the July sun promised another hot day, Mattie thought it perfect: perfect for making bread, perfect for a sit in the cool orchard, perfect for a moment to herself, which was next on her list.

It had been a while since she had reason to be lighthearted. Mexico's revolution was as hot as the summer day. As they vied to fill the vacancy of the Mexican president they had ousted, generals came and went as easily as one, two, three, shoot. With each political rise to power, military loyalties shifted according to personal advantage, or worse, a new political faction was thrown into the melee. The revolution was no longer "in their backyard" as Parley McCrae had prophesied. It was knocking at their front door.

With so many soldiers and so few resources, regardless of their political views, generals stopped at nothing to support their cause, which included helping themselves to the community's herds and stores. What would it be next? A life? The threat was ever looming every day at the forefront of Mattie's thoughts.

But not this day.

She had banished life's ugly apprehensions to loiter harmlessly in the emptiness of her boudoir. Mattie smiled. *Armoire, boudoir, indeed,* she thought—words bandied about by California's highfalutin society, words that rolled off the tongue but were difficult to spell.

When restricted to the written word, she safely surrendered to plain old English—wardrobe and bedroom.

Humming "Amazing Grace"—her voice so soft and slow, it passed for a lullaby—she kneaded the large yeasty blob of dough: lift, push, roll, lift, push, roll. Shaping it into a large round mound, she smoothed it over with a thin layer of pig lard, covered it with a clean dishtowel, and left it to rise in the hot kitchen.

Giving her hands a quick wash, she grabbed the saltshaker and surrendered to the shady refuge of the orchard. The trees were heavy with fruit waiting for the autumnal frost that would make them sweet. Sitting with her back against a tree trunk, Mattie rubbed two freshly picked green apples to a sheen. Salting each bite, it was mouthwateringly tart, just this side of bitter. With a proper frame of mind, taking care not to eat too many, it was the perfect summer treat on this perfect summer day. Mattie giggled.

When she missed her first flow, she hardly dared to hope. Having missed her second, she knew. Finally, she would have her own little sweet touch of innocence to snuggle—February, by her calculations.

In the cool shade, the expectant mother was immersed in happy speculation. It would be a boy, naturally, to perpetuate his father's name. He would be called Sevey in honor of her father. Their son would look like Ene, but have just a little of his grandfather Sevey— maybe the eyes, or patrician nose, a long beard.

Mattie laughed.

Ene will be ecstatic at the happy news, she thought. She had almost told him this morning before he left for town, but she wanted the telling to be a special occasion: after his favorite meal, perhaps standing by the tree where he had proposed. "It will be our secret," Mattie announced to the magpie that scolded from a high branch. *At least until evidence requires otherwise, which is a few months off*, she mused.

Her reverie was abruptly ended by the sound of a horse coming fast and hard. Almost before the horse had come to a stop, the rider swung off and dashed into the house. It was Ene.

Something was terribly wrong.

***

"Leave?" She choked. "This house?

"Not just this house, Mattie. Mexico." Apprehension in Ene's eyes belied his calm voice. "Salazar is evicting us because we won't give up our guns: Colonia Juárez, Colonia Dublán, the mountain communities, Díaz. Everybody.

The anxieties relegated to her room that morning spewed forth in a frenzy and lodged in her chest, making it hard to breathe. The perfect day was shattered.

"When?" Mattie's voice quivered.

"July twenty-seventh."

"One week." Mattie swallowed down the lump in her throat.

Ene hugged her close. "Women and children, a few guards, and any man too feeble to pack out of here on horses will go by train. You will meet up with the mountain folks at Pearson. The Dublán people will join you at the Casas Station. You will wait for the rest of us in El Paso."

"Leuna. We have to tell Leuna."

"I expect she already knows. Cliff was at the meeting." Ene drew back and looked at Mattie, hesitating.

"What, Ene? Don't hold anything back, not now."

He swallowed. "What I'm about to tell you could be our death if it got out."

Mattie nodded.

"President Romney figured that the revolutionaries would try to take our weapons. With nothing to defend ourselves, soldiers could sit on those hills with their Mausers." Ene gestured to the north. "And shoot down on us. There'd be nothing we could do about it. A while back, the stake committee smuggled guns in from the States— US army. Each bishop was given an allotment."[3]

Mattie paled. "How do you know this?"

"I helped deliver them."

Mattie stared. Had Ene and the men been caught with those guns, and if they were discovered now, it would be a bloodbath. "Now what?" she whispered.

"We take them with us when we leave and return them to the US government."

Mattie clung to Ene. She wanted to tell him that he was going to be a father, and she did not intend to raise the child by herself. Truth was, there were no guarantees for either of them. General Salazar was mean and unpredictable. Ene was at greater risk, of course, and from his furrowed brow, Mattie knew the situation weighed heavy on him. She couldn't possibly add to his burden by telling him that she carried his baby.

***

"Tie this to the wagon." Mattie handed Leuna a bottle of thick cream. It would be butter by the time it jostled all the way to Pearson, a welcome addition to their lunch.[4] It was still dark outside, adding to the somber mood. While Ene checked the horses, Mattie and Leuna went from room to room one last time before locking up the house. Except for the beds stripped of bedding, there was little evidence that they were leaving forever. Mattie knelt at her wedding trunk and looked one last time at her dishes and linens. Women and children were allowed to take little more than food for the trip—a hundred pounds of baggage per adult, fifty per child, and a bedroll each.[5] It seemed ironic that the clothes she was allowed to take would be of no use to her in a few months. She would have much rather used her allotted space to take her wedding gifts. But it would have been complicated explaining why she was taking linens instead of clothing.

Reverently closing the lid, Mattie turned the key in the lock. Taking a deep breath, she lifted her chin. If she couldn't manage a smile, at least she would present a brave façade. She was a Sevey, and Sevey women did what they must.

Mattie walked out and didn't look back.

"Que Dios les bendiga," Rafaela Quevedo said tearfully when Mattie reached the wagon. "God bless you."

Mattie gave her neighbor a quick hug. "God protect you," she said with a steady voice.

"We'll take care of everything," Javier Quevedo promised, accepting the key to the ranch house.

"Thank you," Mattie answered graciously, suspecting it was a promise he might not be able to keep no matter how sincerely offered. "Please send our best to Silvestre."

"If we do not return," Ene said, "everything is yours. Looks like there'll be a good crop of apples, and there is still plenty in the garden."

"You will be back in time for the apples," Javier said, "and we will keep your home in good repair against the day that you return."

Ene clapped him on the back. "You're a good man, Javier." Turning to Mattie, Ene said, "I think we're ready, then." He handed Mattie up to the wagon box next to Leuna.

With heavy heart, Mattie took the reins and joined the caravan of neighbors already in route. Ene followed on horseback, driving the stock. The sky had begun to lighten. How the day would end was in God's hands. *If all goes well*, she thought, *we should be in El Paso by this time tomorrow.*

Mattie dared one last look at the ranch house before the wagon disappeared around the bend. Javier, Rafaela, and their two small children, Pablo and Susana, were no more than black shadows. Would she ever see them again? Mattie squared her shoulders. There were no tears, but the old bitterness welled up. Where was God? How had it come to this? Had she married Alonzo, she would be ensconced in a comfortable home instead of fleeing for her life, a newlywed expecting her first child.

Mattie swallowed the lump in her aching throat, ashamed. Had she married Alonzo, there would have been no Ene.

***

Jane Wood, tall and thin, her hair pulled severely back into a low knot at the base of her neck, adjusted her frameless glasses. Stoic and competent, she directed her family with solemn efficiency. Roberta, Rosalie, and Clarence obeyed, putting on their bravest face. Lucy, with her newborn, her dark eyes even darker with worry, kept her emotions buried deep with a visible determination to do what she must without a fuss.

Peter Wood said, "Lee and John will stay here with the stock until we get back from Pearson. Then I 'spect that tomorrow morning we'll head for the meeting place at the base of Pajarito Mountain."

Ene said, "When we and the mountainfolk catch up to the rest of them, we're going to make quite the expedition. Hope those people in Dog Springs are ready for us." What Ene didn't say, but what they were all thinking, was the possibility of running into revolutionaries before getting to the New Mexico border. The meeting place had been kept a secret. Whether Villistas or Carranzistas, at the very least the men would lose livestock—unless their precious cargo of US military–issued weapons were discovered. In which case, they would all be executed.

Mattie was not at all sure she would even reach Pearson without incident, much less El Paso. Having turned the reins over to Ednar, Lucy's husband, she sat in the back of the wagon with the other women and children lulled into a stupor by the continuous grind of wagon wheels. Rivulets of perspiration made muddy lines in her dusty face. Peter Wood drove the other team and the wagons bumped along. Ene rode alongside on his horse, Midnight, his eyes constantly scanning the trail. As usual, he was armed. *That's reassuring, but surviving a shootout might be the beginning of something worse,* Mattie thought.

Clouds of dust from distant wagons could be seen ahead as well as behind. Where were Lola and Minerva on the trail? Mattie wondered how her family from Chupe was faring, if they were already en route on the train. Glancing at Roberta and Rosalie, she couldn't imagine what the children must be feeling. They were asleep. Maybe they saw this as nothing more than a grand adventure. Maybe she should follow their example.

Just as Mattie began to relax, the wagon stopped. "What's wrong?"

"A man just stepped out of the bushes," Leuna whispered, her green eyes wide.

A ragged-looking soldier raised his pistol. Mattie's pulse quickened. Had it not been for his gun, he would have elicited only sympathy.

"Here we go," Ene siad, his voice tight. "Everybody keep to your places." Ene dismounted. "Ednar, you come with me." Mattie held her breath as the gunman trained his gun first on Ene, then on Ednar, ignoring Ene's polite greeting. She couldn't make out the words, but from the tone of his voice, she knew Ene was keeping up a friendly conversation. He said something to Ednar who headed back to the wagons.

"What's he want?" Peter asked, his rifle surreptitiously covered with a blanket on the seat of the buckboard within easy reach.

"What else? Money and guns. Ene's offering him food. What can we part with?"

"I have bread and cheese," Mattie volunteered quickly, saving her mother-in-law from offering her food, which she would need for the children. "It isn't much, but it's something."

Ednar took Mattie's offering.

"Be careful, Ednar," Lucy said.

Ednar nodded, glancing appreciatively at Lucy.

Jane's thin lips moved in silent prayer.

The soldier waved his weapon and rambled belligerently until he saw the food. Thrusting his gun into his waist, he grabbed at the offering. Looking more haggard than dangerous, he sauntered off. Accidentally dropping his bread, he picked it up, gave it a shake, and ate wolfishly, disappearing among the tall mesquite.

Mattie let out a long sigh.

Ednar took his place on the wagon seat and picked up the reins. "Let's go before he runs out of food."

Ene lifted himself easily into the saddle and rode back to Mattie.

"You could have been killed," she said.

"On the contrary, ma'am. I had to talk that rebel out of being dead." He winked.

"Ene Wood, you are incorrigible."

Lucy and Leuna laughed.

Jane almost looked soft. She said, "Ene could talk a tiger out of his stripes."

"Only to shut him up," Mattie said, not knowing whether to laugh or cry. She laughed.

Peter Wood's grin, under his white bushy mustache, was evidenced only by the deepening wrinkles at his eyes.

***

Shading her face with her hand, Mattie searched for Phoebe. She was several car lengths away standing on something that put her head and shoulders above the crowd. Mattie waved, working her way toward her sister with Leuna close behind. They found not only Phoebe but also Anna and the four of the oldest Sevey nieces and nephews. No one smiled and eyes shone as they hugged each other.

"We came off the train to get some fresh air," Anna said.

"If you can call this fresh air." Leuna waved her hand in front of her face, fanning the dust.

"Compared to inside," Phoebe said, "this is wonderful. Where's Ene?"

"He'll be along. Have you seen Minerva and Lola?"

"They arrived about a half hour ago," Phoebe said. "They're traveling with their in-laws."

"And how are all of you?" Mattie asked.

"Isabel is a brick," said Anna. "She's organized us. Bessie's baby is only a week old, and Keturah is expecting any minute. She'll be lucky to make it to El Paso."

"Poor dear," Mattie said with feeling. "What's the general attitude in the mountain settlements?"

"Our Mexican neighbors don't like us much," Anna said. "One or two folks are sympathetic, but they won't be able to stand against the others. We expect nothing will be left of our homes when we return."

Mattie noticed that Anna said *when*, not *if*, and drew comfort from it.

Behind her hand, so the children could not hear, Phoebe said, "George and Lem shot our dogs so they wouldn't starve to death."

Leuna pulled a face. "How awful!"

"It seemed the kindest thing to do," Phoebe said.

"We hid our valuables in a cave," Anna said. "As for our store, we just had to walk away."

"And leave the men behind." Phoebe sniffed.

The women fell silent. As with her sisters and sister-in-law, Mattie's throat was too full of tears to speak.

Anna broke the silence, lifting her chin. "But then, here we are, safe for the moment." She tried to smile. "Faith, sisters. In no time we will be in El Paso, and before you know it, we will be reunited with our menfolk."

"*If* we get to El Paso," Phoebe said. Anna shot her a warning look, and Phoebe became silent.

"What?" Mattie asked.

"To talk about it might show a lack of faith," Anna said.

"Talk about what?" Mattie looked at each woman in the eye. No one spoke. "For Pete's sake," Mattie said in a foot-stomping tone. "Talk . . . about . . . what?"

Anna glanced at the children to make sure they were not listening, then she whispered, "The soldiers have threatened to blow the Cumbres tunnel."[6]

***

All totaled, eight hundred women and children from Colonia Juárez boarded the train, joining the five hundred from the mountain settlements who had boarded at Chico early that morning.

Mattie wondered how many women knew about the tunnel. Did Lucy and Jane? Minerva and Lola? She wanted to find them, to give them a hug. To weep. To wail.

Mattie had parted with the Wood women, who agreed that they could handle three children easily between them, that Mattie and Leuna were more needed by the Seveys. Mattie was glad she had kept her own condition a secret. The women who needed her most would have only fussed over her.

Traveling arrangements settled, the women began boarding the train. Mattie hung back for a private moment with Ene. The usual glint of humor was absent from his eyes. He pulled her to him, kissing her forehead.

"There are ugly rumors, Matt." Only in tender moments or impending doom did Ene speak in a soft voice. Or call her Matt.

What had once rankled, Ene calling her Matt, had become dear to her. Another time, she might have smiled.

"I know." She swallowed hard. "Anna told me."

The train whistle blew the warning. It was time to go.

"Don't be getting into trouble." Mattie meant to make Ene laugh. Instead, he hugged her tight and wept. The dam in her own eyes broke and tears flowed freely.

Had Mattie noticed, she would have seen that many men wept openly and unashamed, tears coursing down their weathered faces, able to let their women and children go only on faith in their God to keep their loved ones safe from harm as promised by the stake president. The men had a perilous journey of their own to make. That they would never see one another again weighed heavily in each of their thoughts.

Without speaking, Ene kissed Mattie again and helped her into the train. She took her place with the seven Sevey women, who traveled with eight children from newborn to ten years old, another newborn threatening to appear before they arrived at their destination. She was grateful for the distraction that kept her from dwelling on the fear lodged in her heart like a never-melting piece of ice.

The train lurched forward. "Shouldn't we close the windows?" Mattie said.

Isabelle shook her head. "Can't. The guards broke the windows out with a steel bar." She smiled weakly. "They were stuck, and we were suffocatingly hot."

As the train picked up speed, Mattie was grateful for the cool breeze, not realizing that in a few minutes the open windows would not be welcome at all.

Reaching the mile-long Cumbres tunnel, the train was plunged into blackness. Smoke and cinder from the engine poured in. Her own violent coughing blended with the raucous chorus of crying children and desperate mothers gasping for air. Mattie fought to keep her stinging eyes open as she groped at her hem and threw her skirt over several of the children's heads. Never, in all the commotion, did Mattie forget that the tunnel might instantly erupt into a ball of fire.

Emerging into the sunlight, coughing and wheezing and covered in soot, she was grateful to be in one piece.

They had survived the second crisis of the trip, only to hurtle toward the next.

***

Despite the evening breeze, the heat was unrelenting. It was nearly midnight, and still there was no hope that the train would be leaving Casas Station. General Salazar used every pretext to hold 2,300 passengers, all women and children except for the few guards and old men.

While waiting, there had been a chance to wash faces and hands, removing much of the black soot that covered them. Mattie looked around at the other languishing passengers and longed for another splash of cold water to her hot face and neck.

She stiffened when two soldiers entered the car followed by Cecil Brown, one of the guards. They walked to the front.

"If we are willing to leave our water and lanterns behind," Brother Brown said, fighting to hide his disdain, "we'll be free to go."

If anyone objected, they did not say so aloud. No one dared complain for fear that by doing so they would not leave at all. The soldiers collected the few lamps aboard and watched as container after container of water was poured out the windows. The soldiers poked around until they were satisfied that the water was gone.

Mattie pursed her lips. At that moment, she hated General Salazar. She hated these soldiers. Glad for the dark, Mattie let her angry tears slide down her hot, sooty face.

The train finally pulled away. In unspoken agreement, the passengers, even the children, held their heads high, backs ramrod straight, in quiet dignity.[7] It stirred the hearts of many of the soldiers. They hung their heads in shame.

If all goes well, Mattie thought, *we should be in El Paso by morning.* Exhausted, she was just dozing when the train began to slow.

"Don't be alarmed, ladies," Brother Brown spoke from the back of the train. We're stopping for water. Take your containers and drink your fill.

On her third trip by the light of the moon to the clear, cool stream that fed into the Casa Grande River to refill her containers, Mattie took a moment to splash her face, suppressing the temptation to plunge in, clothes and all. Returning to her car, she was surprised to find a single coal oil lamp burning brightly, arranged in some contraption that hung from the ceiling. Mattie looked at the guard, eyebrows raised.

"We bought one for each car in that little town over there." Cecil Brown motioned behind him, then smiled. "Don't tell General Salazar."

Mattie grinned.

Now in the dim light, and the dead of night, the passengers swayed with the movement of the train. The children whimpered in turn. Two children leaned heavily against Mattie, one on each side. Younger children slept on quilts on the floor. Next to Leuna, Keturah squirmed on the straight-backed bench.

"Hold on, Keturah," Mattie whispered just before her eyes closed in troubled slumber.

***

"Rest stop," announced Cecil Brown. "We'll be here for a few minutes. Don't wander. Each of you is responsible to make sure that all in your party is on board before we leave. We don't want to have to come back for anybody." This brought a low chuckle from the passengers.

Outside, the dark night allowed privacy—women and small children to the left, men and boys to right. Phoebe and Anna stayed with the babies while the others took their turn and then helped the children. Mattie rose from her seat and made her way to the exit. Her legs were stiff, and her swollen ankles pushed against her boots. Not for the first time, the bile rose in her throat. This time, under the cover of night, she retched. She hoped the sickness would be gone soon.

Mattie rejoined her family who were stretching and walking as long as they could before getting on the train.

Keturah suddenly doubled over, her blue eyes reflecting pain. "I'm afraid this baby is not going to wait," she panted.

Isabelle took charge. "It's time for the birthing car. Mattie, you go with her. We'll take care of things here. Minnie Stark and her sister have offered to help if we need them."

It was not far to the birthing car just behind the engine. Keturah paused once, leaning heavily on Mattie for support. Finally arriving at the car, they found it had most of its windows except for a few in the back and was sparsely employed. The passengers were women, some with infants born since their departure, some like Keturah, who was about to deliver, and one in labor.[8]

The guard, Brother Harris, the only man allowed in the birthing car, ushered Mattie and her patient to one of several vacant seats arranged to make room for a bed.

Mattie glanced at Keturah and saw that her jaw tightened. Her wide forehead glistened with perspiration, her blonde hair damp around her face. Spreading several layers of quilts that had been heaped on them by the other Sevey women, Mattie helped her sister-in-law to her makeshift bed.

A hanging quilt that shielded the woman in labor from prying eyes did nothing to block her agonizing moans and then a scream. Mattie and Keturah both jumped. Suddenly, all was silent except several quick slaps followed finally by the sweet cry of new life. As if on cue, the women in the car exhaled simultaneously, smiling at each other in the dancing shadows of the coal oil lamp.

"It's a girl," Sister Hardy said from behind the screen, happy relief in her voice.

Keturah began panting. "Mattie," she whispered, "the baby is not going to wait much longer."

"Heavens to Betsy, why didn't you say something?" Mattie gently scolded.

"Sister Hardy's been a little busy." Keturah tried to smile, but it looked more like a grimace.

Mattie called out, "We got us another baby on the way!"

The midwife pushed the blanket aside. In a crisp tone, she said, "Do you think you can make it up here?"

Keturah nodded. "As soon as this pain passes." It came out a groan.

Behind the curtain of quilts, there was an identical bed across the aisle from the woman who had just given birth—a narrow quilt-covered sheet of plywood stretched between two sawhorses. Sister Hardy helped Keturah take her place.

Keturah moaned.

"Breathe deep, child. I need just a few more seconds." The midwife turned to the new mama. "You going to be okay?"

The woman nodded. "I'll just love this baby for a while, Sister Hardy. You do what you have to."

"Good girl." The older woman turned to Mattie. Dark circles deepened the lines in her eyes, but her voice spoke strength and confidence. "I'll be needing help. Are you up to it?"

Mattie looked at Keturah breathing through another pain. Taking a deep breath, Mattie said, "I'm up to it."

***

Keturah's infant boy was just an hour old when morning's first light appeared, barely perceptible in the eastern sky. The birth had been quick, allowing just enough time for hand washing. The baby's healthy cry brought the usual sighs from the other women, despite their exhaustion and discomfort. After helping the two new mothers to makeshift beds, Sister Hardy sat heavily in the straight-backed seat and dropped instantly to sleep, her chin resting on her ample chest. Mattie, a woman from Colonia Dublán, and the guard who hefted the water buckets managed the cleanup.

Too keyed to sleep, Mattie held the swaddled infant while Keturah slept. As the day grew lighter, mesquite bushes emerged from the darkened landscape. In the distance, short yuccas looked like vaqueros in sombreros watching the train rush by.

Thoughts swirled like misty clouds in Mattie's mind. Women had suffered indignities and inconveniences, not to mention possible death. They had left their homes as suddenly as if they were going for a pleasure walk. Lives had been disrupted, families torn apart and the future uncertain. Where was God?

"Mattie." Keturah smiled up at her sister-in-law. "You're shaking your head. Are you losing the argument?"

Mattie blushed. "Miserably. It's hard to understand all of this." Mattie moved her arm in a small arch.

Keturah reached for her baby and hugged him close. She smiled at Mattie. "It's been hard, but lots of things have gone right. We're safe. Salazar let us leave instead of shooting us all. And if that's not miracle enough for one day, we got us four healthy babies and four happy mamas without a single complication. I don't think its coincidence, Mattie." Keturah reached for sister-in-law's hand and patted it. "Joy born of travail, Mattie."

Mattie's eyes glistened. "Thank you, Keturah." Would the day ever come when she would be able to see the blessings without having them pointed out to her?

***

The monotonous clack slowed as the train crossed the Rio Grande from Ciudad Juárez to El Paso. It seemed the whole city reached out with a helping hand. The lumberyard was transformed into a camp. Sheds were divided into cubicles, allowing privacy for each family. Emergency plumbing was volunteered. Food and quilts were donated. Taxis and restaurants offered free services. Doctors volunteered. Businesses dropped handbills advertising employment that would allow families to remain at the lumberyards until other arrangements could be made.[9] The only dark spot on such overwhelming kindness was the photographers and journalists who clawed unrelentingly at the outer gate to get interviews with "refugees."

Mattie bristled at being called a refugee and was grateful for American soldiers guarding the complex, keeping the reporters at bay.

Keturah and Bessie rested peacefully with their newborns in their makeshift home.

"We're the lucky ones," Isabelle said. "The Cardons and Whitings have been assigned to army tents."

"No, the lucky ones are in a hotel." Minerva looked pointedly at Mattie.

Mattie flushed. The Wood family was taking her and Leuna to the Alberta Hotel, where they would stay until Mattie could get passage to Bisbee and Leuna to Salt Lake, where she would join their mother.

"I hate leaving you here," Mattie said.

This time, Minerva flushed. "I didn't mean anything. I don't resent your going, but you are lucky."

"I would dearly love to take you with me, especially you, Keturah and you, Bessie, with your newborns."

"Nonsense," Keturah said. "I'm perfectly comfortable. Besides, Bill plans to come here for me, and we'll be off to Arizona."

"And I wouldn't think of leaving either," said Bessie. "Don't worry about us. We're right where we want to be for the moment."

"It's not like Bessie and Keturah don't have all of us to help," Isabel said. "And the people here have been wonderful."

"I'll think of you every day." Mattie hugged her sisters-in-law, and Minerva and Lola.

***

Arriving at Nellie's where she was to stay, Mattie was grateful that her sister and husband had moved to a new home. There were no reminders of that awful night when a crazed man meant to kill her. Those were nightmares of the past. Now her nightmares concerned Ene, who was somewhere on the trail between here and there that was fraught with danger. By day, she hung tenaciously to hope. It had been a week. She was sure that he would arrive any day.

Mattie sipped her lemonade. Comfortably situated in a wicker chair, she swatted at the daring flies as she superintended Jack, who had grown into a boisterous two-year-old, playing on a patch of grass at the base of the porch. Naomi, who was nearly as much boy as Jack, preferring the wood carved horses to dolls, played just far enough from Jack that he could not interfere with her make believe.

Parley McRae came through the gate. "I see Nellie has you busy watching the crew."

Mattie smiled.

Parley handed her a letter. "It's from Leuna, posted in Salt Lake. I suppose that means she got there."

"I imagine so." No news from Ene. Mattie hoped her disappointment did not show. "Have you heard if our men arrived at Dog Springs?"

Parley frowned, as if searching for the right words.

Mattie sighed. "I can already tell it isn't good news, so you might as well tell me."

Parley cleared his throat. "Rumor has it that a band of Mexican revolutionaries have been spotted heading to the border."

"As in Dog Springs border?"

Parley nodded.

"A band of revolutionaries?" Mattie stared. The implication hung like putrid air between them. Mexican revolutionaries at Dog Springs could only mean one thing. They had found the expedition. Mattie fought the rising bile that welled up inside her.

***

The soldier wiped his brow. Dog Springs, New Mexico, was not a comfortable place to be any time of year, much less July. For hours, while the sun beat down, he and thirty other United States soldiers had tracked the cloud of dust that came ever closer from behind the rocks where they waited. Finally, nearly two hundred men slowly materialized out of the dust, driving a herd of horses numbering close to five hundred.

The private adjusted his hat. He was surprised that the rebels did not use more stealth in crossing the border and shook his head at their insolence. Rigid and grim, with his gun ready, he waited for the captain's command to open fire on the hapless raiders.

***

The company of Mormon colonists—hats pulled low against the sun, grizzled, and covered with dust from too long on the trail—looked rough and hard. Hidden in their wagons were the smuggled guns that they were returning to the United States military. Miraculously, they had traveled without accident or sightings of the Mexican revolutionaries.

Ene was in the lead with Ammon Tenney. He grinned at Ammon. "You could use a bath," he said.

"You're no sweet-smelling rose yourself, old man."

Ene guffawed. For the first time in more than a week, he relaxed, unaware that at least one gun was aimed at his heart.

***

Mattie tried to keep busy, but even playing with the children brought little relief. All she could do was wait.

And hope.

Seeking refuge in the large vegetable garden behind the house, she began picking tomatoes that hung red and heavy on waist-high vines supported with stakes and twine.

The first time she had reached for a tomato down low, she had recoiled when her hand had touched a web so tightly woven that it sprang back with no apparent damage—black widows, Nellie warned. After that, Mattie never picked tomatoes without a long stick to stir up the webs and frighten off lingering spiders.

Gathering the corners of her apron, creating a deep pocket, she began to fill it, her mind crowded with fear, leaving no room to be persnickety about passing through gossamer traps so deadly to an unsuspecting insect.

It had occurred to her that the band of reported rebels might be the men. It brought little comfort. There had been several forays by the Mexican soldiers into the United States to steal guns from the very army put there to keep them out. And that army was on high alert. How would US soldiers know a dust-covered revolutionary from a dust-covered farmer?

It was the makings of a massacre.

"Please, dear God," Mattie prayed. "Protect our men."

***

"Ready," commanded the captain in a voice just loud enough for his men to hear.

This is not going to be pretty, the private thought, *but these rebels need to learn they can't plunder our borders without a price.* What was the captain waiting for?

"Aim."

The soldier found his man and took aim. Suddenly, his target removed his hat, wiping away some of the grime from his face. The soldier blanched. He knew that face. It was his friend, Ammon Tenney. These weren't Mexican rebels at all. They were the refugees!

"Don't shoot, don't shoot!" he screamed, jumping from his hiding place. [10]

***

It was the excitement in Nellie's voice coming from the front porch that first got Mattie's attention. Then she heard the familiar baritone chuckle. Her heart leapt. With little recollection of how she got to Ene's tight embrace, she sobbed shamelessly.

Even Nellie wiped at her eyes, and Parley coughed to cover his emotion.

"I hope those are happy tears." Ene laughed to hide the tremble in his own voice.

"We thought you were dead," Mattie whispered.

"I almost was," Ene whispered back. "I almost was."

After a much appreciated bath, and over a sumptuous supper of fried chicken, white gravy over biscuits, and of course, sliced tomatoes doctored with vinegar, salt, and sugar, Ene recounted the incident at Dog Springs. It solicited a shudder from both his wife and his sister-in-law and an appreciative whistle from Parley. When dinner was over, Nellie forbade Mattie to help with the cleanup.

"The two of you have some catching up to do." Nellie looked pointedly at Mattie, who in her grief had let Nellie, who was well into her own pregnancy, in on her secret. "Parley will help me with the dishes," Nellie insisted.

In the cool August evening, Ene put his arm around his wife as they walked to nowhere in particular.

"Colonia Díaz was burned to the ground before we ever left the Pajarito," Ene said. "I expect the other communities will get the same."

"What do we do now?"

"Maybe get work in the copper mines. If Parley and Nellie don't mind, we can live with them until we can get our own place."

"I can't believe we are talking about never going back to Mexico, but I do enjoy not having to look over my shoulder every minute worrying about soldiers robbing us blind or killing us."

"You afraid somebody will knock me off?" Ene was trying to make light of the matter.

"I don't want to raise our baby without a father."

Ene stared. "Baby?"

Mattie grinned and nodded.

"*Our* baby?" he asked, emphasizing our. "As in now?"

Mattie nodded again.

"When?"

"February sometime."

Ene whooped, and twirled Mattie off her feet. Silently she acknowledged her wisdom in not telling her husband such happy news with anyone in the near vicinity.

Abruptly, Ene stopped. "I didn't hurt you, did I?"

Mattie laughed and shook her head.

Ene grinned. "We'll name him Enos Sevey."

"And if he's a girl?"

Ene guffawed and kissed his wife. As they continued walking, he listened to her account of the grueling train ride, grimacing and smiling alternately.

The evening had turned to night when they arrived at the gate of McRaes' wood-frame house.

Mattie turned to Ene and placed her hand on his chest. "I think I would die if I had to face life without you." Her voice wavered.

Ene took her in his arms and kissed her. Tenderness washed over her like a warm bath. For an instant, all the doubt and uncertainty of life melted away. She wanted to freeze the moment and live within it forever.

***

"We can't live with the McRaes forever, and me with no job," Ene insisted. "Why waste any more time here when I have a living in Mexico."

"I'm not talking forever," Mattie said, "just until the baby comes."

"That's four months away."

"Fine. Go now, but we go together."

"It's not safe yet for families," Ene said. "The Bentleys tried it and came back because it was too dangerous."

"I'm not the Bentleys," Mattie said.

Ene looked at his wife. "You are a spitfire, but I can't let you, Mattie, for your sake and the baby's. Until families are allowed back, it just doesn't make sense to be taking my wife and child and plant them in harm's way."

Mattie knew his argument had merit and hated that. She stared at the yellow moon just cresting the hill and pulled her shawl close against the October evening. Any other time, a full moon might have inspired tenderness. Now, it served only to antagonize.

"You'll write often," she commanded. "I'll go crazy if I don't hear from you often."

***

November 6, 1912

Dearest Mattie,

I hope you are taking care of our little son.

Mattie smiled. "It'll serve him right if it's a girl."

I arrived safely. Had no trouble. Alma Spilsbury is in town. We are the only white men. The soldiers no longer use our schools for their headquarters, but they come riding into town on occasion. The schools are going to need cleaning, but other than that, they are in pretty good shape. Many of the homes, both here and in Colonia Dublán, have been well cared for by the Mexican neighbors. The Quevedos have been true to their word. They have given me garden produce that Rafaela put up using your equipment. Not much money was made from the orchards. Soldiers pretty much help themselves. Martha's dishes are still in the cupboard, and her rocker sits in the front room. Your wedding trunk is gone. It seems it served as a bribe.

The linens and dishes were gone. Somehow, the news did not upset her. It had been harder to leave them behind than to learn that she had lost them all together. Mattie continued to read.

I love you, miss you, and look forward to the day when you will join me.

***

"You need something to lift your spirits, Mattie." Nellie was almost cross.

Mattie watched the flames dance in the fireplace as she rocked back and forth in Nellie's rocker. November had flowed slowly into December, and Christmas was two weeks away. Ene had been as good as his word, writing often—not that Mattie had received his letters regularly. The mail system lacked. Sometimes she went several weeks without a letter and then received them all at once. How forlorn it would be to live, as Ene did, in a town of vacant houses, windows staring out at her. She shivered.

"Why don't you dress up a bit and go to the Hermitage for lunch. I know Mrs. Abernathy would love to see you."

"It's so busy at lunchtime." Mattie tucked the lap quilt more tightly around her legs.

"Today is Saturday. There will be few customers, and even fewer if you go a little late," Nellie insisted.

Mattie looked at her sister, who grinned back at her. Mattie smiled. "Perhaps you're right, Nellie."

Mrs. Abernathy was delighted to see Mattie and insisted that lunch was on the house. The two women visited comfortably in the nearly empty County Home Bar and Hermitage. Mattie did not notice the appreciable glances from the few male customers finishing a late lunch. Her hair, wound in thick ropes, was pinned appealingly at the base of her neck, and her jade green eyes shone, animated in conversation. She blushed when the older woman's discerning eye discovered that she was with child.

"Not that it's evident to the casual observer," Mrs. Abernathy said, "but I'm no casual observer."

Careful to avoid the subject of Mr. Dyer, Mattie's previous employer had no compunction grilling her about "that young man" she had gone to marry in California and did not give up until she had learned every detail of the whole unhappy affair.

"In the end," Mattie said, grinning, "I went home and married my childhood nemesis. You know, every rose has a thorn. We can't agree which of us is the thorn." Both women laughed.

"My, my. Life does have an interesting way of turning out, doesn't it?" Mrs. Abernathy said, rising. "Thank you for coming to see me, Mattie. It's means a lot to me. If you need work, I can use you."

Mattie expressed her gratitude for the kindness, and Mrs. Abernathy brought her a large piece of hot apple pie and left her to eat it. She chewed slowly, savoring the sweet cinnamon-flavored apples, cooked to perfection. Casually, she glanced at the customer who had just entered the diner. Mattie stared. Looking back at her was Alonzo Skousen.[11]

***

"My son, Lem, got in from El Paso today." Alma Spilsbury looked over his cup at Ene. Alma had been a young married man when he had first arrived in Mexico; he felt strongly about defending the life he had made, wanting to leave nothing to chance and admired Ene for having a like notion.

"Did he bring Allie?" Ene asked, looking for good news to pass on to Mattie.

"Nope, but he 'spects to soon. Bishop Bentley feels purty strong that the Mormons belong here, and Lem says that Elder Ivins backs him. He's encouragin' anyone who wants to, to come back. He says we'll be safe if we mind our p's and q's. Should be a nice parcel of folks arrivin' next month."

"What about Dublán?"

"Same. Lem says Bishop Call should be arriving any day."

As soon as Alma Spilsbury left, Ene took up his pen and wrote to Mattie. "You can come as soon as you are able to travel after the baby is born," he wrote. He paused. Two months seemed an eternity.

***

The pie barely made it down Mattie's throat without choking her. Her face grew hot as Alonzo made his way to her table. He was dressed in an expensive pinstriped suit, his overcoat draped over his arm.

"Hello, Mattie," he said, with a lopsided grin, like he half expected to see her.

"Alonzo," Mattie stammered.

"You're looking radiant."

"What a coincidence." Mattie hoped her voice sounded steady.

"Oh, not such a coincidence. I went to El Paso to check on my folks. Mother told me you were staying with Nellie and Parley. I'm passing through and after a bite to eat at your old stomping grounds, if I still had the courage, I was going to drop in at the McRaes'."

Mattie said, "Oh. How nice."

Alonzo nodded. "I'm on my way home to Tucson. I opened the business there for my uncle."

"And you're doing well?"

"There're no earthquakes." Alonzo smiled.

Mattie gave a nervous laugh and stared at the twisted napkin in her hand. But for the earthquake that had given her time to think, she might be sitting here as his wife. "And your family?"

"Just me and the wife," he mumbled, glancing away. "Children aren't a possibility for us. Something to do with a bad case of the mumps when I was a kid."

Mattie's shade deepened when she realized the mistake. "I . . . I was asking after your parents."

This time, Alonzo turned red, and Mattie wished she had not tried to explain. The waitress arrived, saving them from more awkward apologies. The server took Alonzo's order—a large bowl of beef stew and generous portion of hot raised bread.

When they were alone again, now composed, Alonzo picked up the conversation. "Dad's planning to go back to Mexico as soon as he can.

Mattie hardly realized that Alonzo had spoken. She was stuck back in the conversation, the part about *no children* because of some cruel fate of childhood.

"So you married our archenemy." Alonzo grinned.

Mattie tried to think of something clever to say. In the end she just smiled and fussed with her pie.

"I was more than a little surprised when Mother referred to you as 'the poor girl Alonzo jilted on her wedding day.'"

Mattie knew Alonzo was grinning again. He was trying to put her at ease, joking about the past, showing that he had put it quite behind him. "I thought you would prefer being the rogue," she said.

"I thank you." He nodded gallantly. "There is something manly about being a rogue."

Mattie blushed again.

Alonzo's meal arrived. "Let me know if you need anything," the waitress said.

Alonzo thanked her. When she was out of hearing, he asked, "Do waitresses really mean that?"

"Most of the time." Mattie was finally able to look at him. She relaxed enough to carry on a normal conversation, even laughing over stories from her days as a waitress.

Alonzo grew serious. "How are you coping with the war and all this?" He waved his hand as if to take in all of Bisbee.

Mattie went back to scrutinizing her pie. "Fine," she said a little too quickly.

"You leave your home at a moment's notice, you have a hellish ride on a train, your future's uncertain, and you say 'fine'?"

Mattie's face burned. Had she been anything but bright red since the moment Alonzo walked in the door? Alonzo looked at Mattie for a long moment and then mercifully changed the subject. "How's your mother?"

"Mother was already in Utah when we evacuated, thank goodness."

"Moe married yet?"

Moe was a safe topic, and Mattie relaxed a little. "Not that I know of. He doesn't write much."

"I thought Moe would tie it up with Ruthie."

"She had other plans. It broke his heart." Mattie could have cut her tongue out for her choice of words. "So when does your train leave?" She hurried on, trying to sound casual, hoping it didn't sound like she was rushing him off, which she was.

Alonzo took out his gold pocket watch. "I have just enough time to finish this bowl of stew and a piece of apple pie."

Mattie tried to hide her relief. "Nellie and Parley would love to see you." Propriety demanded that she invite Alonzo to the McRaes', but she was loath to do it. When she stood, he would certainly see that she was expecting, and it was suddenly important to her that he not know.

"Thank you. Maybe another time." Alonzo was no more successful in hiding his relief than Mattie had been. He finished his last bite of pie, then shook Mattie's hand. "It's been a great pleasure, Mattie. I wish you every happiness."

"Good luck, Alonzo." She meant it and watched him leave, feeling only sorrow for having hurt a good friend so deeply. He could hardly say Ene's name, much less ask after him. Compassion filled her. Touching her belly that might never have been, she shuddered.

Many honorable women were denied the privilege of bearing children. Perhaps God knew that she would have suffered too deeply and prevented her from such a fate.

"You don't always know why God does what He does. But you know that God is there." Grandmother Thomas's words came to Mattie.

Mattie sighed. At least she had spared Alonzo the pain of knowing that she was with child.

***

As she left the diner, Alonzo stood in the shadows and watched her walk away. Grave and pale, he nodded. Just as he thought. Mattie had been right not to marry him. All his money could not have given her what she wanted most. Children.

1913

O N THIS COLD JANUARY DAY, THE SUN SHINED IN A desperate effort to deceive, but the naked trees and the brown grass evidenced the truth. Mattie ambled up the walk to the McCrae house, holding a letter. Entering, the warmth of the wood stove caressed her face.

"A letter from Ene?" Nellie set the iron on the ironing board.

Without taking off her coat, Mattie sat in the comfortable chair and grinned at Nellie as she ripped open the envelope. The letter was dated January third.

Dearest Love,

How I miss you. Christmas was just another day without you. I hope that you are taking care of yourself and our little one.

More and more families are arriving, and things look too nearly normal here. Tom and Isabel arrived last week. Too many rebel soldiers hide out in the mountains, and it's not safe for families to move back yet, so they'll be in Colonia Juárez for a while. Their valuables are safe.

General Villa is in command now. He has the Red Flaggers on the run. We don't see much of them any more. That has subdued the Fierro brothers some. General Villa keeps a tight rein on his men, which is good for us. There is less lawlessness and we feel safer with him in charge. After the baby is born, you can come home.

I will be in El Paso on a business trip the tenth of January. Send a telegram to the Alberta Hotel if you can meet me.

"Nellie, Nellie." Mattie heaved herself from the chair and lumbered toward her sister. "I'm going to El Paso to meet Ene."[1]

Nellie situated the shirt just right to give the collar a finishing touch with the iron. "You're doing no such thing, Martha Ann Sevey. You're going to have a baby any day now."

"It's Martha Ann Wood, and you're spoiling it for me. It's eons before the baby is due."

"A month, Mattie. That's four little weeks, or less, and from the looks of you, I'd say less."

"I'm going, Nellie, but I'd much rather go with your blessing. It's only for a few days."

Nellie put the shirt on the hanger and added it to the other ironed clothes hanging from the doorframe. "Can't say I'd do differently." She smiled.

Mattie grabbed her sister impetuously and swung her around. "Thank you, Nellie. You're the best."

***

Ene kissed Mattie hard, and she clung to him, already dreading the day she had to leave. She must not think about it. Why ruin the only two days they had together?

"You've grown a mustache," Mattie said.

"You like it?"

"You look like Pancho Villa."

"That's the idea." Ene grinned. "How's Junior?"

"You know it's a girl," Mattie teased.

"I hope she doesn't mind being called Junior." Ene laughed and Mattie was sure that the whole station turned to look at them. She didn't care.

"How's Nellie and Parley?"

"Nellie wasn't too happy about me coming."

"Have you heard from your family?"

"Phoebe and Moe got married." Mattie smiled.

"To each other?"

Mattie laughed. "Brother and sister? Be serious."

"Son of a gun, that old man. I didn't think he'd ever tie the knot."

"He's the same age as you practically, you old man."

Ene laughed and hugged his wife.

She wondered if he would mention Alonzo's visit. He didn't. Having shared her deepest sentiments on the topic in a letter, she let it go.

As they dashed from depot to cab, and from building to building, the biting winds stung Mattie's nose and ears. Late afternoon on the second day, they kept to the warmth of the hotel.

"This is no good, Matt," Ene said quietly. "Two days is too short."

Mattie was silent. In Ene's tender embrace, she felt complete. She hated the separation.

"Let's stay here a few more days, Ene."

"What would you say about coming home with me?"

"What about the baby?"

"I don't mean for you to stay," Ene said. "Come home for a couple of weeks. I'll bring you back to have the baby."

Mattie considered the suggestion unaware that her eyes, bright and smiling, had already given Ene her answer.

"Nellie's going to kill me," she said with a laugh.

***

The train ride from El Paso to Pearson resembled nothing of the last time Mattie had taken this route. She grew silent as memories flooded back. Ene put his arm around her and drew her close. "You are a force to be reckoned with. I knew it the first time you bested me that night we were playing hide-and-seek."

"I was only eleven," Mattie said.

Ene's jolly, baritone laugh turned several heads.

Leaving Casas, unsmiling soldiers, grizzled and smelling like something out of a slop bucket, could not dampen Mattie's excitement when familiar landmarks told her she was nearly home. Two days in Pearson and then Colonia Juárez.

Mattie's heart quickened when the train made an unscheduled stop at the mouth of the Cumbres tunnel. The soldiers mumbled surprise among themselves. Well armed, they left to investigate.

"I'm going to see what's going on," Ene said.

"Be careful, Ene. I didn't come home to bury you."

Ene grinned and patted his gun concealed under his coat, tucked at the back of his waist. It brought little comfort to Mattie who feared that carrying a gun would cause more trouble than it would prevent.

Time seemed interminable before steam hissed, the great arms churned, and the wheels lurched, inching forward. Mattie looked for Ene and saw him standing by the track waiting for the car. He gripped the long metal handle and hefted himself up to the step.

"What happened?" Mattie asked

"The engineer thought he saw someone in the tunnel. We checked things out but didn't find anything. Doesn't mean he didn't see somebody. They could've been leaving instead of entering."

The train entered the tunnel and sudden darkness. Ene fidgeted. Mattie grew quiet. The windows had glass now, saving them from the black ash and choking fumes Mattie remembered. She was not saved, however, the terror of knowing that anything might go wrong in the mile-long tunnel: the worst, being trapped under tons of rock and earth. As the car grew light again, Mattie relaxed and smiled at Ene. He squeezed her hand.

***

Mattie spent most of the next two days sleeping while Ene took care of business. Her dreams, like a dark omen, always returned to the train, rocking deep within the tunnel with no way out. Each time, she awoke trembling.

The winter sun was low on the horizon when Mattie rose to ready herself for dinner. She would surprise Ene and meet him in the café below. Dressing with care, she unraveled her thick braid and brushed through her long hair. Braiding it again, she wrapped it at the back of her head. A distant rumble shook the window. *An early thunderstorm*, she thought, dismissing it with a shrug as she placed the last hairpin.

The diner lacked the flair of the Hermitage, but it was clean, and the food was delicious. Mattie searched the menu. Enchiladas, tacos, desebrada, burritos, posole, tamales, and chile rellenos made up for the absence of Mrs. Abernathy's apple pie. Tonight, she would indulge with a healthy portion of flan. Almost, she could taste the caramelized sugarcoated custard, and her mouth watered.

The diner door opened, and Mattie looked up to see Ene. His ashen face and pursed lips made her heart lurch. So distracted was he that he didn't see her, taking the stairs two at time. She called to him, but he didn't hear. Mattie hurried after him, arriving just as Ene was coming out of their room.

"What's happened?"

"The train," he said hoarsely.

"The train?

"The Cumbres tunnel . . . blown up."

"Passengers?" she whispered.

Ene nodded.

"The silhouette in the tunnel when we came through?"

"I . . . I think so. Some fellow down at the mill bragged that it was meant to blow a couple of days ago."

Mattie sat hard on the edge of the bed, the horror of it too immense to absorb. It could have been her and Ene. She tried to block the mental picture of carnage.

The tiny life within her moved gently. Another thought struck her. Without the train, she would not get back to Bisbee to have her baby.

***

Mattie's disappointment, being cut off from Bisbee, was short lived when she saw the small adobe house Ene had built. The isolated ranch house was risky for wartime, and their new little home had been built next to his parents' place.

A two-room affair—a large kitchen and one large bedroom— was nothing fancy. With Mattie's touch, it became a comfortable haven. Furniture from the ranch house—beds, bureaus, table and chairs, the cupboard with Martha's dishes, pots, pans, the stove, and Martha's rocking chair—were installed. Colorful rag rugs graced the hewn-wood floor, contrasting pleasantly with whitewashed walls.

Mattie loved being mistress of her home again. With being so busy and with the joy of being with her husband, the past month had flown by.

It warmed Mattie to see Ene happy and content. Between freighting and the butcher shop, they did okay considering the hard times, and she was fiercely proud of her husband. Tom and Ene went in together on the butcher shop, and they hired a loyal man named Rudolfo to run it, allowing the men to tend to the other irons in their fire.

Needing to make a trip to the butcher shop, Mattie threw a heavy cape over her shoulders that fell below her knees, covering her heavy protrusion. Stepping into the cold, she trundled the few steps to her in-law's home. In another couple of weeks, the frozen path would become a bog. Perhaps a thick layer of hay would be just the ticket. Otherwise, Jane would go mad trying to keep the floor clean.

Mattie knocked lightly on the door and let herself in. Her mother-in-law sat at the kitchen table, darning well-worn socks. "I'm going to get some cheese." Can I bring you anything?" Mattie did not say that she hoped the walk would begin in earnest the intermittent pains that had robbed her of much-needed sleep during the past week.

Jane adjusted her glasses and shook her head. "Thank you kindly, dear."

"I was wondering," Mattie said, "if I could borrow some helpers to come with me."

Jane's mouth turned up at the corner in a half smile, letting Mattie know that she recognized the plea for help as merely a way to pleasantly occupy a couple of pent-up children. Mattie no longer thought about the irony of these children being her brother- and sister-in-law or aunt and uncle to her newborn.

"Can I go?" asked Rosalie, her brown braids bouncing as she jumped up and down. "I'm eight. I can be lots of help."

"Me too," said Clarence.

"You're not eight," Rosalie said. "You're only five."

"But I can help." Clarence poked out his lower lip in defiance. "John says I'm lots of help."

"If your big brother says so," laughed Mattie, "then I'm sure it's true."

Clarence's blue eyes barely visible under a shock of brown hair, beamed at Mattie. Addressing his mother he whined, "Please, Mama. Can we?"

"If Mattie wants the bother of you," Jane said, "you both may go."

Clarence and Rosalie turned expectantly toward Mattie. They used every excuse to spend time with her, often escaping to her house when their mother "soaped the floor," which she did frequently with lye soap and scrub brush—which would happen even more frequently without a nice path of hay.

Mattie nodded. "Get your wraps." The children whooped.

"How about you, Roberta?" Mattie invited her dark-haired sister-in-law. Deep brown eyes flashed, bordering on disdain. Mattie grinned. She had expected it. Roberta considered herself above children's play, at least most of the time. She was a beauty, even for a twelve-year-old. Like Ene, she and sixteen-year-old John had dark complexions like their father. Rosalie and Clarence were the fair ones of the family, brown hair and blue eyes, taking after Jane.

"We'll be back for supper," Mattie said, taking each child by the hand. "I'll visit awhile with Isabelle."

It was uncharacteristically quiet as they passed the Harper Hotel on Main Street—a reminder that life had not returned to normal since the exodus. Left, then down a dirt path, the swinging bridge spanned a trickle of water snaking down the dry Piedras Verdes River. Holding tightly to the braided cables, careful not to look down, Mattie kept her focus straight ahead, never releasing her grip until her feet touched firm ground. She smiled as Clarence and Rosalie jumped up and down and rocked back and forth with abandon. As a child, she had played for hours on the bridge. Now her equilibrium hardly allowed her to walk across without assistance.

"That's enough, kids. Let's be going."

The children scrambled easily to the other side in synchronized step with the movement of the bridge. They followed the trail to the canal, six or seven feet across with a proper bridge, one that did not sway. This was Ene's canal. Mattie smiled with pride.

It was then she saw the man following behind them. She knew him only as Treviso, angry and malicious. Quickening her pace, she lumbered down the street as quickly as her discomfort allowed. Treviso quickened his pace as well. Mattie shuddered.

One lot from Tom and Isabel's house, just before the pursuer caught up with them, John Hatch stepped out into the street just as Mattie passed his front gate, intercepting him.

Arriving at her brother's home, she offered a quick prayer of thanks. She could hear that Hatch's polite conversation was met with anger. She turned to look as Treviso lunged forward with a knife.

Mattie blanched.

The children stared.

"Come," she said. She pushed the children through the door without bothering to knock. Isabel, long sense having lost her girlish figure, came from the kitchen, wiping her hands on her apron.

"A bad man is fighting with Brother Hatch," Clarence blurted, eyes round.

Isabel's hands froze, still wrapped in the apron.

"Treviso," Mattie said.

Isabel headed for the butcher shop that abutted their house. "I'll get Rudolfo."

Mattie deposited Clarence and Rosie in the parlor with Isabel's children, Julia and George. Returning to the front door, Mattie saw Rudolfo in a blood-smudged butcher's apron. The irony was not lost on her as he ran toward the fighting men. Their Mexican friend made good time despite being squat and round.

John Hatch kept Treviso at bay, throwing rocks in his direction. Rudolfo shouted, and Treviso turned to look. The rock that hit him was not intended for his head. Treviso dropped to the ground and slowly rolled to his back. Rudolfo picked up Treviso's knife.

A crowd had gathered. Mattie held her breath, waiting for the fallen man to get up. Treviso did not move.

He was dead.[2]

***

John Hatch's explanation that it was an accident was met with menacing threats of death at the "gringo" who dared to attack one of their people. While Hatch retreated to his house, Rudolfo tried to calm the mob.

It was then that Mattie felt the pain beginning in her lower back, spreading to her abdomen. It was nearly a minute before it slowly receded and Mattie could breathe again. There was a popping sensation deep inside. A gush of warm liquid puddled at her feet. She was grateful for her long skirt.

"Isabel," Mattie said. It came out calm and commanding.

Isabel tore her eyes from the drama down the street to look at Mattie.

"I need to go home." Mattie stepped to one side.

Following her gaze, Isabel saw the damp earth. Her eyes grew wide. "The waters." Down the street, the crowd was growing fast. Grabbing Mattie's arm she propelled her toward the house. "It's not safe right now. We'll have to wait for Tom."

***

An hour passed before Rudolfo reported that he had dispersed the crowd, saving Hatch's neck, at least for the moment. Emotions ran high, and the streets were dangerous. He agreed to take a message to the Woods so Jane wouldn't worry.

Between pains, Mattie wished for Ene who was not due until tomorrow sometime.

It had been several hours since the sun had set when Tom finally came in. Rudolfo agreed to go with him to take Mattie and the children home. The ride was uncomfortable. Another pain. Mattie gritted her teeth. Inhaling through her nose, she exhaled through her mouth as Sister Hardy had coached Keturah.

Tom lifted Mattie gently from the wagon. "Rosie, better get your ma and pa," Tom said.

"Is Mattie going to be okay?"

"I expect she'll be fine as goose feathers in a few days." Tom smiled. Rosalie darted off and within seconds, Jane and Peter appeared as Tom helped Mattie to the door.

"Thank you, Tom," Mattie panted.

Jane readied the bed and made her daughter-in-law as comfortable as possible.

"Is it time for Grandmother Spilsbury?" Mattie asked. Three generations called Prudence Spilsbury grandmother, even those not related. She wasn't a midwife, but she knew her way around the birthing bed.

"I believe the pains have to get much harder and closer together before we can expect a baby." Jane was apologetic. "The first one always takes longer."

Mattie wanted to cry. Keturah's baby had been born within twenty minutes after the waters broke. Already, she had been in labor for hours.

The night dragged on. Mattie roiled in pain. She was unaware of the dawn, unaware that Mexican mobs threatened to kill every white man, woman, and child, and burn the town to the ground for what happened to Treviso. That Jane Wood slept in the chair at her bedside, that Grandmother Spilsbury attended her, seemed just a dream. Not until Ene took her hand and spoke her name did she know he had come.

Groaning with a tremendous urge to push, Mattie rolled to the side of the bed and threw her legs over, determined to get up.

"Where're you going, Matt?" Ene said.

"To the outhouse," Mattie said.

"That's not what ails you, child." Prudence Spilsbury said gently, pushing Mattie back into the bed. "If you aren't careful, that baby will drop right out on the floor."

Ene was no longer at her side, having been peremptorily dismissed. Minutes dragged into hours as intense pain peaked and waned inexorable as the waves of the sea, Mattie groaning with the exertion, then panting in exhaustion. Conventional modesty ignored, the drapes hardly covered her body, but she was oblivious to the indignities.

Lamps were lit when the sun slid behind the mountains. While the death of a man threatened the destruction of a community, in the dim light of the little room, the ravages of birth threatened the destruction of one woman and her unborn child.

It had been over twenty-four hours since the waters had broke. Pale as death and barely conscious of the cool cloths on her brow and chipped ice at her lips, Mattie's strength ebbed. Voices of instruction and encouragement were lost in the pain. She prayed for the sweet release of death.

***

Mattie felt like a hovering wraith. She saw herself on the bed, pale, weak, and exhausted. Oddly, she felt no pain. Below her, Ene and Peter rushed into the room. She drifted higher and higher. The room became a pinprick of light far below. Then it too was swallowed up in the darkness.

***

On the mahogany bureau, stark against the whitewashed adobe wall, a single daffodil in a jar of water spoke of spring and new life. That it was early morning, Mattie learned from the rooster's flagrant crow. In the next room, a fire crackled and someone swished about. She swallowed and winced, her throat raw and dry.

She was not dead. Had she dreamed it?

Mattie tried to lift her arm—deadweight, as if it belonged to another. Even her legs felt heavy and useless. She willed them to move. Nothing happened. With difficulty, she turned her head and focused on a slumped figure in the rocking chair beside her. Chin on his chest, hands clasped in front, Ene breathed deeply. Mattie wanted to touch him.

Her eyes searched for a cradle and found none. Had she heard the cry of an infant or had she dreamed that too? It seemed she had dreamt a great deal.

Ene's head flopped back against the rocker. His eyes blinked open. He reached for her hand and pressed it to his lips, trying unsuccessfully to choke back escaping sobs. Mattie wanted to stroke his head, but her hand would not obey.

"I thought I lost you, Matt," Ene finally said, speaking softly.

Mattie smiled weakly. "Can't get rid of me so easy." The words came out in a hoarse whisper.

Ene smiled tenderly. "I love you."

"The baby?"

"A valentine baby born two days ago."

"A son?"

Grinning through his tears, he said, "Junior is the most beautiful little girl you'll ever see." [3]

Mattie's dry lips twitched. "Water," she whispered.

Ene raised her head. The cool liquid felt delicious on her throat. "Name?" Mattie asked.

"You'll have plenty of time to come up with something."

"Where is she?"

"She's sleeping by the fire. Mother's keeping an eye on her."

"I want to hold her," Mattie whispered.

"And you shall," Ene said.

On cue, Jane came in the room with a small bundle wrapped in flannel. "It's about time you came back to us." Although Jane tried to sound cheery, her eyes looked sad. Ene's too. Something was wrong.

The baby? Was something wrong with the baby?

Ene helped Mattie to sit, positioning himself behind her, supporting her arms so she could hold her little one. She started, tiny hands spread delicately in momentary spasm.

"You're okay, sweetie," Mattie crooned.

Jane said, "If you need me, I'll be over at the house. There's wheat mush and hot bread on the stove, Ene. See to it that Mattie eats."

"Thank you," Mattie said, grateful not only for the food, but also for her mother-in-law's sensitivity to her need to be alone with her little family.

Jane waved her away.

Mattie stroked the velvety cheek and the thatch of black, soft-downy hair. In that moment she knew the meaning of pure love. Although she had felt the innocence of her sisters' babies and had been touched by their purity, this was different: a powerful bond reserved for mother and child, two intimate friends reuniting, not like strangers meeting for the first time.

She checked the baby, relieved to find that the miniature ears, nose, and mouth were perfectly formed, as were the feet and hands.

The baby was fine, so what were they not saying, Ene and his mother?

The little pink face squinched fitfully, finally giving way to a squawk. Instinctively rooting, she latched firmly to her source of nourishment and comfort. Mattie gritted her teeth. It hurt. When the pain subsided, she laughed at her little black-haired valentine, nursing so vigorously.

"I dreamed this," Mattie said.

"It was no dream. Mother and Isabel saw to it that the baby began nursing right away."

The infant grasped Mattie's finger. What a tragedy to never experience the miracle of life. Sadly, after such a difficult birth, she doubted she would ever experience it again.

The baby opened its eyes. Mattie stared. The glazed, newborn expression had become intelligent awareness looking right into her soul. Was that a smile?

Unbidden, words came to Mattie's mind. She didn't know how she knew it, but there was no doubt that her daughter was speaking to her.

"Grandfather told you, Mother."

"Grandfather?"

"Grandfather Sevey."

Mattie's eyes misted. So that had not been a dream either. "Yes," she whispered, kissing her daughter's tiny, veined hand, "he did tell me."

***

It was July again, and the day was blazing hot. The door opened, preceded by a weak knock. "Mattie, I'm going to the pond to catch fish for supper. You wanna come?" Clarence looked at her with big hopeful eyes, barefoot and dressed in nothing but coveralls rolled up to his knees.

Mattie glanced at the bottle of cream she was about to churn to butter and then looked back at Clarence. The cream could wait. "I'd love to." Mattie was rewarded with a toothless grin. "You go ahead," she said, laughing. "I'll be there in a minute."

Still requiring more rest than she cared to admit, lying out by the pond would be a welcome break. Putting the cream in the icebox, she grabbed five-month-old Maudie and the picnic quilt and headed for the pond.

Actually there were two ponds, one for bathing and the other for catfish purchased from the States. Clarence was setting up the hook with a fleshy worm. Mattie arranged her baby girl on the quilt. The infant kicked her feet and flailed her dimpled arms in vociferous delight.

Clarence scowled pointedly at Maudie. "We gotta be quiet or the fish won't bite."

Mattie nodded, handing her little daughter a piece of wood to chew on that Ene had carved and smoothed for that purpose. Maudie quietly scrutinized her toy while the two fishermen wordlessly took up their poles and tossed in their lines. Since she was forbidden to speak, Mattie let her thoughts stray. She had received another concerned letter from Nellie, and one from her mother.

Although Nellie had been furious with her for going to Mexico, and furthermore, being stuck there, her sister had long forgiven her. It seemed a travesty then, but now Mattie was glad. She would not have had Ene with her.

She was filled with love and appreciation for her industrious husband. How could she have guessed, during those many years of her antipathy, what a gentle and kind man he was?

Ene had cried when he finally confirmed her suspicions that he was keeping something from her. Because of complications, their baby girl would be their last. He had been surprised at her calm smile and confident assurance that five more children were waiting to come to them. In response to his quizzical expression, she recounted her experience.

During the arduous labor, she prayed for death. The pain mercifully slipped away, and she found herself in a spacious hall, drawn toward an iridescent entity of overwhelming love. Six personages, four women and two men dressed in white, approached her. She had never seen them before, yet she knew them. Tenderness in their eyes spoke a deep love and reverent respect. None of the personages spoke aloud, but she understood as clearly as if they had. She reached out to touch them. A voice stopped her.

"It is not time, my little Mattie. You must go back."

Mattie turned to see her father. He looked the same as she remembered, soft green eyes and long gray beard. She wanted to run to him, to embrace him, but her feet would not move.

He waved toward the personages. "Your children. You have a mission not yet complete."

At that point, Mattie heard Peter Wood's distant voice commanding her to live, and the searing pain of labor returned. She had thought it all a dream until that miraculous moment when her infant child snuggled in her arms was allowed to communicate to her.

She wondered if the next baby would be a boy. Or would the boys come much later? Ene would dearly love a boy, although he showed no regrets that his first was a daughter, who he called Junior from time to time and then guffawed when Mattie rolled her eyes.

She missed Ene terribly. Worrying about him took its toll during the long absences with the freighting business. It helped to have Isabel and Tom close by, and she ate most of her meals with Ene's family. Clarence and Rosalie checked Maudie's availability several times a day. John checked on Mattie.

He had been smitten with Mattie since her first visit during her courting days, and it was the family joke as to who loved her best: John or Ene. When Ene was away, Mattie woke every morning to a crackling fire in her stove and cut logs stacked neatly in the wood box. Every evening, John brought a fresh bottle of milk and several eggs gathered from the chickens. It was John's adoration of his older brother, as much as his innocent affection for his sister-in-law, that led him to appoint himself guardian in Ene's absence. Mattie found comfort in it.

Nevertheless, her little daughter was her greatest source of comfort during Ene's absence. Mattie enjoyed a sense of peace and renewal when she held her baby. Life took on a proper perspective.

Now in the July sun, she smiled at Maudie arching this way and that to get a good look at her world from the quilt where she lay cooing and gurgling. In the shade of the weeping willow, surrounded by the constant twitter of sparrows and the occasional mournful call of the dove, Mattie could hardly believe that a war raged.

The Treviso crisis seemed years away instead of a mere five months. Bishop Bentley, by the grace of God, had averted a massacre.

Mattie smiled. God had been very busy that night.

"Look," Clarence whispered. "There's one nibbling at my worm." He crimped his mouth willing the fish to bite. Just then, Maudie burbled at her clasped hands, and the fish swam away. Clarence gave Maudie a withering look, then settled in for another long wait.

Mattie grinned, handing the smooth carved toy to her baby, trying to keep her quiet to appease her young uncle. Little chubby hands gripped it absently as she followed life around her. Bees hovered over sweet honeysuckle. A fat robin flew to a higher perch in the blossoms of the bird of paradise. A large monarch butterfly fluttered close and then flew to the rose-covered trellises artfully placed to cover the unattractive cement embankment of the irrigation canal.

Mattie smiled, remembering her surprise when she learned that the beautiful flowers were Peter and Ene's handiwork, not Jane's.

A further monument to her father-in-law's skill, potatoes, carrots, green beans, onions, and radishes grew in long, straight rows, recently weeded. Ears of corn, topped with golden silk, clung to stocks well over seven feet tall. Cucumbers and green chili peppers hid camouflaged in the leaves. Red tomatoes accented the weighted vines with bright color. Round pumpkins sat shaded in a patch of broad leaves and orange blossoms.

In the orchards across the road, peaches had already been harvested and apples looked like little green balls. Mattie's eyes swung back to the vineyard showing clumps of purple grapes, not quite ripe, but still inviting to the birds, or to any poor beggar or marauding rebels that happened to pass by.

Such a garden to a starving soldier was manna from heaven. One soldier was not a problem. It was the ten or twenty who trampled underfoot that they did not want. Soldiers passing through town with no intention of returning cared little what they destroyed or maimed. Mattie understood fighting for a cause. She could even understand raiding a garden. But she could not understand pillage and plunder.

"I got one, Mattie! I got one!" Clarence shouted. His pole arched downward. He gave a quick yank, pulling his line out of the water. A big catfish flopped desperately at the end of it.

Mattie was smiling when she walked through the door of her home.

1914

ENE WAS HOME. MATTIE SMILED AND BUTTERED A HOT biscuit and poured a cup of Postum, a new hot drink Ene had discovered in Deming. Grabbing her shawl, she went out to meet him, into the February twilight. Ene's breath clouded each time he exhaled.

"You know a man's heart," Ene boomed, reaching for the cup. He drank greedily.

"I know his stomach." Mattie grinned.

Wiping his mouth, he kissed his wife. "Thanks."

"It's my way of trying to get a dust-free kiss," Mattie said, noticing the grimy powder on his face.

Ene laughed heartily and reached for the biscuit." This hits the spot. Hope there's more where this came from."

"Supper will be on the table by the time you get the horses put up."

"How's our little valentine?"

"She took two steps by herself today and is proud of it. She's with Aunt Roberta."

Ene grinned and kissed his wife again. "Before you know it, she'll be riding a horse."

"How'd the trip go?" Mattie asked.

"I met another general. He's setting up housekeeping in San Diego at the Terraza Hacienda. From the looks of things, he plans to be around for some time."

"Whose side?"

"He's one of Villa's, Miguel Hernandez from Zacatecas. His daddy's rich. General Hernandez has Lem Spilsbury and Arnold Bennet hauling lumber for him from Pearson."

"How convenient."

"If I'm willing to include San Diego in my mail run, General Hernandez will pay me and give me two teams of horses."

"You'll end up dead, Ene Wood, going back and forth between the Red Flaggers and the Villistas."

"Can't see how I can turn it down."

The extra route meant more time away from home, but wages were hard to come by, and time away from home was time earning a living. It had been the way of life even before the war, except for the lucky few who had factories or businesses in town. Since the revolution, most of those were defunct. The soldiers of each faction drew heavily on their resources, some promising to pay later, and some outright stealing. Either way, the results were the same.

"Are you up to making a trip to Columbus?" Ene grinned. He knew she was expecting another baby, just past the nausea. By wagon, she would be on the road for most of two weeks.

"Me and Maudie?"

"Maudie can stay here with her aunties and her grandmother," Ene said. "It'll make things less complicated."

"You just want a cook and bottle washer," Mattie teased.

Ene chuckled low in his throat.

"What's in Columbus?" Mattie asked.

"John Wilson has hired me to oversee a delivery, two freight wagons driven by his men. You and I will lead in a comfortable little buggy with a top for shade."

Mattie considered the offer. The awkwardness of pregnancy was not yet upon her. The ride would not be too bad in a buggy. She would insist on a cot for sleeping, of course. The ground was just too hard, pregnant or not. But her comfort was not the real worry; it was the possibility of crossing paths with the Red Flaggers

Ene had met Pancho Villa in Ascención on the last peach-selling trip. He told Ene to never leave Mexico, that it was as much his home as Villa's. He assured Ene that if he was taken prisoner by one of his men, he had only to say that he had a special message for El General Francisco Villa and demand to be allowed to give it to him personally. Villa promised that by doing this, Ene would be given safe conduct to his camp.[1]

The Red Flaggers, on the other hand, would not be so easily dealt with. Mattie did not doubt that to a starving soldier their cargo was more valuable than gold. Not to mention that she herself might be marked as a valuable item.

***

Leaving her baby was harder than she expected. With two days behind her, the pang was less acute. Today, Mattie's thoughts were dominated by the need for a bath instead of marginal washings in the freezing river. There was no advantage to riding in a buggy when choking dust billowed around them, as it was wont to do crossing the flats from Colonia Dublán. Horse and traveler, monochromatic from head to toe with fine powdery grit, looked like ghosts. Even so, it was better than the alternative—mud thick as clay that would stop their progress altogether.

Mattie reached for the canvas water bag and drank deeply, offering some to Ene.

"Thanks," he said.

It struck her how relaxed all three drivers appeared, considering the bad news Delbert Taylor handed them just before leaving Colonia Dublán. He had lost two wagonloads of commodities to the Red Flaggers along this road, commodities meant for Wilson's store.

"Three men will hardly be able to fight off the Mexican army," Mattie said.

"It's not about fighting." Ene looked at his wife. "We aren't going to die over beans and corn."

Mattie grinned. "And that's why all three of you are packing guns?"

Ene laughed. He had no good answer and gave none. Both fell silent, trying to keep the grit out of their mouth.

Approaching mountainous terrain north of Ascención, the horses strained against their harnesses. The rocky road made less dust, but still enough to mark them for miles. Ene constantly scanned the horizon. Stopping at the mouth of a narrow draw, he handed Mattie the reins and jumped down from the buggy to confer with Ernesto and Juan.

"Ernesto is going to go have a look to make sure we don't blunder into anything," Ene said when he returned. The wait seemed interminable although it couldn't have been more than fifteen minutes.

"No hay nadie," Ernesto said.

"Bueno." Ene clucked at the horses, bringing the reins down sharp on their backs. The buggy lurched forward. As Ernesto reported, there was no one in the draw and no one on the ridge. Mattie's sigh of relief was short lived when a thunderous cloud of dust grew ever near.

Red Flaggers!

Ene swore. "Keep rolling."

Juan passed the message to Ernesto. Mattie's heart beat in her ears. "There must be thirty of them," she breathed.

"Buenas tardes," Ene said, trying to sound amiable while looking down the barrel of their guns. Mattie suppressed a shudder at the cold fierceness in the eyes of ones so young. They were practically children.

"Your guns," commanded the man, who looked a few years older than Ene, wearing the insignia of "Capitan." Ene and the two teamsters removed their guns. A soldier jockeyed his horse close to the wagons to collect them.

"Where are you going?" The question was directed at Ene, but the eyes never left Mattie. She pretended not to notice the insolent appraisal.

"Columbus," Ene said, a little too fiercely.

"What do you have here?"

"Beans and corn."

"Follow," the leader commanded.

Ene tried to keep his voice friendly. "We would be happy to share what we have with you and be on our way."

The captain leveled his gun at Ene's chest. "Follow!"

"This isn't good," Ene whispered to Mattie.

"Shut up!" said a vicious looking soldier, poking Ene in the ribs with his gun.

Five miles off the road, they entered a canyon. Armed men looked down on them from the canyon walls that opened abruptly to a small valley that was wall to wall with tents and makeshift shelters.

"A battalion," Ene hissed under his breath.

"Get down, señores."

Ene helped Mattie out of the buggy. Juan, Ernesto, and Ene were promptly tied, hands at their backs.

The leader approached Mattie. "Come." Mattie glanced at Ene. He stepped forward. Immediately, two guards grabbed him.

"If she gets hurt," Ene hissed, "you're a dead man."

The leader sneered. "You, señor, are the dead man."

Ene bolted but was quickly apprehended.

"My husband has done nothing." Mattie sounded braver than she felt. "Why kill him?" Although not fluent in Spanish, Mattie had no problem getting her point across.

The leader grinned. His insolent gaze made Mattie shudder.

She tried again. "We'll give you our goods."

He laughed, showing yellow teeth. "They are already ours." The captain pulled her after him. Mattie looked desperately over her shoulder at Ene. With primal rage in his eyes, he strained against the hands that hauled him off in the opposite direction.

Her arm hurt where the captain gripped her. She fought down hysteria, hoping that a calm façade would be to her advantage.

They stopped at a dilapidated shed, windowless, about twice the size of an outhouse.

The captain grinned. "Mas tarde, reina." He pushed Mattie in and closed the door. The sound of chains clinked together, and Mattie was alone.

The shed smelled musty but not filthy. Her eyes grew accustomed to the dim light. An old, rusted cast-iron skillet and a couple of broken two-by-fours were scattered on the dirt floor. A rat the size of a baby rabbit scampered cross the floor. Mattie gasped. It exited through a small opening near a stack of dusty horse blankets in the far corner.

That brought to mind a far more dangerous rat. The captain had called her "his queen" with a promise to return. His depraved objective was not lost on Mattie. Tears she had bravely held in check spilled down her face. She dropped to the stack of blankets. There was no room for worry about insignificant problems such as fleas.

The sun sank behind the mountains, taking with it the last light of day, leaving her in complete darkness except for glimpses of distant firelight that danced between the slats of her prison. It was then she heard footsteps.

Waiting in the dark, memories of another time rushed in. She wanted to scream, to thrash her way to freedom. She rose. A weapon. She needed a weapon. Her hand fell on the cast iron skillet. He would not take her without a fight.

The chain rattled. A lantern preceded a sombrero too wide for the door. It was removed. The captain's smile sent shivers down her spine. He closed the door.

Mattie waited for just the right moment, then swung with all her might. She missed his head, landing a wallop on his arm. It hardly slowed him. Easily he wrested the weapon from her hand and drew her close in an inescapable grip around her waist.

"A woman with fight lights a man's fire. You are such a woman, no?" He touched her hair and then lifted her chin to meet his eye. His crocodile smile made her shiver. His stench made her sick, bile racing up into her throat. She didn't fight it, letting it erupt like a fountain in his face. In a stream of unutterable blasphemy, she was slammed into the wall. She fell to the floor.

"Jorge!" a voice commanded from outside.

"Que quieres?" the captain growled, frozen in mid-kick meant for her stomach.

Mattie quickly rolled, giving him her backside.

"Te habla el general," said the voice on the other side of the door.

The captain hissed. "No te preocupes, perra," he whispered to Mattie. "No te olvido." He laughed, leaving with the skillet.

All grew dark again. Mattie felt terribly tired.

And helpless.

Mattie

***

She had no idea how long she had lain on the cold, damp earthen floor. Was Ene alive? Had she missed the gunshots?

Carefully and slowly she sat. She smelled of vomit. Patting her barely protruding stomach, she was quite certain no harm had been done to her unborn child. There were no broken bones, but for sure she had a few beautiful bruises. Her ribs would be sore for a day or two.

Pulling her shawl close around her, she considered the horse blankets. They would make an adequate bed for her aching body. Taking a deep breath, feeling her way around the floor, she cleared a spot. Making her way to the stack in the corner, one by one, Mattie arranged the blankets three long and four high.

She was about to try out her bed when the staccato of gunfire made her jerk.

"Eeeeeene!" She thought she had screamed, but there was no sound. Mattie's teeth chattered uncontrollably. Her throat ached. A sharp pain pulsated in her head. She hated these soldiers who gave airs of patriotism to their senseless bloodthirsty murdering.

The chains rattled. Prickles ran up into her scalp. Mattie gripped the two-by-four and positioned herself beside the door. It squeaked as it swung out.

"Señora." It was not the captain's voice.

Mattie hesitated. This soldier sounded very young. Seeing her poised for battle, he jumped, almost upsetting the lantern. Hardly able to support the ammunition strapped across his chest, Mattie figured he could be no more than thirteen, though his eyes seemed much older. Mattie lowered her weapon.

"Cobijas, señora," the boy said meekly, holding two quilts that she immediately recognized as her own. Cautiously, he placed them on the floor along with a lantern, never taking his eyes from her.

"Comida." The soldier boy motioned to someone outside. It was a woman. She carried a large bowl of beans and something wrapped neatly in a clean cloth that she placed on Mattie's makeshift bed— probably tortillas from the smell of it.

"Agua," the young soldier commanded imperiously.

The woman nodded and left, throwing Mattie an unfriendly glance. She returned with a bucket of steaming water and rags.

For a minute, Mattie thought the boy soldier might salute. Instead, he bowed.

Left alone with the shadows that played over the walls, Mattie looked absently at the warm water, then at food on her bed.

Who had sent it? Surely not the captain they called Jorge. Did she have a benevolent ally, someone higher in command—a general perhaps? Would he allow her to leave with Ene's body? And Juan? Ernesto? Or was he currying favor, saving her for himself.

She could not eat. "Please, dear God."

It was a prayer that had been on her lips the moment she saw the Red Flaggers. God did not seem to be listening. "I know you have mysterious ways, but with all due respect, dear Lord," she whispered, "they can be most vexing and most grievous."

***

Opening her eyes, the gray light of morning peeked through the slats. Mattie stood, ignoring stiff muscles and an aching back. Before finally falling into exhausted sleep, she had washed herself as best she could. Daylight and being somewhat clean brought new courage and a ravenous appetite.

She drank from a gourd and fell hungrily on the food. The cloth held tortillas. Mattie spooned beans into one, topped it with green chili, and rolled it up. Even cold, it had been a long time since food had tasted this good. The spicy green chili piqued her lips and tongue deliciously.

Reaching for another tortilla, Mattie thought of Rafaela Quevedo and the hot tortillas she shared with the Sevey family. The peaceful life at the ranch seemed a lifetime away. She wondered if she would ever know such carefree days again.

The sound of approaching voices stopped Mattie in mid tortilla, her third. Gripping the board, she took a stance. The chain rattled. The door swung open.

"Mattie?"

Mattie stared.

"Mattie, it's me, Silvestre Quevedo. Are you alright?"

Silvestre Quevedo. Except for the voice, she would not have recognized her old neighbor and friend behind the drooping mustache and smart uniform. She wanted to throw her arms around him and weep. She whispered, "The food came from you."

"The boy did not tell you?"

Mattie glanced at the board in her hand. "I think I may have frightened him a little."

Silvestre glanced at Mattie's crude weapon and grinned. "Yes, I see."

"Thank you for the food and the quilts, and especially the water."

Silvestre looked down, chagrined. "I apologize profusely to have kept you locked in this shabby little place, but as Captain Maldonado has demonstrated, you were much safer here than in a tent."

"The man they call Jorge?"

"The same. The pig used you badly. For this I am truly sorry."

"Just bruises, Silvestre. Not the worst."

"He is a dog!" Silvestre hissed. He motioned to the boy soldier, the same one who had come last night to pick up the quilts.

He saluted smartly. "Si, General."

"General?" Mattie asked, surprised.

"I am not the only general who commands here," he said to Mattie. "My brother Rodrigo too is a general. And the other one is General Orozco. He was hard to convince, but Rodrigo and I finally won him to our side."

But not soon enough, Mattie thought, thinking of Ene's cold body lying somewhere near.

"If you are ready, I will take you to Ene."

Mattie braced herself. She would be strong.

***

The walk from prison to morgue was short. Arriving at a large tent, Silvestre deferred to Mattie. She entered. There were five men standing. Rodrigo, who smiled at Mattie and shook her hand, and another officious man who Mattie assumed was General Orozco. Her eyes grew big when she saw Juan and Ernesto grinning at her.

And Ene.

Mattie's brain swirled. "Guns . . . I heard . . . I thought . . ."

In two steps, Ene was at her side just as her knees buckled under her. The resolve to be strong dissolved into hiccups and sobs as she clung to her husband who held her tight, his own emotion choking his words.

"The guns were for the captain that brought us in. "Ene's voice trembled. "He was executed for insubordination. Did he hurt you, Mattie?"

"Bruises, that's all." That he intended more caused Mattie to shudder. Still, she did not wish him dead.[2]

Suddenly aware of the other men who stared at the floor to allow husband and wife a little privacy, Mattie stepped back and wiped furiously at her face.

Silvestre turned to Ene. "Amigo, your wagons are ready." He handed Ene a letter. "If you are stopped again by Red Flaggers, show them this." It was an order to let Ene pass without being searched or his supplies confiscated. The letter carried General Orozco's signature.

***

The wagons were untouched, tarps still in place. Fierce-eyed soldiers, gaunt and ragged, stared coldly. Mattie's heart ached for the young boys, hardened by life's darkest moments. She wondered at what cost Silvestre and Rodrigo had rescued her and Ene.

Ene handed his wife into the buggy. She whispered, "We must give them something."

Ene nodded and turned to the generals. "Will you accept a few bags of corn and beans?"

They smiled gratefully, glancing at their fierce subordinates. "You are kind, my friend." Rodrigo motioned a few men to unload the bags. Mattie noticed that sullen faces softened. After five bags of corn and three bags of beans, Silvestre said, "That is plenty. You are very generous." The men shook hands and embraced, gently thumping each other on the back. While shaking Mattie's hand, Silvestre surreptitiously slipped her a neatly folded square of paper.

"Please," he whispered, "for my family. If it should fall into the wrong hands, it will not go well for you and could mean death for me and Rodrigo." He did not say who the wrong hands might be. It did not much matter. She owed the Quevedo men.

Little did Mattie know that the name of Silvestre Quevedo would one day save her again.

***

The Columbus trip, now nine months behind them, was no more than a bad memory that surfaced now and then in her nightmares. Ene's mail delivery business gave him connections in high places among the warring factions. He walked a tenuous line fraught with danger no less threatening than what they had already suffered. Mattie hated the war. She found solace in her bright-eyed little girls, unsullied by life's harsh realities. And it was good to have her mother back too.

The two women were putting supper on the table. It was nearly dark, and a cold, furious wind whistled about the house, forcing its way past loose-fitting window frames. Ene stepped into the kitchen, face scrubbed clean, hair smoothed back, having stopped at the wash pan outside the door.

"Time we was bringin' in that wash pan before that frozen mustache of yours breaks off," Martha said.

"Just what I was thinking." Ene's eyes twinkled as he reached for Mattie and kissed her soundly. Mattie pushed away from the cold, wet bristles, and laughed.

Ene sat down to the table, helping himself to a thick slice of bread, which he broke into bite-size chunks. He dropped them into a bowl. "Sure is nice to have you back, Mother Sevey," Ene said, topping off his bowl with thick cream, a generous spoonful of sugar, and a dollop of strawberry jam.

"Like I said, war or no war, I'm here to stay. Let 'em shoot."

Ene looked at Mattie and grinned. Neither of them pointed out that for all her bravado, Martha did agree to stay in town instead of the ranch. She rented a two-story house from the Romneys, practically next door to Tom, and invited Ene and Mattie to move in with her. Shortly after Hannah was born last August, they accepted the invitation.

Assisted by Fanny Merrill, an excellent midwife, little Hannah made a less-dramatic entrance into the world on the twenty-sixth, just before sunrise. Ene found it ironic to have Sister Merrill's expertise when it was so little required.

"Good cooking," Ene said, picking up his spoon.

"A hungry man ain't hard to please," Martha laughed.

"Have either of you heard that Mexico has another president?" Ene made a small mound of salt on the tablecloth next to his bowl. Mattie handed him several green scallions, washed and trimmed.

"Zapata?" Mattie guessed.

"Carranza." Ene dipped an onion in the salt.

"I say Pancho Villa should be president." Martha made her own mound of salt.

"He'd like that, but the United States will never back someone so rough around the edges. They are going to throw in with the high-class gents educated in the States, like Carranza."

Ene sprinkled salt and sugar over his vinegar-drenched tomatoes. "Maybe this Carranza fellow will put an end to the war."

"I certainly won't miss the Red Flag Movement," Mattie said, shuddering. "It seems to me their soldiers are the most cruel, Silvestre and Rodrigo excepted." Since she had delivered the letter to Javier Quevedo, she had heard nothing of his sons and wondered if they still lived.

Ene wiped at his mouth. "Nothing like bread and milk and onions, especially your bread, Mother."

"Humph! Flattery gets you nowhere, Enos Flake Wood."

"It sure can't hurt to try." Ene's laugh filled the house.

Martha chuckled, shaking her head as she left the kitchen.

Mattie knew her mother had come to love and respect Ene.

Generosity to friend and foe alike was Ene's greatest obstacle to any lasting fortune. But there was food on the table and a little silver in his pocket, and he was an excellent husband and father. And he took care of Martha as if she were his own mother.

"Okay, Mr. Flattery," Mattie said, cleaning up the supper dishes. "You've made your conquests with the adult women in your life. Let's see how well your charm works with your little women."

Eyes dancing, Ene embraced his wife and spoke softly. "If truly I have charmed *thee,* Mattie, oh formidable challenge of my heart, then surely any other shall be powerless to stave my charm. Young or old, I shall triumph victorious."

Mattie laughed. "You're incorrigible."

Ene grinned. His kiss was tender. Mattie's stomach fluttered. She whispered. "Your daughters await you, oh victor."

***

The fierce pounding at the front door was not a dream.

"Ene! Señor Wood!" a man's voice called.

In the dark, Ene threw on his pants. "Aye voy. I'm coming." Lighting the coal oil lamp, he replaced the glass chimney.

Mattie sat up. "Who is it?"

"Not sure. If anything happens, slip out the back and go to Tom's." Ene pointed to the loaded 30-40 rifle. "And take that with you." For a frantic moment, they looked at each other in perfect understanding. Ene stepped out the front door. Mattie latched it behind him.

Staying in the deep shadows of the front room, Mattie peered out of the large bay window. A hundred mounted soldiers silhouetted by the full October moon brought a tingle to her spine. The low rumble of animated conversation was unintelligible. Had they come for the guns hidden upstairs? Her heart pulsated in her ears. What seemed like forever suddenly ended when, as if on cue, the soldiers turned their horses and rode away, leaving a thick cloud of dust visible in the moonlight.

Mattie unlocked the door.

"Villistas," Ene said, answering the question in her eyes. "General Hernandez wanted the location of the Red Flaggers' camp."

"My heavens, how did you get out of that?"

"I told him I mind my own business and wanted to be left out of politics."

"Just that?"

"Well, I played on his sympathies a little, told him I had good friends on both sides and refused to play informant against either one of them.

Unease gripped Mattie like a giant, cold hand. "Something tells me this isn't over yet."

***

John and Ene mopped up the last of their eggs with a hot biscuit and washed it down with cold milk. John Wood had dropped by early, bringing parts that Ene would use to repair his wagon.

"You sure make the best biscuits I ever ate, Mattie."

"Well, you had better have another or I won't believe you," Mattie said.

John grinned and helped himself to his sixth biscuit, drowning it in butter and peach preserves.

"I heared a man at the door," Martha said, coming into the kitchen. "Looks rough. You better get it, Ene."

Ene found a dusty, unshaven soldier who he recognized as a Red Flagger. "Muy buenos dias," Ene said. Hard black eyes met Ene's friendly smile. *This guy looks like he hasn't a friend in the world*, thought Ene. *I expect he might challenge anyone who dared to disagree.*

"El General sent me to borrow a few guns."

Ene was not fooled by the word *borrow*. "I have one I can loan you. Espérese, por favor." Ene was back at the front door in a few minutes with an old pistol kept for just such an occasion. The soldier accepted it, never taking his eyes off Ene's face, then left.

"What's that all about?" John asked when Ene returned to the kitchen.

"Red Flaggers asking for guns.

Mattie jumped in. "It's been a long time since they bothered us for guns. I'd bet my bottom dollar it has something to do with the Villistas who were here the other night."

"The Red Flaggers can't pin anything on me," Ene said.

"You know Gutierrez. He'll make something of it."

"Maybe I should stick around," John said.

"No need." Ene slathered jam on his thickly buttered biscuit. "We'll be okay. Besides, Pa needs you."

"Guess I'll head home, then," John said. "Thanks for breakfast, Mattie."

Mattie smiled. "You're welcome anytime."

Ene saw John to his horse that was tied to the maple tree at the gate and waved him off. Grateful for the cool October morning, Ene set to work making repairs on the wagon. Not twenty minutes past before the same soldier as before showed up again.

"Que hubo, how's it going?" Ene said, his voice more friendly than he felt.

"El General waits for you at the saddle shop," the man said, unsmiling.

"The gun was not good?" Ene asked.

"He waits." The soldier turned his horse and left.

***

About fifteen armed men loitered outside the whitewashed adobe building that showed too many seasons without paint. Under wide sombreros, grizzly mustached faces stared at Ene. Ernesto Martinez, an old neighbor for as long as Ene could remember, leaned against the wall as if he had come for an afternoon gossip. He did not meet Ene's eye. Ene recognized four others he had known since grade school. Greeting each by name, they nodded in return, but there was little friendliness in it. Ene entered the shop, his misgivings mounting. He wished he had brought his letter from General Orozco.

General Gutierrez sat at a workbench using it as a desk, shuffling papers importantly. Ene's boots marked his staccato progress as he crossed the board floor.

"Buenos días," Ene said.

Never taking his eyes from his make-work, the general raised an insolent hand, indicating silence. Ene might have laughed at the officious manner, but the import brought an angry knot to his chest. He kept his face passive.

A little to the right of his superior, Ricardo Lopez, another school friend, now captain, stood officious and erect. He sneered. In sharp contrast to the lean soldiers outside, Ene could see that neither man looked as if he sacrificed much at the table.

The long silence in the unheated room punctuated Ene's cold reception, conspicuous as the pungent smell of leather. New bridles and leather quirts, displayed on the wall, hung over a tall stack of uncut leather precariously balanced. In the back room, Elwood Cardon, owner, was working at making saddles, Ene presumed, and probably praying for his life. Obviously, the leather craftsman had been ordered not to show his face.

Finally, Gutierrez motioned imperiously for Ene to sit. Ene remained standing.

"*Don* Enés," Gutierrez said, mocking. A true Don was a Spanish landlord despised for his wealth and power and the very cause of the revolution. Ene was no Don. "You help my enemy, I am told."

"You are misinformed." Ene hoped he sounded calmer than he felt.

Gutierrez hissed. "Mentiroso. Liar. The Villistas attacked us the day after El Señor Bloom saw them leaving your house."

Ene's jaw clenched. Trust Bloom. Ene wondered if the old newsmonger got something for his trouble or he was just plain mean. Ene opted for the latter. "They came," Ene's said, his eyes never wavering. "I told them nothing."

Gutierrez stood, letting his contempt show. "You will see how we deal with lying traitors." The general jerked his head at Ricardo Lopez. "You know what to do."

The captain clicked his heels and saluted at the retreating generalissimo, who stomped out, yelling commands. Luiz Martinez and a second soldier entered as ordered, saluting Ricardo.

"Tie his hands," the captain barked.

Ernesto looked apologetic at Ene. Ene nodded his forgiveness as his hands were tied in front leaving a long piece of rope to act as a leash. The other soldier threw a poncho over Ene and put a round sombrero on his head, pulling it low. To anyone who might see him leave, Ene looked just like another soldier.

***

Heading upriver in the direction of the Sevey ranch, Ene walked briskly behind the horse of the soldier who had helped Luiz. At last, the procession stopped. The general dismounted and made a large X in the dirt with his boot. "Bring the prisoner," he barked.

Ene was pushed to the spot. Gutierrez gave another command, and six men lined up shoulder to shoulder about fifteen paces out while the others watched still mounted on their horses, their guns drawn.

One by one, Ene looked each of his executioners in the eye. Four of them had gone to school with him, raced their horses against him, swam in the same waterhole when they were children. Over the years, Ernesto Martinez had been the recipient of Peter Wood's generosity with sacks of beans and corn.

"I would never betray you," Ene said with little hope of being believed. These men lived in a world of suspicion where even generals changed their loyalties on a whim, where too often, advancement came by backstabbing and subterfuge.

Although he too had gone to school with Ene, the captain, Ricardo Lopez, had done little to mask his resentment since they were teenagers, allowing his bitterness to fester like an angry sore that poisoned his soul.

Ene refused the blindfold and looked down the barrels of six muzzles.

He thought of Mattie—the indomitable, green-eyed Mattie. He hardly had to bend to kiss her. Just by turning his head, he could bury his face in her thick brown hair smelling of sunshine and soap. That first day that she had run into him blind with panic, he had felt an innate desire to protect her and quash the evil that haunted her. It had not been easy winning her affections. He had agonized over the possibility of failure.

Now she would be a widow with two baby daughters to provide for, daughters who would grow up with no memory of their father. He could almost feel their hugs, see their smiles, hear their delighted squeals.

He prayed for a miracle.

***

"General! General!" shouted a soldier. "Allí viene un gringo."

A burro rounded the bend, carrying an old man whom Ene knew well. The guns lowered. The old man's eyes grew wild with fear.

Gutierrez cursed. "Oye Gringo Viejo, you want to join him?" He pointed at Ene.

The man shook his head vehemently.

"Then get out of here," the general commanded.

The intruder paddled his donkey into action, disappearing through the brush. Ene didn't blame him.

Gutierrez smirked. "You must choose braver friends, Señor Wood." He gave the signal and six guns rose to position.

Ene said evenly, "There are braver witnesses who know that you have me. Too many people, Gutierrez. Your superiors will not be happy."

"Shut up!" Purple rage crept up the general's neck as he grappled with his indecision. The soldiers stared coldly at their leader, the executioners lowering their guns. Leather rubbed leather as men shifted in their saddles. A horse stomped impatiently. Somewhere, a hawk screeched.

Ene knew that a witnessed incident seriously jeopardized the chance of gaining recognition as a viable government from the United States. It was one thing to kill a gringo, but it was another to be found out bby your superiors. A bloodthirsty executioner could become the executed.

Ene held his breath, hoping.

"Capitan!" The general finally spoke. His voice made a

high-pitched sound that might have been funny had the situation not been so grave.

Like a puppet, the only militant who wished to see Ene dead jumped forward, saluting smartly. "Si, mi general."

"Before you let this dog go, sword whip him until you have no more strength to raise your arm." Gutierrez turned swiftly and threw himself into the saddle. Spurring his horse toward Ene, he pulled up at the last moment, turning sharply. The horse was so close, its tail swept across Ene's face.

Ene never moved.

"Get out of Mexico, Señor Wood, or you are a dead man." Shouting a command, the general galloped off followed obediently by the mounted soldiers.

***

When the dust cleared, Ene was alone with his would-be executioners and their hate-filled captain.

Ricardo flashed an imperious grin. "It shall be a long time before my arm grows tired," he said. Stripping Ene to the waist, he shoved him against an old cottonwood. A soldier on each side of the trunk grabbed Ene's wrists and pulled him stomach first against the rough bark. Metal scraped against leather as Ricardo pulled his sword from the sheath. Two quick whooshing sounds told Ene that he sliced an invisible X in the air.

Ene braced himself.

Whack! The captain grunted with exertion as the sword landed broadside on the prisoner's back.

Ene lurched involuntarily.

Whack!

Ene eyes closed against the pain.

Whack! Whack!

He slipped to his knees, scraping his chest against the bark. Rivulets ran down his back, sweat or blood Ene could not be sure. Suddenly, filled with indignation, with strength he did not know he had, he exploded to his feet sending the two soldiers sprawling into the dirt. He turned quickly to one side, and the sword came down harmlessly on the tree trunk. Ene grabbed the captain's wrist.

Ricardo winced.

Ene said in a cold, calm voice, "I command you to stop."

Ricardo looked stupidly at Ene. Finally he squeaked, "Take him."

Nobody moved.

Ricardo looked around. Five guns were leveled at his chest.

Martinez said in a low voice, "It is enough."

The captain's eyes grew hard. "The generalisimo will hear of this."

"No doubt we will be punished," said Martinez, "but it will begin with you, mí capitan."

***

Her mother provided warm clean cloths, and Mattie cleaned and treated the angry flesh on Ene's back. He flinched. She willed away the nausea, not from the sight of blood. Heavens, she could snap a chicken's neck, cut its head off, quarter it, and throw the entrails to the hogs as easily as cutting into a loaf of bread.

No. She was afraid. For Ene to be at the house another minute was insane.

Ene said, "I'm not running, Mattie."

"Then at least hide for a while," Mattie begged.

"I want you and Martha to take the girls and stay with Tom and Isabel."

"I'm not leavin' my home," his mother-in-law said.

"I'm not going anywhere, either." Mattie lifted her chin.

"Yes, ma'am, you are," Martha said. "And you're leavin' now. You got babies to consider."

Ene looked gratefully at his mother-in-law.

Fear pressed against Mattie's chest.

"Just until this mess blows over," Ene said to Mattie. "General Gutierrez can't stay in Colonia Juárez for long or he'll lose his war. I'll find someplace to hide as soon as I can."

Where could he hide? Who could he trust? Someone in the community had betrayed Ene once. They might again.

Ene gingerly pulled on his shirt and grimaced. He said gently, taking Mattie's hand. "I'll try to send word."

***

The last of the evening meal was put away, and Hannah and Maudie were tucked safely upstairs in one of the rooms evacuated by the oldest of Tom and Isabel's children. Mattie's throat ached with the effort of keeping her emotions buried from the moment Ene had straggled in, shirt blood-soaked and torn. She needed fresh air. Grabbing her shawl, she slipped out the back door.

"Just to the orchard," she said in answer to Isabel's quizzical look.

Isabel nodded, compassion shining in her eyes.

Hidden in the dark of night, deep in the leafless orchard where she would not be heard, Mattie buried her face in her shawl to muffle her racking sobs.

She cried for Ene's pain, for the horror of it all. She cried in gratitude that Ene was still alive. She cried for the men so full of hate and vengeance.

War seemed to expose and exacerbate the flaws of human character. Even Silvestre Quevedo had certain hardness to him. Mattie did not readily admit that war also exposed good character, even cultivating strengths—gratitude and appreciation for what is important in life, none of which had to do with things. Her faith was evolving—not perfect, by any means, but stronger. (Affliction was more tolerable when one believed they did not have to suffer it alone.)

Mattie sniffed, smiling in spite of herself. She was sounding like that little girl in the book that she read at Nellie's. What was her name? Oh yes, Pollyanna.

Reminded that she need not take on the burden alone, Mattie offered a sincere prayer and felt better.

***

It hurt to move. It hurt not to move. Ene was still at home, still on the cot where Mattie had doctored him. Even if he had a place to go, he didn't think he could get there, not before he rested. Finally, sheer exhaustion rendered him to fitful sleep and nightmares.

The first sign of dawn showed gray through the bay window of the sitting room, outlining Ene's form. The smell of baking biscuits evidenced Martha's activities in the kitchen.

At the sound of jingling spurs and neighing horses, Ene's eyes flew open. He got painfully to his feet. Peering cautiously through the window, he counted six riders, none of them soldiers of rank, all strangers to him. The red flag told Ene they were Gutierrez's men.

And they meant to kill him.

"They're here, Mother," Ene said, removing evidence of his night's accommodations. "And they're out for blood."

"They shan't want mine. Hide yourself. I'll take care of things."

Hating to leave his mother-in-law, Ene headed for the small enclosed room under the staircase as they had planned.

"Not there," Martha said with such command, that Ene stared. "Up there with them guns."

Ene hesitated.

"I got me one of those feelin's, Ene. Just do it."

Ene gave his mother-in-law one last apprehensive look before taking the stairs two at a time. He had failed to convince her of the prudence in going with Mattie. "If I'm around like nothin' happened, maybe they'll think you ain't here and just leave," she had argued.

The second floor was an unfinished single-windowed room equivalent in space to the entire floor below. The soldiers were pounding at the door as Ene picked his way to the far side around empty canning jars, dusty trunks, and old furniture. Falling to his stomach, he squeezed into a two-foot space, nearly knocking over a pair of boot forms that looked like wooden legs from the knee down. The six-foot crawlway made a ninety-degree turn into an opening tall enough to stand—and to store a small armory.

Ene strapped on two belts of ammunition and loaded a 30-40 US rifle. He cocked it. Even if the sound carried to the room below, it was lost in the confusion.

Through cracks in the floor, Ene saw only four men, faces concealed by their hats. The other two must be guarding the doors, he decided. The tallest soldier ordered Martha to sit and motioned to the short, stocky man to search the kitchen. Swagger and Limp, as Ene labeled them, were sent to search the other rooms. The tall one went straight for the closet under the stairs, plan A's hiding place. For an instant, Ene thought Martha might look up at him. He willed her not to.

As the men helped themselves to what they could carry, including Ene's breakfast, Martha clucked at them. Ene felt a stab of regret when they discovered two blankets that were gifts to Mattie from the Villista general.

When they found the money, one hundred thousand pesos, in the mahogany hutch, Ene mentally kicked himself for not remembering to take it with him.

Swagger and Limp disappeared from Ene's sight when they started up the stairs.

"No nada. No nada," Martha said in broken Spanish. "Just viejo cosas."

"Silencio, mujer!" the tall one commanded.

Martha fell silent.

Ene pulled his eyes from the scene below. From a narrow slit in the partition, he commanded a view of the entire upper room as well as a portion of the stairs that rose up through the floor. A large, round hat appeared followed by a second, then a third and a fourth. Guns drawn, the men fanned out into the dim light. Swagger headed toward the partition. Ene glanced away, afraid that his enemy would feel his stare. The gunman walked to the partition and stooped low, peering into the crawl space.

Placing his hat on a dusty trunk, gun in hand, the soldier dropped to all fours and disappeared into the narrow access inching his way forward. It was a careless move for a seasoned soldier. He would die without seeing it coming.

Ene blinked away the sweat that trickled into his eyes. He held his breath, steadying his shaking hands. "Please, God," he prayed, "let no life be lost here today."

"Manzanas! Apples!" It came from across the room.

Within seconds, Ene saw feet, then legs as Swagger backed out of his precarious situation, in a hurry to claim his portion of the find.

Ene closed his eyes and let out his breath slow and easy. As the men rode off with their precious find, the wounds on his back throbbed, keeping time with his pounding heart.[3]

**

"He's hiding safely at Daniel Skousen's home until we can get him to Pearson," Peter Wood said, informing Mattie the whereabouts of her husband.

She didn't think there was anything safe about the Skousens' place. Next to the gristmill, soldiers randomly came and went each day, helping themselves to what they needed. Keeping that thought to herself she said, "Thank you, Father Wood."

Three days later, Mattie breathed a little easier when she learned that Ene had been successfully smuggled to Pearson hidden under a tarp in the back of Delbert Taylor's supply wagon. Insisting that she return home, and against everyone's wishes, she left Isabel and Tom's after expressing her deep gratitude for their hospitality.

Life returned to normal, as normal as a life gets with a husband on the run in the middle of a war. And political unrest had heightened, hanging over Colonia Juárez like a guillotine. Still, meals had to be prepared, the wash done, butter churned, the mending, and of course, tolerating impertinent visitors.

Mattie and Martha sat across from Alice Templeton who looked down her ample nose at each of them in their turn.

"Perhaps it would be safer if the soldiers delivered their own mail. It is appalling," Alice said with affected sweetness, "the danger Ene has brought upon us all by consorting with the revolutionaries. I do hope for your sakes, poor dears, and for good of the community, that Ene will be sensible and leave Mexico."

Mattie nearly choked. So the town was blaming Ene. How she wanted to wipe Sister Templeton's phony concern off her fat face. Mattie glanced at her mother, who was as rigid as the straight-back chair she sat on.

Mrs. Templeton continued, her smile tight. "You know, Ralph Bloom said that he could have helped Ene the day the Red Flaggers took him, but he thought perhaps Ene needed to learn a lesson about rubbing shoulders with both sides of the war."

Mattie flushed an angry red.

Martha jumped up, pulling herself to full height. "Thanks to that self-righteous, meddling Ralph Bloom, Ene suffered terribly and t'was nearly kilt. Any human bein' wishin' such cruelty on another human is no better than the soldiers who done it. Tell that to Ralph Bloom, and tell him he should be hangin' his head in shame."

Mattie hid a satisfied smile at the startled look on the Alice's plump face. The visitor opened her tight little mouth to speak, but Martha was not finished.

"And what's more, if there's any danger to the town, it comes from the greed and jealousy of the likes of him who accuse Ene falsely. If you're goin' to point fingers, point them at that poor excuse of a spineless man."

Alice Templeton harrumphed and swished out in pious indignation.

Mattie stared at her mother. "Poor excuse of a spineless man?"

Martha sat down hard, practically wilting in her chair. "What've I done?"

Mattie grinned. "I expect she's taken the most direct route to Ralph Bloom to repeat your every word, and probably in your very tone of voice." Daughter and mother stared at each other then burst out into a fit of laughter.

Catching her breath, Martha said, "T'will the good Lord ever forgive me."

***

The kerosene lamp, wick turned low, cast shadows about the room. Letting the rancor of the day seep out of her, Mattie rocked Hannah until she fell asleep, then placed her in her crib.

"Okay, your turn," Mattie whispered to Maudie. Maudie smiled and snuggled on her mother's lap. Rocking rhythmically, Mattie sang softly. Maudie's heavy eyelids closed and opened, each time staying closed a little longer, until finally they opened not at all.

Angelic in repose, the little face lifted slightly toward Mattie. A smile—one of few in the last week—played at the corners of Mattie's mouth. Four months from turning two years old, Maudie was anything but angelic.

Baby fires, Martha had called it.

While her mother restacked the firewood in the sitting room, Maudie toddled into the kitchen. Curious about the pan on the table, she tipped it toward her, drenching herself with yeasty sugar water. After a change of clothing, Maudie went in hot pursuit of the resident mouser. The cat escaped easily, jumping over a mud puddle. The pursuer was not so adroit.

This day, Mattie's active little daughter had two Saturday-night baths, and it was only Tuesday.

Cuddling her little mischief-maker, Mattie forgave all, finding humor and gratitude in the many "baby fires" she had extinguished. Maudie and Hannah were the spice of life that brought normalcy to her world, where her husband not only circumvented assassins, but also had to deal with likes of Ralph Bloom and Alice Templeton. Nonetheless, Mattie was glad that this little "dash of spice" finally slept.

Martha appeared in the doorway. "Brother Taylor is come with news," she whispered.

Mattie put her daughter in her bed, covering her with a heavy quilt, and went to find Delbert Taylor dreading what he might have to say.

"Good evening, Delbert."

"Everything's fine, Mattie. The doc in Pearson was more than happy to help out." Delbert paused. Anger flashed in his eyes. "If I'd been in town when Gutierrez come, none of this would'a happened. I don't know what goes on in some people's heads. I reckon Ene's business is risky, but he's been doing us a favor, befriendin' both sides of the war. I've set a few folks straight on that point."

Mattie glanced at the floor. So Sister Templeton had done her work. "Thank you, Delbert, for everything."

"Don't worry none," Delbert said. "This'll blow over. I've come to tell you that Alma Spilsbury plans to fetch Ene from Pearson. He should be home by Saturday."

Mattie smiled her gratitude, not trusting her voice.

"I wouldn't be tellin' that around. Wouldn't want nobody waitin' for him on the road because some spineless man spilled the beans."

Mattie blushed.

Delbert grinned.

***

Ene returned home without incident.

He ran a few scales on his harmonica. "It's no beauty contest," Ene said, when Mattie came out of the bedroom dressed in her best frock, her hair beguilingly stacked on her head and interlaced with ribbon.

"Dances are always a contest," Mattie snapped, wrapping her heavy shawl tightly around her.

Ene grinned. "Then you're sure to win."

Mattie glared.

From home to the academy was a ten-minute walk. They covered the distance in silence. Ene had brushed away the town gossip as one would flick at a bothersome fly and would not be talked out of taking his place with his family at the dance. Mattie dreaded the humiliation with which they were sure to meet, thanks to the likes of Alice Templeton and Ralph Bloom, who bandied about the community contentious and smug. What if she and Ene were asked to leave?

Pausing at the hall entrance, Mattie took a deep breath.

"It'll be okay," Ene said, reaching for her hand.

Mattie realized that for all his bravado, he was nervous too. She felt suddenly guilty for letting her ire spill over to him. She squeezed his hand and squared her shoulders. Heads held high, they entered the assembly hall.

Every eye swung in their direction.

Silence.

Mattie's heart went still. Chairs lined the walls for the old folks. The younger generation stood in intimate circles, waiting for the music. On stage, each member of the Wood family held their instrument, watching.

"Well, don't that beat all." It was Ralph Bloom. "It's Ene Wood, come back to get us all killed."

Only Mattie's indignation kept her from fleeing. She gripped Ene's arm, unaware that she stood ramrod straight, her gaze steady. What happened next, she least expected.

As if on cue, the crowd cheered. Chanting Ene's name, they surged forward, young and old, shaking his hand, welcoming the hero home. They embraced Mattie warmly, congratulating her on her good fortune to have her brave husband back.

Ene grinned broadly behind his mustache.

Mattie's eyes shone.

Ralph Bloom stood alone.

1915

A THICK BEEF STEW SIMMERED ON THE STOVE AND SALT bread cooled on the sideboard beside an applesauce cake heavy with chocolate fudge.

"You expectin' company, daughter?" Martha looked askance at Mattie.

"Ene's coming home today." Ene never knew when he might return home, what trouble might keep him on the trail, but Mattie had an uncanny ability.

She loved Ene with such fierceness it frightened her. True, he could be vexingly stubborn. But how could she deny him the very characteristic that won her heart? She had married for love, certainly not for money. Generous to a fault, Ene was not, nor ever would be, rich beyond being able to provide her with the necessities and a few extravagances like chocolate and, on occasion, linens.

She reveled in his knowledge of her, that she was partial to strawberries with heavy cream sweetened with a dash of sugar; that she delighted in the sound of rain falling on the tin roof; that she was afraid of the dark; that she agonized over unanswerable questions; that when deeply troubled, she found solace in holding her babies.

Martha shook her head. "Well, if Ene don't get here soon, your stew will be ruint and the bread hard."

"He'll be here." Mattie grinned.

***

The silhouetted mountains cast the valley into shadow that crept wraithlike up the eastern slope where a freight wagon screeched and moaned down the meager dirt road into welcome shade. The manhunt quite forgotten, Ene had resumed freighting. Not that it wasn't dangerous. All political parties were cranky. Orozco's liberal Red Flaggers were losing to Villa and Carranza, each of whom vied for US support that was paramount to the succession of the next Mexican president.

Amber fingers streaked the sky when Ene finally reached the bottom of the hill. August monsoons had begun and the promise of rain hung in the air. By the next week, the dry lakebed north of Colonia Dublán would be a bog keeping him close to home until late September. He welcomed the change.

"Whoa there," Ene said unnecessarily to his team that had already stopped.

The kitchen door flew open, and Maudie ran toward her father. "Papa, Papa."

"Careful, sweetheart. Not too close." Mattie smiled at him from the doorway, one-year-old Hannah on her hip.

Securing the reins, Ene jumped down from the wagon and Maudie flew into his arms.

"How's my girl?" Ene said, whirling his two-year-old daughter. Maudie squealed with delight. "Have you been good for your mother?"

Maudie nodded vigorously. "Not Hannah. She cry."

Hannah reached for her father. "Dada."

That's what Ene heard, but to the casual ear, it was not so easily discernible. He took his baby daughter in his other arm and leaned toward his wife, kissing her tenderly.

"Welcome home, husband. I've got dinner ready for you."

"How do you do that?"

"How do I do what?"

"Know when I'm going to arrive when I hardly know myself."

Mattie grinned and shrugged. "Just do."

"Well, I'm so hollow, I think I could touch my backbone through my stomach." Ene put his little girls down, and they ran off to tell Gramma that their papa was home. Ene kissed Mattie properly this time. "Mmmmm. You smell like soap and sunshine."

"After a kiss like that, even you smell good." Mattie laughed.

Ene grinned. "I hear Hannah's been difficult?"

"A few nights with an earache. She's fine now."

"And you? You look spent."

"Nothing a good night's rest won't cure." Mattie smiled. "If you're going to stand here and kiss me all night, your food's going to get cold."

"Some things are just worth it." Ene kissed her again.

Mattie laughed, shooing him back to his work.

Ene suspected that the strain in his wife's eyes came from worry about him on the road more than being up nights with the baby. Deftly unloading the wagon, he checked each item as he placed them in the storeroom—wheat, corn, beans, a bolt of cloth, five pounds of chocolate. Mattie would be expecting the chocolate. He never forgot. She would feign surprise, but her appreciation was genuine. However, the bolt of cloth would be unexpected.

Ene grinned. He knew her every expression. Lost on the casual observer, it was obvious to Ene the warning glance, the angry glint, the gleam of humor, and the soft glow of love. Their bond transcended imperfections, allowing tolerance and forgiveness to placate tempers and willfulness.

He hoisted himself effortlessly over the rail, landing gracefully on his feet.

That's when he saw the man.

Ene stiffened. Even in the dim light, he recognized Captain Ricardo Lopez.

***

He must have been hiding in the long grass, Ene thought, looking for his rifle. It leaned against the wall of the storeroom, too far to be of any use.

As if reading his mind, Ricardo said, "I am unarmed." He was gaunt, dressed in rags.

"What do you want?" Ene asked, his voice flat.

The Captain glanced furtively around. "I need a place to hide."

"Hide?"

"The Carranzistas," Ricardo said. "Please, just one night."

A simple request fraught with risk. Could Ene trust the man who had vowed to kill him? Trust aside, if discovered harboring a fugitive, Ene was signing his own death warrant. He looked long and hard at the haggard, haunted man that stood before him beaten and fearful. No revenge could impose a worse punishment. What had it cost his enemy in pride to come begging for help?

Ene was decided.

Convincing Mattie was another matter.

***

"You aren't serious," she said. It was not a question. "If he doesn't kill us, the Carranzistas will." Her whisper was low.

"My gut instinct says it'll be okay. The last place anyone will look for Ricardo is in the house of the man he nearly murdered. Besides, he has no weapon. Even if he did, I doubt he has the strength to use it."

Mattie wouldn't turn away a vicious dog without giving it something to eat, but putting it up for the night was insane. "May the Lord protect us," she breathed.

Ene nodded. "We'll wash up and be right in."

"You'd better lock away the pitchfork and the ax," Mattie said. "I'll send mother and the babies to Tom's for the night."

Ene returned with their school chum once full of vitality and bluster, now hardly recognizable.

"Pase. Pase," Mattie said in broken Spanish, hoping that she conveyed more warmth than she felt. "Come, sit." She motioned toward a place at the table.

"Gracias." The Captain did not meet Mattie's eye, uttering his thanks when she served him mounds of food. The silence was broken only by the sounds of voracious eating and Mattie's offer of more.

After supper was cleared and the visitor comfortably situated on the floor in the kitchen, Mattie retired to her bedroom. Reaching into the deep pockets of her apron, she removed a butcher knife, an ice pick, and a meat cleaver. Ene hid his smile.

Lying beside his wife in the soft glow of the coal oil lamp, Ene squeezed Mattie's hand. "What a homecoming," he said wearily. "Not exactly what I had in mind after three weeks on the road." He yawned and fell instantly into deep sleep.

One foot on the floor and one eye open—compassion doing little to mitigate apprehension—the night dragged on for Mattie. Outside, the rain fell. Several times, Mattie got out of bed and creaked toward the kitchen. She found a measure of security in the storm, now a considerable howl. It would discourage a manhunt that would bring serious trouble to their door. Dozing fitfully through the nightmares, she finally fell exhausted into a slumber so deep that dreams could not reach her.

She jerked awake.

The room faintly lit with morning's first light, showed Ene fully dressed bending over her. "He's gone."

"Did you check the outhouse? Maybe he's in the orchard?"

"I checked everywhere. I could find neither hide nor hair."

***

It was just after lunch when Tom came riding into the yard. Dismounting, he tied the reins of his sorrel to the low-hanging branch of the mulberry tree.

Mattie set the slop bucket down. Straightening, she raised her hand to shade her eyes from the sun. "What brings you over in the middle of the day?" She enjoyed Tom's visits.

"Just came from Turley's. Bad news."

The familiar tingle at the base of her neck made Mattie shiver. "Come in for some cake and a cool drink, Tom? Ene will want the details."

Tom followed Mattie through the back door, hanging his hat on the peg.

"Tom." Ene's booming voice filled the kitchen. "Good rain last night. What brings you?"

Tom pulled up a chair. "The Federales found Ricardo Lopez hiding in Turley's orchard this morning."

Mattie and Ene glanced at each other.

"Did Turley know?" Ene asked.

"Not until they shot Lopez trying to escape." [1]

Ene grimaced. "It seems a man marks himself for a violent death when he sets out to harass the innocent in the name of the revolution." [2]

Mattie clutched her throat. After what Ene had suffered at Ricardo's hands, still carrying the scars to prove it, she should be jubilant.

She felt only sadness.

1916

POKING AND STIRRING AT THE CLOTHES IN THE BIG COPPER tub with a tree limb carefully trimmed for just this purpose, Mattie let the rising steam warm her hands. Her skirt was tucked at the waist so as not to touch the glowing coals. *Men's britches*, she thought, *would be a sight more convenient and certainly more flattering than my skirt all pulled up to look like a giant loose-fitting diaper.*

She straightened, rubbing at her aching back, glancing at the girls playing quietly under the leafless peach tree. Maudie, three years old next week on February 14, understood *hot* and played at a safe distance. Hannah, tethered to a tree, strained against the rope toward the steaming cauldron oblivious to the dangers.

Leaving the delicates to soak in boiling water, Mattie turned to the dirty clothes requiring harsher cleaning methods. Deftly, she passed a bar of lye soap over a little dress spread out on the tin washboard. Suds foamed as she repeatedly moved the dress quickly up and down over the corrugated surface. Giving the garment a thorough twist, Mattie tossed it into a tub of cold rinse water.

"Mama," Maudie called. "Look at Hannah." Mattie turned. The rope lay limp where it had fallen from Hannah's waist. Frozen in silent terror, Mattie watched helplessly as her baby stumbled, lost her balance, and plunged into the tub of scalding water.

Hannah screamed, breaking the spell.

"Hannah!" Mattie shrieked. In seconds, she pulled her daughter from the boiling cauldron, submerged her in cool rinse water just steps away, hardly noticing the searing burns on her own arms and hands.

"Mother!" Mattie prayed that her deaf mother would feel her urgency and come. Maudie had begun to cry. "Honey, baby, I need you to be brave for mama. Can you go get Grandma?"

Maudie hiccupped and nodded.

"Please, dear God," Mattie prayed, as she stripped the lye-soaked clothes from her unconscious child. "Don't let my baby die. Don't let my baby die."

"She will not die."

Mattie turned, expecting to see her mother. There was no one, yet she heard the voice as clearly as if someone had been standing at her shoulder. Calm came over her, clearing her mind and giving her strength.

Mattie cringed at the angry, red skin already covered with watery blisters. She knew there would be ugly scars, like Jane Wood's. Carrying scars from a similar accident, Jane hid them under long sleeves and high-necked dresses. Hannah would not be able to hide her scars so easily.

Martha appeared at her daughter's elbow. Her face grew white. "Dear God in Heaven." It was a prayer.

Mattie faced her mother so that she could see her lips. "Clean out a tub with scalding water and put it on the kitchen table. Fill it with cool water and call me when you've finished."

"Clean tub, clean water, and cool." Martha limped to the house as quickly as her rheumatism allowed.

"Hannah, my little Hannah," Mattie breathed, wondering if she would ever be able to forgive herself for not checking the rope.

"Got the tub full," Martha called from the back door.

Scooping Hannah into her arms, Mattie carried her to the kitchen and gently placed her in the clean water. It lapped at Hannah's half opened eyes as Mattie supported her head just above the waterline. Hannah hated water on her head and face, but now she accepted all that Mattie imposed as if she knew her life depended on it.

"Go for Tom, Mother. If he isn't home, send for Peter Wood. Tell them to bring oil."

"Let's go for a walk, Maudie." Martha grabbed her shawl and took her granddaughter by the hand taking no time to remove her apron.

"Please," Mattie prayed again, "please, let my child be whole." Mattie wondered if God might think her selfish, asking for more than the life of her daughter. "Thy will be done," she added quickly, just in case.

Olive oil! The thought had come as clearly as if it had been spoken. *What about olive oil?* Mattie wondered. She knew it served symbolically as part of the ordinance when blessing the sick. She had never heard of any healing capabilities.

"Sarah keeped Maudie," Martha said, coming into the kitchen. "Tom is coming. I sent word to the Woods. How's the baby?"

"It looks bad, Mother."

"And you?" Martha searched her daughter's eyes. "How you doin'?"

"If I had just checked the rope again," Mattie said.

"Don't go blamin' yourself, now, you hear? Things happen."

Tears pricked at Mattie's eyes. She could only nod.

Jane Wood arrived first, taking the shortcut across the swinging bridge. Peter had gone with Ene.

"You did good, putting Hannah in water like that," Jane said. "Now you need lard on those burns. That's what my mother did for me."[1]

"It keeps coming to me that I should use olive oil," Mattie said.

"Don't think we got enough of it around here," Jane said, "and it's frightfully expensive."

Tom walked into the kitchen. Seeing Hannah swollen and blistered, his eyes filled with tears. "Poor child."

"Will you give her a blessing, Tom?"

Tom nodded. "I brought Brother Taylor to help."

For the first time, Mattie saw Alonzo Taylor. "Thank you for coming, Brother Taylor."

Tom's voice was strong and confident. "Your mother was directed that you might be born . . ."

Directed? Mattie wondered at the word, making a mental note to pursue its meaning later.

"You will realize full recovery." Tom said the words, but deep in her soul, Mattie knew the words came from God. "Those who minister unto you will be directed and guided in their care and should look to the healing properties of olive oil."

Mattie looked at Jane.

Jane smiled.

Mattie's eyes glistened.

"What do you know about olive oil?" Mattie asked Tom as soon as the prayer ended.

"Nothing much," said Tom, "except that we use it to administer to the sick."

"It was used like medicine in Bible times," Brother Taylor said.

"Have you ever used it in that way?" Mattie asked.

"No," said Brother Taylor, "but somebody," he looked skyward, "knows something that we don't."

***

Hannah finally slept. Next to her bed, Mattie sat in the rocking chair, still as death, exhausted but unable to sleep, staring at the shadows that played on the walls in the dark hours before sunrise. Her own hands barely burned now.

From the snores that never came from the next room, Mattie knew that Ene didn't sleep either. He had cried at the pitiful sight of his little daughter and was tormented at her pain.

The Wilsons' store had only one small bottle of olive oil and that meant a trip to El Paso, which Ene readily agreed to. If he took two horses and slept in the saddle, he could make it in two or three days. However, at one dollar and thirty-five cents a pint, they needed an exorbitant twenty-five dollars to buy enough for Hannah's needs. That could take months.

Except for five dollars in the jar, they had no cash. Selling a horse would give them the amount. Because of Ene's freighting business, that was not an option. It took her a good hour to talk Ene out of it.

Mattie shut her eyes. Tom's voice came unbidden to her mind.

"Full recovery . . . healing properties of olive oil . . ."

Though she couldn't see how, she knew God, in His mysterious way, would provide. Comforted by that thought, Mattie contemplated the other portion of Tom's prayer.

"Your mother has been directed that you might be born."

Interesting how many times opportunity and deeper understanding are born of heartache, despair, and disappointment. Telling Alonzo that she could not marry him had been a painful ordeal. She had not understood then, having no objections to Alonzo, not until his visit that day in Bisbee when she learned he was unable to father children.

Why had God spared her the agony of barrenness? Many noble women were barren. Could it be that in God's great scheme, it was important that she be the vessel through which particular spirits came to earth?

Did God mete out challenges to his earthly children for their own good?

As a parent, she could never purposefully make her child's life difficult. She could not fathom that God would do less, which brought her thoughts full circle—Hannah's little burned body.

Surely that was not God's doing just to teach a lesson. As a matter of fact, it seemed that God had been at her side, directing her every decision and comforting her baby through the pain. But wouldn't it have been more compassionate for God to prevent the whole terrible business in the first place?

How she wished that she could turn back the clock and start the day over.

***

The sun shined through the window before Mattie's eyes fluttered open. She could hear her mother in the kitchen. Hannah slept the sleep of exhaustion, the linen strips still intact.

Mattie went to the kitchen where Ene ate his breakfast.

"Did you get much rest?" he asked.

"I'm okay. And you?"

Before Ene could answer there was a *halloo* at the front door. "Anybody home?"

Ene looked up. "Mornin', Pa."

"Father Wood," Mattie said.

"Sit and eat," Martha invited.

"I've had my breakfast, Martha, thank you. But I will sit."

Peter put a cloth sack on the table. Mattie sucked in her breath. She knew it was silver.

"Now I don't want you saying nothing," Peter said when Mattie and Ene began to object. "I'm doing his for my granddaughter, not for you."

"But Pa . . ."

"I sold old Barco," Peter said. "Tom found me a buyer."

Neither Mattie nor Ene could speak. *Barco*, Spanish for boat, was a big bay with a smooth gait. Mattie knew the horse was a family favorite.

"Don't you worry none," Peter said. "This way, I don't have to see Barco get old . . . or get stole by no ragamuffin soldier."

"How can we ever thank you, Father Wood." Mattie wept as she hugged her father-in-law.

"Now, now. Don't go mushy on me. You're doing me a favor."

***

Moving deftly, Mattie collected what she needed to make cheese—a bit of lye for a tangy flavor, wood molds, pressing stones, and curdled milk. A bouquet of summer sunflowers brightened the kitchen, as did Hannah's smile as she played with a string of jangling canning rings.

Mattie smiled at her little girl. Never a day went by but what she offered thanks to her Heavenly Father. Perhaps He had not spared Hannah the ordeal, but He had spared Hannah. Grateful she was for the miracle of the olive oil, for the generosity that purchased it, that she could do what she had to do in doctoring Hannah, who not only was spared death, but was spared horrid disfigurement.

Mixing the ingredients, Mattie pressed them into wood molds and put them in the pantry. She reveled in a profound sense of equanimity until she turned to see Ene at the kitchen door, his expression cold as stone.

***

Instinctively, Mattie picked up Hannah and held her close, then checked on Maudie who played quietly with a little sock doll she had received for her birthday.

Ene's news was worse than she expected. It appeared that the US rejected Pancho Villa in support of Carranza, who they thought would be less likely to throw in with Japan and Germany, who were all too eager to win back everything the States won in the Mexican war.

Pancho Villa hated Carranza, who beat him out of the presidency. And now he hated Americans.

In open hostility, Villa held up the train near Pearson, killing every gringo passenger. Taking four hundred men, he made a surprise attack in the early hours of the morning on Columbus, New Mexico, a sleepy little town where the army camped. The Villistas robbed and pillaged, stealing horses and ammunition then vanished back across the border. Villa lost nearly eighty men in the skirmish, while only eighteen on the American side were slain, mostly civilians.[2]

And now, full of rage, vowing to kill every white man, woman, and child, Villa was due that night in their little community—first Colonia Dublán, then Colonia Juárez. Instead of preparing to defend themselves, they had been advised by their ecclesiastical leaders to go home, turn out the lights, and go to bed.

Life was difficult enough without this infernal war. "I'm afraid," Mattie said to her mother. Ene was out hiding the horses.

Martha straightened her shoulders and set her jaw. "A miracle will save us, just like the children of Israel were saved from their enemies when the good Lord parted the Red Sea."

Mattie replied, "It wouldn't be the first time God allowed good people to die."

Martha took her daughter's hand and patted it. "No doubt, death'll surely come at the appointed hour, but 'tisn't going to be tonight, dear. We've got Elder Ivins's promise.

"God keeps a promise, Mattie. Now, you go 'head and load your guns, hide your horses and such, and walk the cedar swamps. I'm goin' to pray and then get to my bed as I been told. Be sure to put out the lamps, dear."

***

Tree branches scratched at the tin roof. Mattie jerked awake. She and Ene lay on top of the bed, fully dressed, guns within easy reach. Ene snored lightly. The outhouse door slammed.

Mattie slid from bed and went to the window. The moonless night proffered nothing except black shadows. She heard, rather than saw, the trees swaying in the fury of spring winds. What did she expect, burning homes? Were the soldiers marching toward Juárez? Would a miracle save them?

Mattie shook her head. Just when she declared her faith unshakable, along came another test.

Returning to bed, her mother's words came to her mind and Mattie prayed again for faith in the promise.

***

Gray light was showing at the window. Ene was gone. She didn't remember falling asleep. Mattie picked up her gun and went into the kitchen. A fire burned in the wood stove. Stepping to the back door, she was met with a palpable calm that permeated the little valley. Birds chirped, horses whinnied, and across town, a dog barked. Even the March wind was subdued.

"Sleep good?" Mattie turned to see her mother. Martha eyed the pistol.

Mattie looked sheepishly at the gun in her hand. "It's not over yet," she said weakly.

"Oh ye of little faith," Martha harrumphed, bustling about the kitchen.

"Do you know where Ene's gone to?

"Went to the school to find out what he could."

Mattie put the gun away and went to dress her daughters. Returning to the kitchen with Maudie and Hannah in hand, she found Ene just coming in the door, a big smile spread across his whiskered face.

"Don't be keepin' us waitin', Ene Wood," said Martha sharply. "I'm in no mood for shenanigans."

Mattie hid a smile. Her mother was more nervous than she let on.

"Villa took his soldiers by way of the lakes, bypassing both Colonia Dublán and Colonia Juárez. By now, they are miles south of us." Ene's sonorous baritone resounded merrily. "President Bentley cannot explain it, except for Elder Ivins's promise and the grace of God.

Martha smiled.

***

"Here, Maudie, take a big handful and throw it over the chicken's head, like this." Mattie reached into the sack of corn and demonstrated.

Maudie disappeared up to her waist and emerged with her hand bulging with the little yellow kernels. Grinning, she looked up at her mother for approval, not seeing the impetuous chicken until it pecked at her hand. Maudie flung the corn aside and batted her hands at the chicken's head. Mattie laughed as she shooed the chicken away.

"Try again, dear." Mattie held the sack open. Maudie looked doubtful. "Throw the corn quickly, then the chickens won't come so close."

Maudie took another handful of corn and threw it wide. The chickens scattered to assure their share. Maudie clapped her hands. "More, Mama, more."

Mattie smiled at her eager daughter and opened the sack. Maudie successfully repeated the process, reveling in her newfound power over the greedy chickens.

"I did it! I can tell Papa."

Mattie smiled despite the tug at her heart. Ene had been gone a week. It was certain that neither Pancho Villa nor the Red Flaggers would continue to honor their promise of safe conduct.

Ene had merely shrugged at the idea. "With a price on Villa's head payable by the US government," he said, "it's very unlikely the general will frequent the north, and the Red Flaggers will be reduced to non-cohesive rebels."

Determined not to torment herself with worry, Mattie dismissed the whole sordid business as she had more than once since Ene's departure. Even the constant spring winds and blowing dust had not helped her with her resolve. One rebel soldier could pose a threat.

Little did either of them know that the threat would come to Mattie instead of Ene.

***

A scream brought Mattie's head up. The sound came from down the block. Not Isabelle—the other direction. Quickly she took Maudie's hand and led her from the chicken coop.

"Take the eggs to Grandmother," Mattie said, handing Maudie the basket. "She's in the kitchen." Maudie nodded and walked carefully, carrying her charge. Mattie hurried to the front gate and surveyed the road. Her heart jumped into her throat. Several blocks away, six horses stood in front of the Thompsons' gate. Even from this distance, Mattie could see their wide sombreros and heavy bandoliers marking an X on their chests. A soldier led the Thompsons' only horse from their corral, laden with quilts and bundles of who knew what. Ruth Thompson ran after them. Mattie could barely make out the words *mine* and *thief.* The tallest soldier grabbed Ruth and pushed her roughly out of his way. She lost her footing and fell to the ground, screaming her fury. The man drew his gun and pointed it at her.

Mattie froze.

Another soldier stepped between the gun and the woman and

slapped her. Instantly, Ruth fell silent. The gun now holstered, Mattie breathed out slowly. Did Ruth realize the soldier who slapped her had saved her life? *If Brother Thompson is at home, he is injured . . . or dead*, she thought.

Next, the soldiers stopped at the Hansen house. Mattie saw the curtain drop at the window. Four men dismounted and went to the back, checking for animals, Mattie surmised. The other two pounded on the front door, commanding that it be opened. When there was no response, they swung at the door with an ax. Mattie could take no more. She went to the house and locked the door behind her, realizing instantly the futility of it.

"Soldiers are working their way up the street." Mattie kept her voice steady.

Martha's eyes grew wide. "Bar the door."

"That won't stop them. They nearly killed Ruth Thompson, and they're breaking down the Hansens' door with an ax." Mattie deliberated silently, wondering what to do. "We'll invite them in," she said suddenly.

"What?" Martha nearly screeched. "We're going to get ourselves killed, or worse."

"Some of that faith of yours would be helpful about now." Mother and daughter stared at each other.

"We'll drown them in hospitality." Mattie knew that by nature, Mexicans are friendly and hospital people. It was their only chance.

"It's crazy."

"We have no other choice. There are six of them." Mattie headed for the pantry. "We'll scramble eggs, fry up some potatoes, and make enough biscuits and white gravy to feed them all."

Martha went to the flour bin. "Best put Maudie with Hannah in the back room."

Mattie knelt in front of her three-year-old daughter. "Maudie, I need you to stay by Hannah. Be as quiet as you can. No matter what you hear, don't come out until I come for you."

Maudie nodded solemnly and curled up by Hannah, who slept soundly. Mattie closed the door on her two little daughters.

"Dear God, protect us."

***

"They're here," Mattie said, glancing out the window. Her whole body trembled. She said another prayer. Taking a deep breath and letting it out slowly, she swung the door wide and stepped out onto the front porch before the last man had dismounted. Six grizzly-faced men stared with piercing black eyes. No one smiled, except Mattie. She was familiar with their gaunt, ragged appearance and thought of Ricardo. What political faction were these soldiers? Suddenly, she did not want to know.

Mattie continued to smile, her heart in her throat. With what she hoped sounded sincere, she said, "Pase, pase. Hace mucho frio. Mi casa es su casa. Please come in out of the cold and warm yourselves. My home is your home."

One by one, the men slowly came to life and moved warily toward the open door. The lead soldier, scowling and suspicious, motioned Mattie to enter ahead of them. Several soldiers positioned their guns for easy access. They suspected a trap. The thought surprised Mattie. She nodded and walked gracefully toward the kitchen, forcing herself not to look over her shoulder.

From the stove, Martha greeted the men with a stiff nod. Mattie motioned toward the table set for six. Coffee steamed from each cup. Six plates were stacked with hashed brown potatoes and topped with two fried eggs. Golden brown biscuits swam in pools of white gravy.

Mattie saw a softening in their grim faces. "Perhaps you'd like to wash," she said. Instinctively, the soldiers looked down at their hands, as if seeing them for the first time. Jagged fingernails and cracked hands were dark with months of rubbed-in grime.

"Si, señora," the leader mumbled respectfully. Setting their hats off their heads to hang down their backs, each man washed and took a place at the table. Hungrily, but well mannered, they ate in silence, helping themselves to bottled peaches and mounds of butter and jam. They drank most of two gallons of milk.

These soldiers, Mattie thought, *surely have wives and children of their own, honorable families like the Quevedos, who, inspired by inflated dreams, had united against rich minority rule to eradicate poverty and establish peace and justice.* Now the common masses fought against each other, led by greedy generals divided in their struggle for political power and prestige. In the end, what would the poor soldier gain for his trouble? Certainly not what was promised. If the soldier survived the war, he would return home, worse for the wear, to be ruled by another corrupt aristocracy pretending to be for the people.

Overcome with compassion, Mattie, with their permission, prepared bundles of beans, flour, sugar, salt, and lard. She looked around the pantry for other items. Bottled fruit would be too heavy. She spied a bag of dried apples and a sack of jerky.

Perfect! Her eyes flickered from soldier to soldier. Respectfully, they kept their gaze on their food, all except for the tall one Mattie recognized as the soldier who had threatened Ruth at gunpoint. He looked at Mattie in the same way that he looked at his food. She felt gooseflesh stand out on her skin.

Not until the last morsel of food had been eaten and the last drop of milk and coffee drunk did the soldiers stand. Mattie was ready with the bundles. Thin smiles stretched their faces as the men accepted her offering.

"Gracias, señoras. Muy amable." Each man nodded respectfully to Mattie and Martha. When the tall one took his bundle, his sneer broadened and he let his hand brush Mattie's. She ignored the gesture.

"Que ojos tan verdes tiene la señora," he said insolently, noticing Mattie's vibrant green eyes aloud to the other men.

"Cáyate, Ramón!" the leader barked.

Mattie looked at the commanding officer with what she hoped was respectful dignity. "Que le vaya bien. May all go well," she said. *Bien lejos de aqui,* she added silently. Far, far from here.

The soldiers strapped the goods to their horses. Without stopping at the next home, they rode out of town. Clouds of dust were whisked away by the wind, and the air became clear again.

It was over.[3]

***

"We done it," Martha said quietly, closing the door. "We not only saved ourselves, we saved Isabelle. She'd a been next."

Mattie could only nod. Her legs suddenly became rubbery, and she fell into the nearest chair. Covering her face, she gave way to great gulping sobs.

Martha squeezed Mattie's shoulder. "You done good, daughter. Real good," she said in a quivering voice. She cleared her throat. "Well, the world don't stop jus' 'cause a trouble. Now you go and check the little ones and I'll make cakes. I 'spect the Hansens and the Thompsons needs a visit 'bout now."

A sentiment originating with Grandmother Thomas, "to lift the spirits by partaking of the good side of life," was a philosophy to which Martha strictly adhered. And cakes and visiting was just the thing after a harrowing incident. "When you're done with them folks," Martha added, "you go on over and see Allie."

***

Though the Hansens and the Thompsons were gracious in accepting Mattie's kindness, it did little to lift her spirits. Brother Hansen was busy replacing his front door, shaking his head morosely for being gone when his family needed him. He had stepped out and was at the Cardons' saddle shop just across the river. After looking down the barrel of a gun, Ruth Thompson was ill and kept to her bed. Ruth's sister, who had come to help, was pale, whispering in somber tones. Richard should have never left, she kept repeating, as if Ruth's poor husband had purposefully left his family at the hands of desperados. Like Paul Hansen, Richard Thompson would feel guilty enough when he returned that evening from Pearson. When they asked whether the soldiers had stopped at her house, Mattie simply said that she and her mother saw them leave town. To tell either family more seemed boastful under the circumstances. Mattie was relieved to get away.

It was at Allie's that her spirits were rescued. Since childhood, Mattie and Allie Spilsbury had been comforting each other through life's injustices, helping the other to laugh at the contemptible.

Both of them freighting widows, they found solace in one another's company.

Allie's well-furnished house was cool, shaded by big cotton-woods, front and back. Clean laundry was stacked neatly on the dining table. In the corner of the room, next to the china hutch, Allie's infant son lay in a cradle. Whooping in the back yard were Allie's two older boys, playing war.

"I'm so glad you came today." Allie hugged Mattie. She forced a strand of black hair escaped from the bob at her neck "I'm so distracted, I nearly turned to the mending."

Mattie laughed. She felt better already. Ever since Mattie could remember, Allie had hated mending. Mattie handed the cake to Allie.

"Woman, you don't have to bring me something to be able to visit, but I sure won't tell you not to." Allie put the cake in the kitchen. "Maybe this will cheer my Lem. He cried over his favorite shirt, bidding it good-bye forever when he put it in the mending bag."

"Instead of a quilting party next Wednesday, Allie, you should have a mending party and be done with it."

"That'd shock Lem, all right," Allie said.

"And that's not an easy thing to do." Mattie grinned.

"No it's not, but he got the shock of his life this week, and I've been dying to tell you." Allie's eyes danced. She motioned Mattie to sit down.

Mattie made herself comfortable. "I'm listening."

"Well, Lem went to El Paso a few days ago on the train. He was on a secret mission for the Villistas. The general paid Lem five hundred dollars to deliver a message to the US government in El Paso. Lem didn't want to, because of the business of trying to stay neutral and all, but the general left him little choice. Lem hid the letter in his BVDs, knowing that if the Carranzistas found it, he'd be a dead man. He steps off the train in El Paso, and who should he run into but one of Carranza's generals."

Mattie gasped.

Allie went on. "He knows Lem and started telling him how he

hates Villa, and if that blankety so-and-so wins the war, it will be the end of hope for Mexico. Well, Lem just nods his head, and then this general asks Lem to come with him to have lunch. By now, Lem is pretty nervous. He thinks that maybe the general knows about his secret mission and he's headed for a trap.

"Lem hummed and hawed and said he'd be happy to meet the General after he takes care of business. The General agrees. Lem figures that the general knows nothing about the message or he would never have allowed him out of sight. As soon as Lem gets away, he goes straight to get rid of that letter. Keep in mind, he has no idea what it says, and what's more, he doesn't want to know."

"Did he deliver it?" Mattie asked.

"Yes. And Lem kept his lunch date with the general, still a little nervous. Turns out, the general wants Lem to accompany a doctor to Casas to treat his wounded brother."

"Is that so risky?" Mattie asked.

"It is if the wounded brother is a Carransista general. You can imagine what the Villista general would think of that."

"Oh! Poor Lem."

"Lem felt like he was walking on thin ice. He goes to El Paso on a mission for the Villistas, and the next day returns to Casas on a mission for the Carransistas. But he can't say no. It's more dangerous than saying yes."

"Well, Lem got back, so everything must have worked out."

"Better than we ever dreamed." Allie clapped her hands. "The wounded general paid Lem five hundred dollars for his efforts."[4]

"A thousand dollars in two days?" Mattie threw her head back and laughed, startling Allie's infant. Quickly, she muffled her giggles, and the baby settled in again.[5]

Although they enjoyed the humor of the situation, Mattie and Allie were careful not to speculate about the horrors that Lem might have faced and still could face if he were found out.

They grew serious when Mattie related her own morning's adventure. Allie was genuinely horrified and impressed by turns. "And," Mattie said, "when it was all over, I cried like a baby."

Allie laughed. "The crying heroine. Remember when you were

nearly crushed by a horse that lost its balance in the sand down by the river? It got up, leaving you in the sand. I was nearly hysterical, thinking you were dead. Calm as a cow chewing its cud, you got on that horse, rode him home, rubbed him down, gave him hay, and went to your room and cried for an hour."

Mattie grinned. "I don't know why I do that."

"All that scare has to come out sometime. What matters is your level head when it counts." Allie gave Mattie's hand a squeeze.

Mattie smiled. "I was sure glad to see those soldiers go."

"I'll bet my bottom dollar they were on the run," Allie said, "Lem found out that Pershing's army is arriving in Dublán any day now."[5]

"American soldiers? Here?"

Allie nodded. "For a manhunt. Pancho Villa. Dublán is the advance base or something like that. It's a great chance to make some money if you're willing to live in Dublán for a while. The soldiers need temporary shelters, they need food, and they pay top dollar." Allie smiled. "And best of all, while they're around, Mexican revolutionaries won't bother us."

There was no doubt in Mattie's mind that Ene would move to Colonia Dublán.[6] Mattie hoped for it but wondered if the blessing of Pershing's army would only bring more condemnation on their heads.

***

Never having seen Chung Lee's name written, Mattie said it the way it sounded, and it came out Johnlee. Chinese, Chung Lee had migrated first to California and then to Mexico. Since April, when they had moved to Colonia Dublán, he served as Mattie's assistant chef. In no time at all, he had become a trusted employee and a family favorite.

Mattie wiped her hands on her apron. "Johnlee."

"Yes, Mees Mattie." He bowed.

"Go over to Taylor's store and pick up the meat." Mattie handed Chung a note. "Tell them it's for Pershing's soldiers. They'll put it on the account.

"Yes, Mees Mattie, I go right now." *Right* came out as "light," but Mattie would never have made fun of Chung Lee. Her own language skills were lacking not only in Spanish but also, from Chung Lee's respectful grins, Chinese as well.

"Can I go with Johnlee?" Maudie looked at her mother expectantly.

"Go. Go." Hannah chanted jumping up and down. Mattie looked at her assistant. His blue-black hair, streaked with gray, was pulled away from his lined face into a single braid that hung down his back nearly to his waist. If he did not want to take the girls along, he would busy himself, careful not to make eye contact, pretending not to understand.

Chung Lee's eyes became pleasant slits, wrinkling at the corners. He showed crooked but gleaming white teeth. "I take Maudie and Hannah for riddo walk."

"Johnlee says yes, Mama."

"Don't be any trouble now, or Johnlee won't take you next time." Maudie smiled big and nodded.

"I buy riddo missies candy?"

"You spoil the little missies." Mattie grinned.

Chung Lee bowed. Eyes twinkling, he said, "Yes, Mees Mattie." He walked out, braid swinging, two little girls in hand.

Mattie grinned. She had never been able to convince Chung Lee that he didn't have to bow. She finally decided that a leopard couldn't change its spots, accepting the show of politeness, which had become endearing.

While the bread baked, Mattie took advantage of a few spare moments to write a letter.

25th day of October 1916

Dear Phoebe,

I hope this letter finds you enjoying good health. I have a few minutes to myself while Hannah and Maudie are gone with Johnlee for their weekly supply of sweets. Johnlee absolutely spoils my girls. He's very grandfatherly.

And speaking of my girls, I marvel every time I look at Hannah.

While my hands still carry slight scars, she has healed without blemish.

Dublán flats is a terrible place to be in the summer. Had Ene not moved us here in April when it was still cool, I would have never agreed to the venture. Mother and Allie are the smart ones.

I was surprised when Allie didn't move, but then I believe it would be more difficult to leave a home that is your own.

I don't see mother often, but I do get her cheeses regularly. She has a Pershing account. It has been a nice little business for her.

The company store is doing well for Ene and his brother Bill. The permit is good until April next year. Between the store and me feeding the soldiers, we have more money than we've seen since we've been married. Ene is on the road most of the time freighting goods, but I get to see him more by living here than if I had stayed in Juárez. We are comfortable in the Wagner home. It took a little cleaning, having been vacant since the exodus. They have been kind to let us use it. The Woods live a few houses down from us. It's nice to have them close.

For the first time in five years, we have been safe from the harassment of the revolutionaries. Villistas and Red Flaggers are afraid to come too close, and Carranzistas are on good behavior because they want the US soldiers to get rid of Villa. Pershing has had no success on that score. It's like Pancho Villa vanished off the face of the earth.[7]

Edward, a lieutenant colonel who takes his meals with us, says that the Mexican poor love Villa like the British poor loved Robin Hood. Villa began as a peon, and he's fighting their cause, so they hide him.

When Pershing pulls out, we fear unfriendly visits from renegades. Many families plan to leave. Don't know what will happen to the rest of us. At best, our business will end. I won't mind moving back to Juárez. I don't look forward to another summer in Dublán.

Mattie rested her hand and read what she had written, then continued.

Pershing's soldiers call Ene "Pancho Villa." There is a striking resemblance because of Ene's broad mustache. He grew it for that very purpose. Ene likes Villa and believes that he is not through yet in spite of his setback. Anything can happen.

Mattie ended the letter, asking Phoebe to forward the letter to Nell, Lola, Leuna, and Moe, and begged for a return letter from each. She was folding the letter into the envelope when Chung Lee returned. Mattie smiled. This diminutive grandfather looked tall only when standing next to the children.

***

Mattie, Martha, Isabelle, and Jane Wood worked miracles getting the children fed, responding to demands for seconds and careless spills in record time. Everyone laughed at little Maudie when she announced apologetically that she was "spillful," having dropped potatoes and gravy on her Christmas dress, a hand-me-down from Rosalie. After they had eaten, the children were quartered in a back bedroom with Roberta, who entertained them with stories and games while the adults took their turn at the lavish feast.

Pies lined the sideboards and windowsills in the kitchen: apple, peach, suet, mincemeat, and pumpkin—twenty all told. Every available kerosene lamp had been employed in the dining room to light the festive table.

Besides the Woods and the Seveys, who came from Juárez bringing Martha, guests included Mattie's soldiers, as Ene called them. Since April, Lieutenant Colonel Edward Campbell had been a regular at dinner when he was in camp and had brought a dozen soldiers with him, rarely the same men twice. What began as a business deal grew into friendship, and the lieutenant insisted that Mattie and Ene drop his formal military rank.

"This is a wonderful meal, Mattie," Tom said. "If anyone had tried to tell me that my little sister would grow up to cook like this, I wouldn't have believed them."

"I practically gave up on her growing up at all," Ene said with a mischievous glint.

"I don't think Tom meant that type of growing up." Isabelle laughed.

"If anybody was waiting for somebody to grow up," Peter put in, "Mattie was waiting for Ene."

"Yep," Tom said. "Mattie had to wait for Ene to outgrow his obnoxious self. There wasn't any of us that thought it would happen."

Edward laughed. "That Mattie would wait, or that Ene would outgrow his faults?"

"Yes," said Jane Wood.

Ene let go with a voluminous, good-natured laugh. "Somehow this conversation has turned nasty."

The soldiers, enthusiastic and handsome in their dress uniforms, grinned from ear to ear at the verbal exchange.

Edward said, "The meal is delicious, Mattie. I don't think I have ever celebrated Christmas so grandly . . . especially under the circumstances."

It had been five months since the Tenth Cavalry had been nearly destroyed by the Mexican Army in an uncharacteristic encounter.[8] The soldiers who now sat around her table had lost friends, and Edward had come close to being counted among them.

He smiled. "You have been kind and hospitable, allowing your home to be our home away from home. We are forever in your debt."

"Hear, hear," the others intoned.

Everyone waited for Mattie to speak. Staring at her plate, she did not, could not, trust her voice. The fire crackled in the fireplace, casting dancing shadows on the evergreen, whose branches were laden with stringed popcorn and cranberries, planted firmly in a bucket of wet earth. Mattie's eyes went from the roast beef to the venison, ham, and sausages, to the mashed potatoes and gravy. Few green beans were left in the serving bowl. The squash had not been as popular, and the corn had been finished to the last kernel. Cranberry and pickle relishes graced the table in small, delicate bowls. In a large basket, a few miniature loaves of sourdough bread, browned to perfection, peeked out from under a clean linen cloth. Homemade butter, cut in fancy curls, was nearly gone.

Mattie knew she had to say something. And sentimentality would open the floodgates. Finally, she looked at her military guests.

"You are very kind, but let me point out that your debt made me a pretty penny."

Everybody laughed, and the mood became light again until the subject turned to the war. It was inevitable, even on Christmas day. Edward initiated the subject, and Mattie silently thanked him for leaving it until the end.

"We've received orders from General Funston in El Paso," the Lieutenant said. "The hunt for Villa is called off. The first troops will pull out in a few weeks."

"So, there's truth to the rumors," Ene said. It was not a question.

"General Pershing hopes to have us all stateside by the middle of February."

"Hope you take no offense," Ene said, "but I'm not at all sorry you didn't catch Villa. I think he's the hope of Mexico."

The lieutenant laughed. "No offense taken. We have a grudging admiration for him ourselves, but we don't shout it about."

"Carranza's soldiers," Isabelle said, "would shoot us for saying as much."

And Carranza's soldiers, Mattie thought, *would be all that was left to protect them when Pershing's army pulls out.*

A dark foreboding sent a shiver down Mattie's spine.

1917

MATTIE BLEW OUT THE LAMP AND CRAWLED INTO BED beside Ene. It had been a long Saturday. She had fed twenty soldiers. Within the week, not a military man would be left, many of the colonists people returning to the United States with them.[1] Mattie was glad she and Ene were not one of those. They would move back to Colonia Juárez and pick up their life there.

"You've been quiet all evening," Mattie said.

"I have something to tell you. You aren't going to like it."

Mattie remained silent.

Ene pulled her into the circle of his arm and clung to her. "I saw General Gutierrez today."

"The one that had you sword whipped? Isn't it a bit risky for a Red Flagger to come here with all these Carranzistas?

"He was Pershing's prisoner."

"Was?"

"It was pitiful, Mattie. Gutierrez was crying like a baby, begging me to do what I could to help him."

Mattie's body became rigid. "You didn't," she said, knowing perfectly well that he did.

"He would have been executed, Mattie. I couldn't have that on my conscience."

Mattie rolled away from Ene and sagged into her pillow.

He said softly, "Don't be angry, Mattie."

Was she angry? Having crossed the line of neutrality by saving Gutierrez, the Carranzistas would come for Ene as soon as Pershing's army had evacuated.[2]

Yes, she was angry. And afraid.

Now she and Ene had no choice but to join the exodus. They would lose everything all for a man responsible for the scars on her husband's back, a man who would have killed Ene, except for an intervening miracle, a man who caused her sleepless nights, a man who caused her stomach to tie up in knots every time Ene left the house.

"No," a voice in her head said, "your sacrifice is for a man's life."

Could she put a price on the life of a human being? War was war, driving desperate men to desperate measures for their cause. Did that make Gutierrez a bad man?

And Ene? Well, he had risen above the very thing she hated about war. That took a noble man.

Shame drained the fire from Mattie's heart. Her throat ached with unshed tears. She returned to her husband's embrace. Swallowing back a sob, she said, "You did a good thing, Ene. I couldn't be prouder."

***

Safely ensconced in a warm quilt on a feather tick in her mother's home in Colonia Juárez, Mattie watched as dawn diluted the cold, February night.

The Second Battalion, the last of Pershing's army, was probably well on their way, mounted soldiers in double file, and wagons bringing up the rear. Ene would be among them. His freight wagon carried her treadle sewing machine, her rocking chair, and other essentials for their new home in Thatcher, Arizona. They had agreed that Mattie and the girls would follow by train in two weeks. Ene would meet them in El Paso.

The light grew brighter in the window. Emotions, which had been buried in the flurry of preparation and farewells, now forced their way to the surface. Mattie's eyes watered.

Saying good-bye to Ene was wrenching. They parted in Colonia Dublán, he not wanting to get too far from Pershing's army. The ride to Colonia Juárez was long and sad as each mile put more distance between them.

Parting with Johnlee was made less difficult when Mattie found him a position with Edward. The lieutenant was due a furlough. He would take Johnlee home to work in his mother's kitchen. She was delighted with the prospects, and Mattie was pleased that perhaps Johnlee's life might become a little easier.

The girls, however, were inconsolable. Johnlee had practically been a grandfather to them.

In two weeks, Mattie would have to bid her farewells again, and it promised to be just as bitter, leaving mother, Ene's family, and Tom and Isabelle and the children.

She loathed leaving the memories of her childhood maybe forever—the place where, as a child, she had first met Ene, where he had come to court her years later, where their names were carved in the trunk of the big cottonwood across the road from the ranch house. They had stood under that tree in the moonless night stealing kisses and planning their future. How futile that had been.[3]

Mattie smiled. *How strange, this life.*

Suddenly, she wanted to visit the ranch one last time. Maudie and Hannah would go with her, and mother too, if she wanted.

"I never heared of such nonsense, and I won't go," Martha said, "and you neither."

"I may never see the place again," Mattie said.

"'Tisn't safe."

"You said yourself that it's been months since soldiers have passed through here."

"They doesn't 'xactly tell us when they plan to come."

"I'll have the Quevedos right next door," said Mattie, like that solved everything.

"And what can they do against a bunch of soldiers?"

Mattie laughed. "Oh, Mother. It's just for a couple of days. I haven't seen the place since Maudie was born, and you haven't been out to check things for a year."

"Don't need checkin'."

"I'll talk with Tom. If he thinks I shouldn't go, then I won't." Mattie gave her mother a quick hug.

Later, reflecting on that moment, Mattie wished she had listened to her mother.

***

"I don't suppose there's any real danger," Tom said, when Mattie had gone to borrow his buggy for the drive to the ranch house. "It's been so quiet that Isabelle and I are talking about moving back to Chupe."

Mattie said, "Ironic, isn't it? We're fleeing Mexico for our lives and you're settling in for the long haul. If only Ene had not gone out to Pershing's camp that day."

"Dwelling on the *if only* will drive you nuts, Mattie," Tom said.

"I know, but I can't help it."

"Sometimes nothing works out the way you hope. You just have to take it a day at a time, do your best, and learn from it."

"You're right, Tom. I don't know why I have to learn that lesson over and over. You'd think I would get it right after a fashion."

"We're all slow learners in one area or another." Tom lifted Mattie up into the buggy. "I'll come out to the ranch in a few days and ride back with you."

***

Rafaela had changed little, except for the strands of gray in her ink-black hair that she still wore pulled back in a practical bob at the base of her neck. And the sadness in her dark, almond-shaped eyes did not disappear when she smiled. War did that, especially if you feared for your sons.

"This one has your coloring but looks like her father." Rafaela pointed to Maudie. Pointing at Hannah, she said, "And the little dark one has her father's coloring, but looks like you."

Mattie laughed. "It is so good to see you."

While Javier unloaded the buggy, Rafaela accompanied Mattie

as she inspected the homestead. The Quevedos had taken such good care of the house Mattie would only have to rearrange a little dust before settling in. The yard was free of weeds, and spring bulbs promised full blooms in another week or two. The kitchen garden was turned and ready for planting.

They had just turned from the garden when Rafaela called to a woman, eighteen or nineteen Mattie guessed, with a boy about fourteen. "Susana. Antonio. Come and say hello to Doña Mattie."

"This is little Susana?" Mattie exclaimed. Susana had metamorphosed from a little mud-lark girl into a dark-eyed, olive-skinned beauty. Despite a slightly overlapping front tooth, her smile was dazzling.

"Buenas tardes, Doña Mattie."

"And Antonio?" Mattie held out her hand. He shook it, grinning sheepishly. He had a hard time finding his voice. When he did, it was lower than Mattie expected.

"Mucho gusto!"

Mattie smiled. *What a handsome young man, Antonio.*

"Doña Mattie." The voice came from the direction of the river. Mattie turned to see a muscular man coming toward her. He sported a mustache, giving him an uncanny resemblance to Silvestre.

"Pablo?" Mattie received his polite handshake. "I thought you were off fighting the cause."

"Father discouraged it, and so did my brothers. They say it is one thing to fight for our country, but it is another to fight for a general."

Mattie understood. The war had become a power struggle among the surviving revolutionaries. "I didn't think you could escape so easily," Mattie teased.

Pablo grinned. "If they don't see me . . ." He shrugged and let the sentence go.

Mattie grew serious. "And Silvestre and Rodrigo?" She feared the answer.

"Silvestre is a general for Pancho Villa now," Pablo said.

"Pancho Villa?" Mattie whistled through her teeth.

"The letter you brought to us from Silvestre a few years back told us of their plans," Javier explained.

Mattie remembered the letter that had been secreted into her possession, the letter that should not fall into "the wrong hands." The Quevedo brothers had been communist generals then, Red Flaggers.

"Do you get to see them from time to time?"

The entire Quevedo family looked at the ground. Finally Javier said, "Silvestre was wounded in a battle with the Americanos. Rodrigo was not so fortunate."

Mattie felt sick at the thought of her good friend Edward and her good friends Silvestre and Rodrigo fighting against each other. Her eyes teared. "I'm so sorry." Controlling the tremor in her voice, she said, "It appears I have dear friends on both sides of the war."

"As do we," said Rafaela, touching her arm. At this, each member of the family smiled and nodded Rafaela's sentiments.

"Thank you." Mattie said. To lighten the moment, she added, "We told the American soldiers that we were glad they did not catch Pancho Villa. He was the best man for Mexico's president."

Pablo was wide-eyed with disbelief, then laughed. "This is treason in our country."

"That's what I told the Americans."

"Come," Rafaela said, pointing toward her own home. "You and your daughters will rest while my family finish up here."

***

When at last Mattie returned to the ranch house, laden with tortillas, tamales, and a dish of beans, she discovered that Javier and his children had been busy. Their food supplies were stored in the kitchen along with several cans of water collected from the well. In the front room, Mattie found her cot assembled and ready. A well-padded bed made up on the floor in front of a crackling fire was for the girls.

She smiled, glad that she had come. The cheery fire added a warm, homey atmosphere. She could almost smell fresh-baked bread cooling on the sideboards and a pot of beans cooking on the stove as the screen door slammed with the comings and goings of children.

Happy and tranquil, Mattie pulled her quilt up close to her chin and slept.

***

The sun was well over the mountain when she took her little girls exploring. She tried to impress Maudie and Hannah with tales of hard work and long hours of milking that she did as a girl. When the girls became more excited about the nest of indolent rats that shared the corral with a couple of milk cows belonging to Javier and Rafaela, Mattie abandoned the effort. She made a mental list to supply her friends with a nice rangy cat.

The children scampered over rocks and played among the river brush that stood as tall as a man. It was too cold for wading in the flow of spring melt. Instead, they floated small, dry branches that had fallen from the cottonwoods. From the banks, Hannah and Maudie chased after their miniature regattas until they swirled out of sight or ran aground.

When they tired of the game, Mattie showed them the large heart on the trunk of the cottonwood tree and explained the E + M carved inside. To her daughters' delight, she added to the carving. When she finished, Maudie traced her fingers over the letters. E + M = M & H.

"There are two Ms, mommy. Which one is mine?"

"You're the second M." Mattie pointed.

"Where's my M?" Hannah asked.

"It's an H," Maudie said.

Mattie took Hannah's finger and laid it on the H.

Hannah giggled. "H."

"Fools' names, like fools' faces," Mattie whispered, "always found in public places." She missed her "fool" and hoped he was safe.

"What shall we do now?" Maudie wanted to know.

They conferred and decided on the orchard where the leafless branches were fat with buds.

"Do you want to play hide-and-seek?" Mattie asked.

"Yeah," said Maudie.

"Hide," Hannah said.

"I'll close my eyes and count. You girls go hide, and I will come and find you." Mattie counted until she no longer heard little feet.

"Here I come, ready or not." A little shoe and part of a dress showed from behind a broad tree trunk. "Where can my little girls be?"

"We're right here." Maudie jumped out.

"Wight heo." Hannah mimicked.

Mattie smiled. "There you are."

"You found us too soon," Maudie pouted.

"Well, if you don't want to be found, you must be very, very quiet and very still."

"Okay. Let's do it again," Maudie said. "And this time, Hannah has to hide by herself."

"No," Hannah whined. "I 'fwaid."

"You can stay by me, Hannah, and help me count." Mattie took her hand and covered Hannah's eyes.

After counting again, the two of them went seeking. Unencumbered with her little sister, Maudie was better hidden this time. Mattie nearly stepped on her before she saw her.

"There you are. What a good hider you are."

"I was very, very quiet." Maudie beamed.

"Yes, you were," Mattie smiled, not realizing how very soon the game would become a matter of life and death.

***

"Doña Mattie! Doña Mattie!" The voice blended into Mattie's dream. "Señora Wood!"

Mattie's eyes flew open. It was no dream. She bounded out of the cot, heedless that she wore only a flannel nightgown.

"Pablo?" Mattie said through the door.

"Sí, Señora, quick."

Mattie opened the door. Pablo and Antonio slipped into the room, quickly shutting the door behind them.

"What's the matter?"

Pablo said. "Drunk Villista rebels. They are camping near. My father heard them. We must hide you and leave no evidence that you are here. We have hidden your horse and buggy."

"But the fire . . . ?"

"Hurry." Pablo cut her off.

Mattie threw on her clothes and with Pablo's and Antonio's help, they had bedding and clothing gathered in minutes. It took two trips to get it transferred to the Quevedos' house. The first signs of dawn showed in the east. Running awkwardly with Hannah bundled in a quilt, Mattie felt sick with fear.

The entire family was up and dressed and Javier took no time for formalities. "Come." He led the way to the shed that shared the back wall of the two-room adobe house. For convenience, it was accessible from the inside as well as the outside.

Mattie stepped in. Cut logs were staked four feet high along the three outside walls. The door leading outside was blocked and a sturdy wedge of wood, forced between door and frame, secured it. Anyone wanting to get in would have to crash the door down— which was entirely possible and frighteningly probable.

"At least you will be safe from bullets," Javier said, sensing Mattie's doubts.

She swallowed and nodded. Wrapping Maudie snugly in a quilt, Mattie placed her in the corner that shared the solid wall of the house, and taking a few extra logs, created Maudie's own little fort of protection where she sat quietly, sleep still in her eyes.

Hannah, on the other hand was inconsolable.

"I will take the dark one," Rafaela said, taking Hannah. "Her cries will give you away. If they see her, they will think she is mine."

"What if she speaks?" Mattie asked.

"Pray she does not," said Javier.

Although Mattie hated to let her baby go, Rafaela was right, and she did not object.

Glancing through the slats of the shed, Mattie saw Pablo walking back to the ranch house. "Where's he going?"

Javier looked somber. "It will look suspicious with a fire hot in the fireplace and no one there."

"I can't let Pablo do this." Mattie was up and headed toward the door.

"Doña Mattie." Javier blocked her way. "It is best."

Mattie watched as Pablo disappeared into her house. Her eyes misted. "Please, dear God," she prayed, "protect him."

Susana took her place beside Mattie on the floor. A beautiful young girl, she was safer not seen by lawless men. Javier handed Mattie a pistol. "I'm sorry I do not have one for each of you," he said. Giving his quickly arranged garrison one last check, he walked into the house.

Holding the gun, cold in her limp hand, Mattie was reminded of Nola Castle. Her father had given her a gun when the soldiers had come to town and hid her in a closet. "If they find you," he said, "shoot yourself. It will be easier going than what they will do to you."

Javier had not given her the gun with that purpose in mind, however. "Between Antonio and me, we can get most of them, but if one gets past me . . ." He didn't have to finish the sentence.

But, could she do it? Could she shoot a man even in self-defense? Cold sweat dripped down her back. She might very well discover the answer within the hour.

Mattie looked at her little daughter and smiled, trying to inspire confidence that she didn't feel. Movement from Maudie would not expose her hiding place, even in broad daylight, but the slightest sound might.

"We are playing hide-and-seek, Maudie," Mattie whispered, "and this is our hiding place."

"And Hannah's hiding place is in the house?" Maudie asked. Hannah had quit crying.

"Yes, and we must be very quiet like we played last night, even if loud noises scare us."

"Loud noises like guns?"

This surprised Mattie. How much did this little four-year-old understand? "Yes, sweetheart, like guns."

***

It was well into morning by the time the riders had pulled themselves into their saddles. Mattie peered through the warped slats. She held up four fingers to Susana. One of the riders shot his gun into the air, yelling to no one in particular. His horse reared and danced in circles.

The blood drained from Mattie's face once she could understand what the men were saying. She had heard that sort of thing before, closed up in a shack not unlike the one she found herself in now. She glanced at Susana. She had heard too. Mattie suddenly wished that Rafaela had hidden with them. None of them were safe.

The raucous troop bypassed the Quevedos' house. With sinking feeling, Mattie knew they chose the bigger place first. And Pablo.

As if her thoughts had conjured him, Pablo appeared at the front door. He pointed down the road in the opposite direction of Quevedos house as if in friendly conversation. Three soldiers dismounted. At gunpoint, Pablo led them inside. The fourth man held the horses.

It seemed forever before the men reappeared dragging Pablo's limp body. Mattie gasped. Jumping to her feet, she pushed through the door that led into the living quarters of the adobe house.

"I've got to help Pablo," she hissed. Her hand was on the handle of the front door. Javier jammed his foot against it, preventing it from opening. He took Mattie's arm. His eyes glistened.

"If you show yourself now, his sacrifice will have been for nothing."

Mattie went limp. With one hand she covered her face and wept softly, the other hung at her side, holding the gun.

"Mirra! Look!" Antonio said in a loud whisper, choked with alarm. Black smoke roiled from the ranch house.[4] It brought little comfort that Pablo's lifeless body was a safe distance from the blaze. The men mounted their horses and galloped toward them.

"They're coming," Javier said evenly. "Quick, Mattie."

Mattie returned to her place in the shed. Wide-eyed, her little daughter remained silent, true to her word. It tore at Mattie's heart. Fervently, she prayed that the soldiers would ride past.

They didn't.

The sound of galloping horses came to an abrupt stop at the front of the house. A loud knock came at the front door. Javier was slow to answer. There was another sound of impatient pounding.

"Abra la puerta." Expletives peppered the command.

Just then, a figure appeared from around the corner. Mattie's eyes flew to Susana's. She saw him too.

"Uno momento, uno momento," they heard Javier say.

Mattie heard the door open. "How can I serve you?" Javier offered politely.

Mattie gripped the gun as the soldier at the back moved slowly and noiselessly toward the shed door.

"We are hungry," a soldier out front said. "Hungry for a woman." There was an enthusiastic whoop followed by malevolent laughter. Hannah began to cry. She sounded far away.

"Mommy," Hannah wailed.

The man outside the shed stopped.

Mattie grimaced.

"Aqui esta su Mommy," Mattie heard Rafaela say. Thankfully, the word was interchangeable from one language to another. Hannah continued to cry. Mattie prayed that she wouldn't say another word.

Looking at her older daughter ensconced securely between logs, Mattie brought a finger to her lips. Maudie nodded somberly and mimicked her mother's gesture.

Hannah's crying stopped. Mattie heaved a silent sigh.

The man was at the shed door. He nudged it gently at first, then a little harder.

Mattie raised her gun, slick with perspiration. Only a short few weeks ago, she could not force herself to put a price on a human life. Now, for the second time, she was ready to kill a man. Bile rose in her throat. "Please, dear God," she prayed.

Javier spoke. "A gun is pointing at your heart, señor. I will not die alone.

"He's bluffing, Beto," said one of the soldiers.

Mattie heard a gun cock—Antonio's. He was just a child. How tragic if he had to kill a man.

"Call for your other man," Javier said. There was a long hesitation. Mattie held her breath.

"Chato. Ven! Ahora!"

The soldier at the woodshed hesitated, drew his gun, and then disappeared around the corner.

"Not now, Chato," the voice at the front said. "Put the gun away. We will be back, señor, and we will leave you as we left your vecino next door."

"Already my son will be unhappy when he hears of the neighbors," Javier said.

"Son?" asked the insolent voice. "What do we care about your son?"

"General Silvestre Quevedo," Javier said.

"General Quevedo?" The voice was stupid with surprise.

"He is my son," said Javier quietly. "Do you know him . . . Chato? How about you . . . Beto?" He emphasized their names.

It was as if all four men had sucked in his collective breath never to let it out again.

Finally, the voice at the front door spoke. "A million pardons, Señor." Mattie wondered if the man bowed. "Vámonos, caballeros." Almost before he had finished saying it, they were gone.

Stillness shrouded the house as the crackling inferno next door tolled the casualties of the encounter.

"Is the game over, Mommy?" Maudie whispered.

Mattie held her arms out to her little girl. She walked into their safe embrace. "Yes, dear, I think so."

"The bad man didn't find us, Mama. I was very quiet."

"Yes, my brave, little girl!" she cried. "You were very quiet."

***

Slipping out of her mother's house, Mattie pulled her shawl closed against the early morning chill. Staying to the high center between the ruts, she worked her way up the road past skeletal century plants still brown from winter's freeze. The wagon trail plateaued in a straight line to the cemetery. She paused, letting her gaze sweep over the tall yellow grass bent by the breeze down to the town below bracketed between the hills. The sun hid behind a ceiling of low clouds, casting a dull shadow. Bare maple trees lined wide dirt roads. Leafless cottonwoods marked the banks of the trickling river dividing the dismal picture equally on both sides. Colorless smoke spiraled from red brick chimneys, punctuating a patchwork of denuded orchards and brown, furrowed rows touched by frost.

Passing through a gate of barbwire, Mattie entered the cemetery and made her way over stony ground. Her eyes moved sadly over the familiar names and stopped at a weathered headstone. Her fingers tenderly traced the engraved letters.

George Washington Sevey
Born - 25 February 1832 - LeRoy, New York
Died - 22 June 1902 - Colonia Juárez
Chihuahua, Mexico

An empty space, reserved for her mother, stretched ominously next to her father's grave. Surely, it would not be vacant when Mattie returned to Mexico—if she returned. Death was only a temporary separation, Mattie reminded herself, a door to a better life, a sweet release from adversity, a welcome step into a life exempt from evil perpetrated by greed and lust, an existence free of the anguish and guilt that tore at her now. Why then, was death so perverse?

"God never answers the whys, dear," her mother's voice echoed.

Mattie smiled ruefully. Yes, she knew better than to ask. Faith isn't trusting God to make all things better. Faith is simply trusting God.

Thankfully, Pablo had not died in the ordeal, but he would be a very long time healing. Mattie could not shake the idea that he had suffered in vain. The mere mention of Silvestre's name had sent the offending rebels off like whipped pups with their tails between their legs. If only Pablo had stayed in his father's house; if only the soldiers had stopped at the Quevedos' first; if only she had listened to her mother and not insisted on visiting the ranch.

Tom was right. There is no end to "if only," and it was driving her nuts.

She hugged herself against the cold. Her husband had fled for his life, they had lost their business, she had nearly lost a dear friend made more poignant by the fact that he had nearly died protecting her and the girls, and tomorrow she would take her daughters and leave behind all that was dear.

She had wondered once if God meted out challenges to test and strengthen her. *No*, she decided. Life meted out challenges. God was the source of strength and support that got her through it.

"I need you now, dear Father," she breathed. "Soften my grief. Grant me peace." The sun peeked through the clouds splaying warm, gauzy paths of light brightening the monochromatic gloom.

"God is there." Mattie heard it as if Grandmother Thomas stood beside her.

Mattie smiled. "I know, Grandmother."

A lilt in her step, Mattie turned toward home. The girls would be awake, asking for her.

Facts

1902

1. George W. Sevey contracted pneumonia and never fully recovered. He died in June 1902. Mattie states only that "When I was just ten years old, our dear Father passed away. He had been Bishop for twelve years and was truly a wonderful man. He was missed greatly by all." (Martha Ann Sevey Wood, as told to Peggy Nelson, granddaughter.)

2. Real names are used for the Sevey and Wood families.

1905

1. "In the middle of town, we had a bandstand above the riverbed where there were huge cottonwood trees and that was where we held our celebrations." (Martha Ann Sevey Wood, as told to Peggy Nelson, granddaughter.)

2. Although Grandmother Thomas did come to live with her daughter Martha, there is no indication from where she moved.

3. "For the town dances, Ene Wood played harmonica and Lucy chorded on the piano as part of the family band. Peter Wood played clarinet and violin." (Martha Ann Sevey Wood, as told to Peggy Nelson, granddaughter.)

4. According to her journal, besides Phoebe, Maudie Crawford and Allie Accord were Mattie's closest friends.

5. Genealogy records show that Leon died at age ten in Chuichupa—cause not known.

1910

1. The County Home Bar and Hermitage was a boarding house in Bisbee and the Mariotte's French Kitchen actually existed. Where Mattie worked is unknown.

2. "Phoebe went to Chuichupa with her brother to clerk in his store—that was our first separation." (Martha Ann Sevey Wood, as told to Peggy Nelson, granddaughter.)

3. According to her daughter Marene Wood Robinson, Mattie was attracted to a banker in Bisbee, although he was no murderer. There is no record of his name or whether or not the attraction blossomed into a full romance.

4. Naomi McRae was Nellie and Parley's firstborn.

5. See note 3.

. Brewery Gulch did burn in 1908. The fire actually started on Main Street with an explosion in one of the hotels.

1911

1. It is uncertain where in California Mattie actually went to meet Alonzo. Mahala Hancock, Mattie's sister, did live in California, but it is uncertain whether she stayed with her.

2. Jack is the second child of Nellie and Parley.

3. The Hancock children appear on the genealogical records.

4. Martha Ann Sevey loved clam chowder.

5. Mattie was never part of the earthquake that actually occurred on March 10, 1910, in the Monterey Bay region; shock recorded seismographically over half the earth and was felt in an area in excess

of fifty thousand square miles. The intensity IV quake location was possibly under Monterey Bay and intensity VI occurred at Hollister, Salinas, Monterey, and Santa Cruz. At Aptos and Watsonville, it was not less than intensity VII. At Watsonville, the excitement reached same proportions. The duration was10–30 seconds.

The Hotel Del Monte was nearly destroyed, and four or five people were killed. Brick and stone buildings in Watsonville were cracked, crumbled, and twisted out of shape. Most of the brick or stone chimneys collapsed. The entire Watsonville-Big Creek Power Company was out of commission. The wharf was destroyed and several warehouses thrown down at Moss Landing. At Soquel there were deep and wide cracks on Main Street from which water flowed up through broken pipes. A six-inch water main extending across the San Alonzo River on a covered bridge was broken, and each end of the bridge moved five and a half inches eastward. At Boulder Creek, not a single chimney was left standing. On Deer Creek, a large landslide came five hundred feet down the mountain, covering twenty-five acres of ground. The slide material, composed of soil clay, and shale was three hundred feet thick. G.B. Griggs, "Earthquake Activity between Monterey and Half Moon Bay, California." http://www.johnmartin.com/earthquakes/ eqpapers/00000027.htm) (October 11, 2004).

6. "[When] I was eighteen, I went to California to marry Alonzo. I had my wedding dress on and was all ready for the ceremony when I burst into tears and said, "I want to go home." (Martha Ann Sevey Wood, as told to Ann Rohrer, author and granddaughter.)

7. Details on the revolution: Clarence F. Turley and Anna Tenney, *History of the Mormon Colonies in Mexico* (Salt Lake City: Publisher Press, 1996), and Enos Flake Wood, as related to his grandchildren.

8. "I came back home to Colonia Juárez from California after calling off the wedding. It was dark, and my girlfriend, Dell, took me to the ranch horseback. As we rode along, we passed Ene Wood and his girlfriend, also on horseback. Dell called, 'Hey Ene, here is Matt Sevey home.' I wasn't particularly pleased to see him, as he meant nothing to me." (Martha Ann Sevey Wood, as told to Peggy Nelson, granddaughter.)

9. "The next day who should come to the ranch to visit, but Ene. He brought his mother up to see my grandmother because Grandma was quite sick. From that day on, he came every day." (Martha Ann Sevey Wood, as told to Peggy Nelson, granddaughter.)

And as Grandmother related to me, she literally did run into Ene one day as she rounded the corner of her home.

10. "My mother wasn't very pleased [to see Ene]. Nevertheless, he kept coming." (Martha Ann Sevey Wood, as told to Peggy Nelson, granddaughter.)

11. Name is changed. Two brothers betrayed the people with whom they were raised and educated.

12. Martha Ann Sevey broke Alonzo's heart but never told anybody but her family the truth for many years, allowing everyone to believe that Alonzo had called off the wedding. There is no record indicating the reaction of the Skousen family.

13. "There was nothing else to do or any way to get rid of him, so on Feb. 12, 1912, I married Ene Flake Wood. We have spent many happy days, more than I will be able to write about." (Martha Ann Sevey Wood, as told to Peggy Nelson, granddaughter.)

1912

1. "We were married in [Ene's] home (Lucy Jane Flake Wood). There were about seventy-five people there. Ene's mother and sister were very good cooks and had a chicken supper with all the trimmings, including ice cream. We received an assortment of dishes and linen." (Martha Ann Sevey Wood, as told to Peggy Nelson, granddaughter.)

2. Grandmother Wood said that if anybody had told her she was going home to marry Ene Wood, she would have jumped off the train. (Martha Ann Sevey Wood, as told to Peggy Nelson, granddaughter.)

3. Account of General Enrique Salazar, Henry Bowman and Stake President Junius Romney: Clarence F. Turley and Anna

Tenney, *History of the Mormon Colonies in Mexico* (Salt Lake City: Publisher Press, 1996).

4. "The cream churned itself into butter and came in handy for our lunch on that sad and lonesome trip on the train leaving the colonies. The train whistle made us think of our husbands and men folk that stayed behind, not knowing if we would ever see them again. We had to ride a wagon to reach the train and on the way a drunk rebel soldier stopped us, wanting money or anything else we could give him. We talked him out of bothering our wagon, which had just a few clothes. Ene was always friendly and could talk people in or out of things as he wanted." (Martha Ann Sevey Wood, as told to Peggy Nelson, granddaughter.)

5. "Adults were allowed 100 pounds and children 50 pounds, trunks included, to travel on the train." Clarence F. Turley and Anna Tenney, *History of the Mormon Colonies in Mexico.* (Salt Lake City: Publisher Press, 1996).

6. "The Chupe people went through the Cumbres Tunnel, one mile long. It was dark and the children were frightened. Black smoke and cinder poured in windows." Clarence F. Turley and Anna Tenney, *History of the Mormon Colonies in Mexico* (Salt Lake City: Publisher Press, 1996).

For the sake of the story, I took geographic liberties and placed the Cumbres Tunnel north of Pearson instead of south.

7. "[Before the train was allowed to leave] Salazar's men bullied Dave Brown and Brother Harris, demanding guns, which were in the baggage car. Guns acquired, the train was allowed to go forward, but without water. The trip was bedlam; windows wouldn't open. Someone got a bar and broke out windows. The wooden seats faced each other. There were no lights nor was there water. A little later into the trip, they were able to get water from a stream."

8. Babies were born on the train.

9. "After reaching El Paso, some were taken to a shed that was separated for each family. My sister, the Wood family, and myself went to the Alberta Hotel. The Wood family then went on to Utah.

Leuna and I went to Bisbee where my sister Nelle lived. I stayed there until my husband joined me in two weeks. That was a very happy reunion. Leuna went on to Salt Lake where my mother was at that time visiting my eldest sister Mahala. (Martha Ann Sevey Wood, as told to Peggy Nelson, granddaughter.)

10. The events at Dog Springs are true. I have no record that Ene Wood was with them. Clarence F. Turley and Anna Tenney, *History of the Mormon Colonies in Mexico* (Salt Lake City: Publisher Press, 1996).

11. Grandma Wood related to me that Alonzo Skousen did indeed visit her, but it was years later. She was sixty or seventy. He appeared at the front door one Saturday morning, just moments before she and Grandpa were to go to the Easter activities. Grandma jokes that at least she was dressed to the teeth, literally. Grandma wore her teeth like a piece of jewelry—only when she dressed up. During his visit, Grandma learned that Alonzo was never able to father children although he never gave a reason. Grandma was convinced in that moment that she had been inspired not to marry Alonzo because it was important that she bear children.

Many honorable and righteous women, who would be noble mothers, marry and never bear children. It is not my intention to suggest that barrenness is a tragic punishment bestowed on the unwary, but simply another trial of mortality. For some reason, it was not meant to be my grandmother's trial, whether it was a burden she could not have borne, or, more likely, that it did not fit God's grand eternal scheme for her and her posterity.

1913

1. "I was expecting my first child, so I thought I had better stay where there were doctors. When I was seven months along, my husband came to El Paso and wrote for me to meet him there. He talked me into going back to Mexico for two weeks. I went and had been in Pearson only a few days when the train was wrecked and the Red Flaggers stopped all other trains. So my first child was

born [February 14, 1913] in a little adobe two-room house across the street form Ene's family in [Colonia] Juárez." (Martha Ann Sevey Wood, as told to Peggy Nelson, granddaughter.)

2. Guadalupe Treviso, a malicious agitator, attacked John Hatch with intent to kill, but he was killed by a rock thrown by Hatch in self-defense. Except for mediative tactics of Alonzo L. Taylor, Bishop Bentley, and friendly Mexicans, the town might have been plunged into a civil conflict by this incident. Turley, Clarence F. Turley and Anna Tenney, *History of the Mormon Colonies in Mexico* (Salt Lake City: Publisher Press, 1996).

3. "Ene and Tom had a meat market, and my husband's parents and family had returned to the colonies. My first child was born in a little adobe two-room house across the street from Ene's family in Juárez. There were no doctors . . . I had a nurse and Grandmother Spilsbury; neither had delivered a baby before. Through the help of the Lord, she finally came into the world after thirty-six hours of labor. I was a lucky mother to get through it under the conditions and to have a beautiful child. I named her Maudie." (Martha Ann Sevey Wood, as told to Peggy Nelson, granddaughter.)

1914

1. "I took a wagonload of peaches into Ascencion knowing that Pancho Villa was camped there, and I asked the colonel to get me a personal interview. . . . We had walked through one room to another when we came face to face with a man with a big Stetson hat, wearing a silk shirt with a knotted bandana around the neck and pair of levis. The colonel said, 'Señor Leña, meet General Pancho Villa.' We shook hands, and he escorted me to a table in the center of the room where we sat down to talk. In less than a half an hour, I felt that I had known him all my life. He asked me all manner of questions and I answered them explaining my beliefs. He said, 'Don't you ever leave Mexico. Mexico is as much your home as it is mine. And if the time ever comes that my army takes you prisoner or threatens you, just tell them you have a special message for El General Francisco Villa and

I cannot give it to anyone except the General himself. I promise you that you will be turned over to me unharmed.' I reluctantly bade him good-bye and never had the privilege of meeting him again." (Enos F. Wood, as told to Peggy Nelson, granddaughter)

After the war, Enos Wood became acquainted with the widow of Pancho Villa who lived in Chihuahua City. He gave her a gift of the Book of Mormon with his signed testimony in it. Years later, a member of my stake who had served a mission in that part of Mexico, told me that he had met my grandfather who had related this story. The elder thought Ene Wood was just a rambling, old man until he was transferred and met Pancho Villa's widow, who showed them the Book of Mormon that Grandpa had given her.

2. Ene and Mattie were captured by soldiers, Red Flaggers, and taken to a canyon where they met up with about five hundred more men. "I was praying for all I was worth as it began to look pretty serious. I can truthfully say I have never been so frightened. Silvestre Quevedo was the man in charge and had gone to our Juárez Stake Academy . . . he was our good friend. They were very polite . . . They gave us something to eat, then gave us back our guns and a written order for no one to [bother] us the rest of the trip." Martha Ann Sevey Wood journal.

Ene's version is interestingly different. Instead of two wagons, he remembers four with him and Mattie in a buckboard instead of a buggy, riding behind instead of leading. I believe a woman would remember best how she traveled because of the comfort issue. After being stopped by the Red Flaggers, Ene tells:

"They took us to their camp where General Silvestre Quevedo, Rodrigo M. Quevedo and Jose Orozco were in command. The first two men were close friends whom both Mattie and I had gone to school with. 'We are going to execute your husband,' General Silvestre Quevedo said to Mattie. Horrified, she said, 'He has done nothing.' They took me on the side of the hill and took Mattie to a shack. After a conference between the generals, they decided not to harm us. I left them two sacks of beans and five sacks of corn." Enos Flake Wood journal

3. "Enos Wood was taken prisoner by Red Flagger, General Gutierrez who meant to have him executed by a firing squad. The appearance of Earnest Hatch seemed to unnerve Gutierrez and he changed the death penalty to a good sword whipping. After about three times, Ene commanded the capitan, Ricardo Lopez to stop. He commanded with such force and authority that Lopez did stop. Several men on the firing squad knew Ene and were grateful they did not have to kill him. Soon after, six Red Flaggers came to Martha Sevey's home to search for Ene. He hid in a false partition in the unfinished room up stairs where '[we] had hidden all our guns and lots of ammunition. I strapped on two belts of ammunition and sat with a 30-40 rifle ready to defend my life at the first sight of a head . . . I could see through the cracks . . . [while the soldiers took] everything in sight. Martha Ann, my mother-in-law, was arguing with them the best way she could because she didn't want them to take two beautiful blankets that General Hernandez of the Villistas had given my wife.'

"The soldiers went up stairs and one of them was in the crawl space." Ene "was ready with [his] rifle raised, praying with all [his] might that [he] wouldn't have to use it." His prayer was immediately answered when one of the other soldiers found a barrel of apples and sent up a shout. The man in the crawl space readily left his post to ensure his share of the fruit. After a while, the soldiers left, taking as much as they possibly could, including about a hundred thousand pesos in Villista money." (Enos F. Wood as told to Peggy Nelson, granddaughter.)

1915

1. One of the men who were present when my grandfather was sword whipped, did come looking for refuge for one night. Grandma Wood was very nervous and "slept with one eye open and one foot on the floor." This man was found hiding in an orchard a day or two later by one of the revolutionary factions and was shot and killed. (Marene Robinson Wood, daughter, as told to author)

2. "It seemed just retribution overtook nearly every person who harassed the Mormon colonists in the name of the revolution; invariably they met violent deaths, usually by execution." Clarence F. Turley and Anna Tenney, *History of the Mormon Colonies in Mexico* (Salt Lake City: Publisher Press, 1996).

1916

1. Jane Flake Wood was badly burned when she fell into a vat of boiling soap. Surviving, she was scarred and wore high-necked clothes, scarves, and long sleeves all her life to hide them. Hannah was never burned, but the incident serves my story.

2. Spring 1916: Villistas raided and looted Columbus, New Mexico, stealing ammunition, wagons, and livestock from the US government. Pancho Villa marched toward Colonia Dublán and Colonia Juárez, promising to burn the colonies to the ground, "kill the men and hold the women and children hostage." With no train service and no trucks, there was no way out to escape Pancho Villa. It was the darkest hour of the revolution as far as the colonists were concerned. "After a very humble assessment of the danger at hand, Bishop Call, of Colonia Dublán told his ward members, 'Go home, get down on your knees, and voice your gratitude to your maker for the assistance and protection received at his hand. Implore him to soften the heart of this determined General and stay his hand . . . 'blow out the lights and go to bed with faith in His power to care for you.'"

The Villistas did come yet no confrontation took place, Pancho Villa took his soldiers east of Dublán by the lakes and on to Chocolate Pass through Galeana and El Valle and south. There are conflicting stories that tell what Pancho Villa saw that changed his mind. That it was divine intervention is accepted unanimously. Clarence F. Turley and Anna Tenney. *History of the Mormon Colonies in Mexico* (Salt Lake City: Publisher Press, 1996).

A popular story I heard growing up and read again in other memoirs, Pancho Villa did come to Dublán threatening to kill every gringo. Arriving, he saw many campfires and assumed that

Pershing's army had already arrived. Frightened, he took his men around Dublán by the lakes and proceeded south, fleeing Pershing's threat.

On my mission to Mexico City in 1969–1971, I met an old man who said he had been a soldier who marched from Columbus, New Mexico, with Pancho Villa. He claimed there were no fires when they arrived in Colonia Dublán. Pancho Villa simply changed his mind and they marched on. Perhaps the vision of fires and soldiers was only for Pancho Villa, or perhaps the story is myth. However, it is fact that something changed the general's mind, an indisputable miracle.

3. Mattie Wood was with her mother-in-law, instead of her mother, when they fed the soldiers who had been working their way down the street, "looting and stealing food, ransacking and con-fiscating anything and everything that might be of value." Mattie was terrified . . . and her husband was away. "Help me," Mattie fervently appealed to the Lord. Instantly, a thought came to her. These soldiers in normal circumstances were a warm, loving, hospi-table people known for their friendly greeting, "Mi casa es su casa." Quickly, the two women mixed up a large batch of biscuits, made thick milk gravy and fried several pounds of potatoes. The first batch of biscuits was just coming out of the oven as the rowdy group of revolutionaries stomped up the little path to the front door. Mattie rushed to the door, threw it open, and calmly welcomed them, "Pase, pase, hace mucho frio." Those rough men showed Mattie and great-grandmother Lucy all the courtesy and respect their mothers had taught them." (Martha Ann Sevey Wood as told to Peggy Nelsen, granddaughter)

4. Lem Spilsbury story. Clarence F. Turley and Anna Tenney. *History of the Mormon Colonies in Mexico* (Salt Lake City: Publisher Press, 1996).

5. "Mexico threatened to join with Japan and Germany to get back Texas, NM, Arizona, and California that was lost in Mexican war with US. . . . [After General Villa's attack] General John J. Persh-ing, and several thousand United States soldiers arrived in Colonia

Dublán from El Paso on the orders of General Freddy Funston who gave the order to seek and destroy Pancho Villa while taking care to preserve the new relationship with the de facto government, Carranza as its president and Obregon . . . It came to be known as the Punitive Expedition. Dublán was advanced base—12,000 soldiers looking for 400 men with 100,000 men on the border against express wishes of Mexican government who, along with some European countries, feared invasion." Clarence F. Turley and Anna Tenney, *History of the Mormon Colonies in Mexico.* (Salt Lake City: Publisher Press, 1996).

6. Colonists helped Pershing's troops by building adobe shelters. Pershing and Aids socialized some with colonists. The Taylor brothers made a beef contract that was very lucrative supplying the army with beef. They also built a bullring and staged bullfights to entertain the soldiers. Clarence F. Turley and Anna Tenney. *History of the Mormon Colonies In Mexico.* (Salt Lake City: Publisher Press. 1996).

7. "Ene and Bill Wood had a company store in the American camp. I cooked meals for the Army on Saturday and Sunday noon. They seemed to enjoy our good old home cooking very much. Among them were several officers. I had a good old Chinese man that helped with the cooking." (Martha Ann Sevey Wood, Journal)

"I met with the [United States] Colonel in charge at Columbus and got a permit to open up a business for [Pershing's] soldiers. It was a regimental canteen where we sold candy, gum, fruits, butter, and other produce from the Colonies. I moved my family to Dublán, my wife and two daughters, Maudie and Hannah, where every Sunday, we had about eleven of the American officers to dinner." From the memoirs of Enos Flake Wood

8. The punitive expedition, as the US army called the nine-month foray into Mexico, resulted in minor skirmishes as far south as Parral in the state of Chihuahua. But on June 21, 1916, the Tenth Cavalry was nearly destroyed in a battle against the Mexican army near Carrezal. Due to diplomatic action, the United States decided not to declare war on Mexico. *Army website, www.army.mil (February, 2003).*

1917

1. "Jan 1917—troops begin evacuation. Feb. 1917 last of troops crossed the border at Palomas. Many colonists went [with] Pershing's army fearing retribution from Villistas for harboring American Soldiers and never returned." Clarence F. Turley and Anna Tenney, *History of the Mormon Colonies in Mexico* (Salt Lake City: Publisher Press, 1996).

2. "One day as I was riding into the camp from Dublán on horseback, I saw several officers of the Carranza Army standing under the cottonwood trees west of the gate. As I entered, I noticed two U.S. soldiers with two men leading their saddled horses. I recognized one as the General Gutierrez who had ordered me whipped and the other was the captain who gave me the stripes. General begged me with tears in his eyes to intervene with the U.S. soldiers who were going to turn them over to the Carranza Army. General Gutierrez knew Captain Zozo . . . Zozo was a friend of mine so the soldiers consented to keep their prisoner until I could bring the Captain. [I] saved the lives of these two men, [and had] mixed in politics. I knew that my family nor my business would be safe now. I must leave my adopted country for a while. When General Pershing's army left Dublán, my family and I went with them to the states. No sooner had I left when Several wagons of Carranza's men came to my place and confiscated everything there was. This was a cheap price to pay for having the privilege of saving the lives of my fellow men. I am thankful that I was not responsible for their execution." (Enos Flake Wood journal)

3. Mattie and Ene left the colonies for a few years, returning in 1919 after several failed business ventures. By then, the revolutionary war was winding down, nearly at its end. In 1920, Mattie discovered she was expecting her third child, a son, who was born while Ene was away on a mission. In 1923, another baby boy died at birth, and in 1924, a healthy baby girl was born on a cool October day. She was perfect in every way except for a small tumor that bulged from her neck. It would not be removed until she was nearly four, leaving her with a scar along the jawline, one inch wide, a scar that would ruin any young girl's life. She, however, was not any young girl. She was my mother. And that is another story.

4. Actually, it was the Samuel Robinson home in Colonia Dublán that was ransacked and burned to the ground. Some members of the family hid in the home of their Mexican neighbors and other members watched from a cornfield.

Ⅱ Discussion Questions

1. Why doesn't God give us what we pray for when the scriptures promise us that if we ask, faith unyielding, we shall receive?

2. What do we learn from Mattie's experiences about the storms of life?

3. Why do bad things happen to good people?

4. Does God send us trial and tribulation, or are they a natural consequence of life?

5. How does adversity bless Mattie's life?

6. Has adversity bless your life?

7. If children are "blessings" from God, how do we account for unwanted babies born to undeserving women? How is it hurtful to women who are unable to conceive?

8. In your opinion, what was Mattie's finest hour of courage and faith?

ABOUT THE AUTHOR

MARTHA ANN ROBINSON ROHRER WAS BORN IN COLONIA Juárez, Chihuahua, Mexico. At age nine, she moved with her family to Toquepala, Peru, South America, where they lived for ten years. After attending Juarez Stake Academy in Mexico her sophomore year, she returned to Peru and finished her junior and senior years through correspondence. In 1965, the family returned to the United States, settling in Tucson, Arizona. Ann served a two-year mission to Mexico Mexico City Mission. She is married to John Rohrer and they live in Pasco, Washington. They have five boys, one daughter, and at present, thirteen grandchildren.